Bruce Taylor

to Sara —
always good to see
you — good luck with
your publishing ventures!
Best Bruce Taylor
November 03

Fairwood Press
Auburn•Seattle

The Final Trick of Funnyman and Other Stories

A Fairwood Press Book
October 2001

Fairwood Press
5203 Quincy Ave SE
Auburn, WA 98092
www.fairwoodpress.com

Cover design by Patrick Swenson

ISBN: 0-9668184-4-X
First Fairwood Press Edition: October 2001
Printed in the United States of America

This collection was first published by
The Ministry of Whimsy Press
PO Box 4248
Tallahasse, FL 32315
Special thanks to Jeff VanderMeer for his invaluable help on this edition

Story Credits: "Naptime," *Aberrations;* "Gregory's Vision," *Figment;* "Altair II," *Horizons Science Fiction;* "Coming Home So Cold," *Kopernikus 14;* "Der Fuhrer as a Bad Kitchen Appliance," *Krauts;* "The Big Brown Satchel of Mr. M." and "The Strange Fate of M. in the Odd Town of X," *Magic Realism;* "Vacation," "The First, Last and Only Painting of Pablo Caso," "The Baker," and "Friends," *Matrix;* "Dr. Frederick's Last Task," *Midnight Zoo;* "The Attendant," *New Dimensions 9;* "The Breath Amid the Stones," *New Dimensions 10;* "Of the Odd Events in Regard to Mr. M.," *Not Yet;* "Oh, Them Dancing Shoes" and "The Coat," *On Spec;* "Onions" and "The Final Trick of Funnyman," *P-I/Northwest Magazine;* "Popcorn," *Pulphouse the Hard Cover Magazine #1;* "Child, Looking at the Moon, Wondering" and "Alternate Reality 578.5," *Pulphouse;* "Cars," *The Silver Web;* "Perfect Disguises," *Twilight Zone.*

To Jack Cady
and to the memories of
Jack Leahy and Avram Davidson,
who said I could do it.
It took a while, but, hey, I did it.

TABLE OF CONTENTS

INTRODUCTION

I'VE BEEN A Bruce Taylor fan since the 1985 Norwescon – a Seattle science fiction convention that attracted about 3,000 SF fans and professionals. Bruce and I had been scheduled to do readings in the same room, one before the other, and I sat in on his. His reading charmed both my eye teeth out; a hard act to follow! This guy, I told myself, is good! I loved the stories, I loved the style, and the way he read them was marvelous!

Bruce and I have run into each other at numerous conventions since then. (In fact, my wife and I even enticed him to an early Spokane convention by inviting him as our house guest.) And unless the program chairperson has me scheduled elsewhere – which is seldom – I attend his readings. Strange and wonderful stuff! So, when he mentioned this upcoming anthology, I volunteered to write the introduction. (For one thing, I'd get to read the stories in advance.) He accepted.

There's a considerable spectrum of stories here: Horror stories some (but by no means all) of which may make you smile. Funny stories that may leave you thinking. Wise stories that can make you nod and say "That's right; that's just how it is!" Or "That's right! Huh! So *that*'s how it is." Love stories. Hate stories. Surprise stories that, at second thought, are exactly what you might have foreseen but didn't.

Clearly some of these stories and insights grew out of Bruce's observations, over the years, as a psychiatric technician at Harborview Hospital in Seattle. Others may bring to mind Hans Christian Andersen, the Brothers Grimm, Lewis Carroll, and Doctor Seuss. And Franz Kafka! There are Edward stories that may bring back your childhood with a different light on it. Sometimes sunlight, sometimes shadowed moonlight, and occasionally the focused and relentless light of the autopsy room.

If reading these stories is an experience, and it is, what an experience it must have been to write them. (Probably I'll never really know. My muse takes me down different paths.)

There are also insights into writing here, if you wish. Insights not explicit but nonetheless clear. Various fine authors have written down the secrets of their successes, too often giving them as the laws of writing fiction, of *How It Must Be Done*. Some of these have become part of conventional wisdom. Here we see them exposed as less that holy writ – formulas, rather than natural law. Formulas with which you can write very good stories indeed, if you choose to follow them. Bruce, on the other hand, has written very fine stories while ignoring those formulas and going his own way, writing what he pleases, galloping across the pages plugged into his own muse, following his own inspirations. In the knowledge that, under the umbrella of the bell-shaped curve of human readiness, there are many who will find much pleasure in what he writes.

Meanwhile, editors for the trade publishers – corporations whose purpose and bottom line is profit – feel uncomfortable with stories so unique. It's like – "Geez, Shirley, this is nice stuff. I'm really tempted. But what's the market? Ummmmm. Ahhhhh. No, I'd better not take a chance." Of course, when such a distinguished author and packager as Bob Silverberg includes them in an anthology, that's different. After all – *Bob Silverberg!*

But as Bruce's credit list grows, Marketing begins to look at things differently. "Frank, we need to try new directions (shudder, tremble). X and Q and those Europeans have been publishing him, and Al and Shirley have pretty good track records. Maybe we could use his German credits as a promotional ploy . . . Now there – yeah."

I won't keep you from the good stuff any longer. Except to say that if you attend science fiction conventions in the Northwest (from Vancouver B.C. to Portland, from Seattle to Moscow, Idaho), attend Bruce's readings. They're an auditory as well as a mental and spiritual delight.

John Dalmas
Spokane, Washington

VACATION

I AWAKEN AS though from a very deep sleep. The light is so bright and I open and close my eyes many times before the blur goes away. I rub my eyes. I feel cool hands on my forehead. I look. Somehow I know that the person touching me is my mother. She grins. "Welcome," she says, "welcome to the vacation."

I hear the words; I don't understand them at first, but gradually their meaning comes clear. And at last, at last I am able to speak. "Vacation?" I say, "Vacation?"

My mother puts her forehead to mine. She smiles and a tear rolls down her cheek. "Vacation."

"Why are you crying?"

"It's nice to have you with us."

Suddenly I don't understand at all what is being said. It makes no sense, for surely I have always been with them. I try to remember back but cannot. I find, actually, that it really makes no difference. I sit up. "Where are we?" I ask.

"Would you like to look about?"

Eagerly I nod. My mother takes me by the hand. I look about. I am in a room. The walls are white. A door opens and a male, who I sense is my father, walks in. He smiles at my mother and I feel warmth flow between them. My father comes over to me. He ruffles my hair. "Hey, sport," he says, "let's show you around."

"Okay."

We go out the door. The light is fearful and I cover my eyes. It is terribly hot. I glance up. I see a very intense light overhead. It is surrounded by blue-black. Other bright lights show also. I see so many strange and wondrous things that I don't know what to think. As we walk, my father points out things and gives them names. And I rapidly learn about where it is we are spending our vacation. And I have so many questions to ask! Some of them my father answers. Some of them my mother answers. And sometimes they simply say, "I don't know."

But I put the information together. We are on a large ship. It is self-contained and perfectly built. The craftsmanship is excellent. And I am utterly fascinated by the ship.

I let go of my parents' hands and run all over asking people about the ship. "Who built it?" I ask. And usually the answer is, "That is not known."

"I want to see the engines!"

An old man nearby laughs. "Ha-ha! No one sees the engines, young fellow, no one!" And he laughs again.

"How fast are we going?" I ask.

He smiles and chuckles. "Very fast." He scratches his beard and, with a beer in hand, sits near the pool, dangling his feet in the water.

"Well – where are we going?"

The old man grins and drains his beer and says, "Here now! Stop asking such questions!" He grabs me and pulls me into the water. "Too many questions. Come here and get your head wet. You're on a vacation, now have some fun." He splashes me and the water is warm.

I crawl out of the pool, sputtering and shaking my head. And I hear gay laughter. "You're silly!" I turn and I look. A young woman, dark of hair and eyes, covers her smile with her hand. I suddenly realize I like her. "Who are you?" I ask.

"My name makes no difference."

The old man nods approval.

"Won't you come into the pool?" I ask.

She stands so tall and bashful but I run up and lightly grab her around her waist. She does not protest and she dives into the water with me and we come up gasping and sputtering.

"Having a good time?" the old man says.

"Wonderful!" I say. And I smile. And the lady places her arms around my neck and we kiss. The kiss is as warm as the water and we walk into one of the cabins and make love. We make love again and again and in moments of repose, I say, "Oh, oh, but it's a wonderful vacation." She giggles and grabs me and we laugh and make love again, again, again and she is all warmth, all movement and her eyes they are bright and I feel that fire within her, within me and we sleep, and we sleep; her head on my chest, her arm around me and suddenly I hear a furious pounding on the door. "Yes," I yell, "what is it?"

It is my mother's voice. "Come quickly! Your father is ill!"

I am horrified. My father ill. My lady friend's dark eyes are concerned and sad. I climb out of bed, hurriedly dress and go with my mother. I am struck by how warm it is outside and the deck plates are hot to my feet. My lady friend runs beside me and we go into a cabin. My father is pale. He touches me. He says no words but his eyes tell all. I hold his hand. "Where's the doctor?" I cry.

My father shakes his head. "I wish I would have taken time to play more," he whispers. "What a fool I was to work and worry so on my vacation."

"You'll be all right," I say, squeezing his hand. My mother answers a knock on the door and the doctor walks in. He looks very serious. He quickly examines my father and then sighs. "The only thing that I can do is to give him some pills to help him rest easy." He digs around in his black bag and pulls out a small brown plastic bottle. "One every four hours," he says.

Outside the cabin I talk to the doctor. "Will he be all right?"

"I don't know." The doctor squints in the bright light. "Sometimes vacations are hard on people."

My first thought is how ironic that sounds. The doctor shakes his head and moves on. My mother exits from the cabin. "Your father is gone." And she weeps. Suddenly I am shocked at how wretched a vacation can be. My lady friend comes to me and I am so glad that she is there for suddenly I feel so very alone and the light, the light, the light is so bright and so keenly intense and the hot deck plates burn at my feet and yet the ship moves on, moves on, moves on and the body is jettisoned into dark space.

For a long time I say nothing. I walk and finally sit on the edge of the pool, my feet in the water. I look to my lady friend. "Some vacation this is. Shit."

She says nothing. The old man comes up to me. "I heard," he says, "I'm sorry."

"I'm tired of this vacation," I say. "I'm fucking tired of it. I want to go home."

The old man sighs. "My friend, you'll be going home soon enough. Just because you're on vacation doesn't mean there's no pain. I lost my wife on a rough part of the trip."

I frown. My lady friend squeezes my hand. I stand and she walks with me in the bright heat. "I guess I should go see how my mother is doing." I look to her. "What about your parents. Didn't they come on the trip?"

"No," she replies. "I was placed on board and left to pretty much fend for myself."

"You've done well."

"You have no idea how much you've helped." And her eyes are so very large and brown and I realize how much I love her. I also realize, as we walk to find my mother, that the old man follows behind.

"Mind if I walk with you?" he asks.

"No, no, not at all," I reply.

We find my mother sitting in a deck chair; her face is still shocked. She looks up to me. "Oh, God," she whispers, "I am so alone! This vacation is so wretched!"

The old man sits in a chair beside her and places her hand in his. He nods and I see tears in his eyes and I decide it best to leave them in peace.

"And so what do we do?" I ask my lady friend.

She smiles. "Explore the ship?"

We explore it gently, a bit at a time. Again I marvel at how so well it is built. "You know," I say, "I've always wondered how this God damn thing works. I want to see the engines."

My lady friend laughs. "As did I when I first came on board. But they cannot be seen. You can spend all your time asking questions and simply forget that you're on a vacation. Just enjoy it."

"I suppose you are right." I nod slowly. "But such a vacation. Such a vacation. I wonder how long it lasts."

"I guess as long as you enjoy it."

For a long time we walk about the ship in silence and then I hear my name announced over the loudspeaker and I quickly go to the paging operator who hands me a telegram. I read it. I read it over and over. "Oh, my God," I whisper, "my mother – " I collapse on the searing deck plates. My friend is beside me. I hold her so close. I mumble, "This vacation is a disaster! I want to go home!"

But my lady friend shakes her head. "Come on, come on, we have to go."

By the time I get back, the body has already been jettisoned into space and I see the old man. He comes up to me and buries his head on my shoulder and weeps and finally he is able to whisper, ". . . we had just made love and she died in my arms. Oh God, but she was a woman so grand!" And he weeps again. Finally he straightens, sniffles, and wipes his eyes. "Such a vacation!" And oh, how he sighs. "Well, got to get on." He shrugs his shoulders. "Got to get on. You know, there are parts of this ship that I've never seen? Do you have any deck that you recommend?"

I look to my friend. She looks thoughtful. "You know," she says, "there's lots of activity a couple of decks down."

He nods. "Think I'll have a look." And he wanders away and I hear him say, "Oh, oh, such a vacation this is."

I nod. "I have to agree with him."

My lady friend says, "Well?"

"I think I've seen enough of the ship for a while. Let's go back to the cabin."

She agrees. We walk in silence and oh, oh, how the heat is intense and the light blinding white and the deck plates so hot and by the time we get to the cabin, I am exhausted. And we stay in the cabin for long periods of time; ever so often we go swim in the pool. And sometimes I watch my lady friend swim, or watch her when she is quiet and realize, realize again and again how much I love her, how much I need her and how so lucky I am. And ever so often she catches that love in my eyes and the message is returned to me by the fire in her eyes. And we love, we still love, in the most gentle of ways. She is beside me, she loves me and I hold her so close and it is then that I realize that the vacation is such a marvelous thing.

And yet, I awaken one morning, a severe pain in my chest. As though by instinct, my friend awakens. "What is it?" Her eyes are dark-wide.

"Such pain!"

"The doctor!"

"No time! Just hold me! Just hold me!"

She does. Oh, God, oh, God, she holds me so close. She lies with me and combs my hair with her fingers and then, and then with fingertips gentle, gentle, gentle as dawn, she touches my face and I know that she knows, yes, she knows that my vacation is over and I am going home.

The Attendant

I OPEN MY eyes. I realize I do not know where I am. I do not know the date. Nor the year. I do not feel old, nor do I feel young. I might be male or female. Looking down, I notice I am dressed in pants. I assume I'm male. I am in a large room with other people, some of whom I recognize. Across the room is a television; since I know what it is and since I am able to recognize people, I must have some previous consciousness. I try to think back, but there is a block. It is as though I have just been born, yet born with some previous knowledge, so that I am able to not only think but comprehend my environment.

I look around. To my right, sitting at a wobbly table and writing furiously, is Gustave Flaubert. He looks up. "How are you feeling?" he asks.

"All right," I reply. The sound of my voice: definitely male. I find myself searching for certainties. "What am I doing here?"

"That's what I'm writing about," Gustave says. "You were leading a demonstration for civil liberties in Uruguay. You were shot."

"Is this then a hospital?"

Someone in the corner, who is painting quickly, stops, turns around, scowls, then smiles, then laughs. It is Vincent van Gogh.

"No," says Gustave, "this is not a hospital. This is a prison."

I shake my head." Prison this is," I say, "but I've committed no crime."

"Neither has he." Gustave points. Thomas Jefferson is smoking a pipe. He is talking quietly with Lenin and Karl Marx.

"Nor has he." Gustave points again, and Beethoven is hurriedly writing a score. Suddenly he turns and places his fingers on the keyboard of a piano. Intensely beautiful music pours forth.

"Then this is absurd," I say, "this is absurd! If we have committed no crime, then why are we here?"

Gustave sighs. "The attendant defines us as dangerous. We think differently."

"The attendant? The attendant! Who's this attendant?"

Gustave points. Beyond the television, a bank of barred windows. Beyond the windows, a vast expanse of lawn. It is hard to see because the light is dim, like you would find at twilight. But then I see the attendant. My breath catches in my throat; I feel suddenly chilled and my hands are cold. "My God!" I say. "My God! What is it?" I stare. I cannot believe what I see. The attendant. It is flame, it is claw, it is smoke, it is scream, it is black, it is white, it is gray, it is beak, it is explosion, it is hands, blood, water, and tooth. "My God," I say again. "My God!" I look around. "What sort of creature is that!"

Beethoven pounds on the piano. "It is elegant!"

Sophocles says, "It is the tragic."

"It is pathetic," says Tchaikovsky.

Lenin says, "It is unity."

Van Gogh whispers, "It is madness." And he screams.

"It is suffering," says Gustave.

"It is the Tao," says Lao-tse.

Everyone becomes silent. Michelangelo steps up to me and says, "The attendant is all of this, all of this and yet still more."

It is very dark; the attendant forever changes. Often it is wracked by explosions of light. Faces around me are white and the shadows severe and bleak, and I notice the television has a commercial on for toilet paper; a beautiful woman has a wad of it in her hand, and to show how soft it is, she rubs her face with it. There is lush music. The commercial abruptly ends in a swirling mass of confused color. Suddenly I am watching a western.

I am seeing the front of a saloon. The planet Jupiter is massive in the sky. The scene is very clear and sharp, although done in black and white. But the black and white fields are reversed as though the scene is shot through a negative. The sunlight is dark, the shadows are white. A gust of wind blows a front of black dust down the street. A man in white (actually black) walks onto the scene. He stops. His legs stiffen. His hands are by his sides; the fingers work. "Dirty Dan!" he calls. "Dirty Dan! Your dirty dealings are done!" A close-up of his face: unclean, needing a shave. Sweat trickles down his cheeks. His shirt is filthy. White flies buzz about. The camera shifts. The doors to the saloon open. A tall male, robust and strong, dressed in black clothes (actually white) with sequins, comes out into the street. He looks immensely strong and virile. "Oh, say, you pretty boy," – and he flips his hand – "aren't you the cute one. Oh, you savage sheriff, you. If anyone is dirty, it's you. My, but I can smell your stink from here, Sheriff Bob."

"Listen," Sheriff Bob says, "nobody in my town performs sex changes on grandmothers without a medical degree or at least a GED and six years experience as a landscape architect! I'm afraid I'm gonna have to ask you to leave or kill ya."

"Oh, you silly boy," says Dirty Dan, his sequins sparkling darkly, "I'm not leaving. And I think you're angry because I didn't tell you about the operations and your morbid curiosity is driving you crazy. Too bad. Tsk." And with an exaggerated turn of the hips, Dirty Dan turns his back to Sheriff Bob. The sheriff shoots. Dirty Dan falls. The sheriff turns and walks away; a woman leaps out from the form of the sheriff and runs to Dirty Dan, and the camera turns and suddenly finds itself focusing in on an image of itself in a black mirror and *wham!* – explosion of color and light.

I jump back.

"Madness!" cries van Gogh, "Madness! Madness! Madness!"

"Nonsense!" snarls Marx. "Class conflict!"

Gustave is standing near me. I point to the television. "What is the purpose of that?"

He shrugs. "The attendant's language. It's rather confused and there is much we don't understand. But it is a way of communicating, and oddly enough, whenever we want something all we have to do is ask."

I scratch my head. I look at the creature. I look at the television. I look at the people surrounding me. I am confused. "I don't understand." I rub my eyes. "I don't understand at all."

"Exactly what is it you do not understand?" asks Gustave.

"What is it about the attendant that keeps you here?"

"It has placed us in here. If we try to leave, it destroys us."

"There's something else! Let us be honest," says Sophocles. "We are of the attendant and it is of us. We cannot be separated."

"Madness! Madness! Madness!" shouts van Gogh, and he stabs a painting with a paint brush.

Slowly I nod. I watch the attendant. All movement, all fire, fur, hands, fin and claw, scales and voice and sob and shriek. I nod again. Something flashes on the television. It is a gear. For some reason, I am afraid. As I look around, I see fear on other faces. "And so," I say, "the attendant is afraid and you are afraid." Something else flashes on the television. I get a fleeting impression of the face of Henry Ford.

"Why should the attendant be afraid of you?" I ask.

"Because," says Gustave, "we see it for what it is."

"And that is . . . "

"Confusion."

"No," says Tchaikovsky. "Sadness."

"Wrong," says Lenin. "Class warfare!"

"Never!" replies Jefferson. "The emergence of rationality!"

There is more shouting and confusion, and the attendant is violent red and flashing, flashing, flashing and smoking and screeching and howling like a creature tortured and maimed. And while all this is going on, I see movement. I run up to the barred windows and look out. Someone is walking toward the attendant. Someone in a long dark robe holding something up in his hand. "No!" I cry, "No! No! No!" I pound on the glass. "No! No!" The person does not turn. In the dusk the figure walks up to the attendant, walks into the smoke and flames, into the howling, the biting, the burning, and suddenly a flash of brilliant blue-white light and we hold our hands up to our eyes. When we are able to see again, we are too stunned to move, much less speak. The attendant has changed.

"Do not you see what has happened?" whispers Gustave. "Do not you see? Confusion seeks structure like water seeks its own level. Do not you see?" Gustave's eyes are wide and his breath comes quickly and he grasps the bars in the window. "While we were arguing what the attendant was, someone came along and gave the attendant a structure. Do not you see? Confusion does not wait for insight! Confusion cannot understand! It wants only structure – now!"

"Madness!" screams van Gogh, and he throws his portrait in the direction of the attendant.

"The *bourgeoisie!*" hisses Lenin.

"History is bunk." We all turn. The face of Henry Ford remains on the television. The face sneers.

Gustave runs from me to Jefferson. "Do not you see? Do not you see? The attendant is now dangerous! It is just as confused! But rather than work through the confusion, it is now able to ignore it. It doesn't have to face it! It feels safe now!" Gustave's eyes are wild and pleading. "Oh, do not you see? We are in danger! We remind the attendant of its confusion. It can well do without us now!"

We stand in silence. We are afraid. We look out at the attendant. We see the new form: the multiple legs made of shining aluminum, the bulbous body black as rubber and slick as though covered by oil. The mouth is gears, the eyes headlights, and on top of the body the figure in the robe. The attendant resembles a vast mechanical spider, and it awkwardly and stupidly moves, and as it does, it tears up the ground, levels trees, and its eyes work and stab the darkness like lasers; and I am watching the television and I see gears and wars, twisted faces and twisted crosses, flags raised, flags burning, and then there is no image. The picture is that of snow, of static. And the attendant moves. It turns. It faces us. The picture on the television clears. I see the room in which we stand and then I see our individual images. And somehow, from the television, comes a feeling of intense rage and also a feeling that we in the room are somehow not only responsible for the attendant's confusion, but also that we have in some way failed. I kneel before the television and whisper, "No, no, that's not true. It takes time. Patience. For we are and always will be part of you."

Gustave kneels beside the set also. "Yes, yes," he whispers, "yes, our ideas are all different, but they are based on the same concern – "

The screen now shows the image of the person in the robe. The figure's face cannot be seen, but what can be seen is that the figure is bloated.

Gustave pales. "My God," he whispers, "it is feeding." Gustave turns away and becomes very ill.

"Oh, God, but you are ugly!" I say. The attendant's eyes flash and suddenly the television picture is flipping wildly and static bursts like gunfire and then I am blinded by light. I hold my hand up to my face and Gustave yells, "It's coming! It's coming!" The attendant attacks, the wall crumbles. And I don't know how I do it. I don't know how I do it. But from somewhere within me, something screams anger, something screams rage, and I run forward into the light. I grab the television and heave it at the light. I fall back. Glass breaking! Shriek of metal against metal! Steel shearing! Explosion! Quaking and rocking! I lie flat and keep my face hidden for a long, long time.

Finally I hear a gentle voice saying, "Come. Come. You must join us, for you are a part of this too." I look up to see the face of Sophocles. I crawl to my knees. I look about. The room is gone. And everyone who was in it encircles the attendant. The attendant is wounded, blinded. The dark robed figure is limp. The attendant knows we surround it. It waits for us to kill. We do not. The attendant wobbles to its legs. We watch. On all our faces, fear yet hope.

And I look about to the faces that I know: to Flaubert to Beethoven, to Lenin, Jefferson, Sophocles, Tchaikovsky. Then we all join hands. I feel movement at my feet. I look down; a white kitten looks up, all gentleness, gentleness, sweet, sweet gentleness. A butterfly alights upon Tchaikovsky's shoulder and a horse with coat as though dappled by sun and shadow nuzzles Michelangelo and the horse watches with gentle eyes and other animals emerge from the forest and silently watch and I feel them within me and distantly I hear the rush of sea and feel the heartbeat of dolphin, of whale. I feel the rhythm of cilia, the movement of protoplasm, and I feel the flowers blooming and the intense energy of seeds waiting their chance to break through their shell, and all life sends that silent prayer, "We live here too. Please, please let us have our life, oh, attendant." Our hands all tighten their grip and the attendant shudders and I hear within me Beethoven. I hear within me Lao-tse. I feel within me the stroke of Van Gogh's brush on canvas and the cool clay worked into beauty by Michelangelo and the hope of Lenin, the desire of Jefferson, and the passion of Flaubert.

Beethoven reaches for and touches the attendant. It shudders, and slowly crumbles into a ball. The sun rises and the rays touch the body of the attendant. The spider-body glows. It glows and melts and we back away. It melts and soaks into the soil. Then a mighty jolt; we fall to our knees and then the incredible: the soil splits and a mighty human fist pushes, pushes, pushes up through the soil and then it stops. The fist turns, and the tightly, tightly clenched fingers face the sun. And Beethoven roars through me; and the horse, it is dancing, its front legs going right and then they go left; the kitten is purring, all rumble and sound, and the animals are frenzied, all dancing and dancing, and the ocean is foamed by flippers and fins, and the dolphins they whistle and leap in the air while the leaves they uncurl and magic! magic! magic! the air so fresh, so clear and so light, and with wonder we watch, with joy we see the fist unclenching, opening like a flower, slowly, slowly until the fingers spread wide and the palm finally knowing the glory of sun.

Child, Looking At The Moon, Wondering

It was 1956, summer, eight o'clock in the evening and Edward and Roy were in Roy's backyard, lying on their backs, looking eastward. "Just about," said Roy.

"Yeah," Edward, age ten, said, "any minute."

"You heard about Old Man Sansdrom?" said Roy.

"No. What about him?"

"He was caught stealing at the A & P."

"Yeah?"

"Yeah."

"What?"

"An onion. Get that." Roy rubbed his crew-cut head and laughed. "An onion. Jeez, if you're gonna get caught, get caught with something good."

"Like what?"

"A *Playboy*."

"Yeah," said Edward. "Yeah, do it big."

The eastern horizon grew brighter.

"So what'd they do to him?"

"Not much. He'd been coming in for years. What a nice guy. Stealing an onion." And Roy laughed again, a high-pitched laugh. "Wow. I guess old Felix, the manager, was really shook about it. I was just in on the tail end of it, but Felix had a hand on Mr. Sansdrom's shoulder and kept saying, 'Mr. Sansdrom, are you all right? Are you all right? Why'd you do that, Mr. Sansdrom?' And Mr. Sansdrom, he was looking to the ground and it was weird – it was really weird – "

"Why?"

"Couldn't answer. He just stared at the ground and couldn't answer."

"Weird," said Edward. Then, "Did you ever steal?"

"Nah," said Roy. "Dad'd skin me alive. God he would. He'd take a belt to my behind and make it shine – wow, he'd kill me if I did that." Then, a pause. "Did *you* ever steal?"

Edward thought a minute and said, "Yeah. Yeah, I did."

"Yeah?"

"Yeah."

"What?"

"Carrots."

Roy laughed gleefully. "Gee. You and Mr. Sansdrom oughta get together – maybe you guys know someone who could steal lettuce, cucumbers, and tomatoes and you could steal a bowl and have a salad."

"Yeah," said Edward. "It was really dumb. God, it was dumb."

"From the A & P?"

"No, from Mr. Jackner's backyard."

"Yeah? Doin' a little early harvest for him, hey?"

Edward shook his head. "You know, I still don't know why we stole them. We ate a couple and then we ditched a bunch of them in Thorndiek's rhododendron bush. And we did it for two or three nights. Under a full moon."

For a few minutes, they lay on their backs and looked at the clear July sky, breathed in the perfume of cut grass and listened to the crickets chirp. The eastern sky grew paler still.

"I remember when what's-her-name – Mary – you know – "

"Mary Jean Allison – Margee."

"Yeah. Boy, she was snitchin' all kinda stuff there at the McKesson's – you name it and she got it. Wow."

Edward had his hands behind his head, looking up as the sky turned from dark blue to black. "What happened to her?"

"Sent her 'way for a while – can't remember where. Some place. Thought she was supposed to come back but I haven't seen her. Boy, wasn't that a mess? Remember all the fights her parents had?"

Edward kept looking at the sky. "Yeah. Everyone was really surprised to hear how she was stealing the McKesson's almost blind – I always thought she was a neat kid. God, stealing when she was seven, jeez, that's too bad."

"Yeah, and when her parents found out, they really let her have it."

"She was in the hospital, wasn't she?"

"I dunno, maybe. I can't remember, but she wasn't at school for a while and when she came back, her arm was in a sling – said she fell down roller skating."

"Oh, yeah," said Roy. "Yeah."

Roy pointed. "Getting close. Real close."

"Yeah," said Edward, and he sat up and ran his hand over the grass, feeling the dryness of it and said, "You never stole anything? Really?"

"Really," said Roy. "Really."

"Ever wanted to steal?"

Roy didn't answer for a minute and finally said, "Uh, yeah, I guess so – "

Edward waited.

"There was this model car at the McKesson's – you know, it was a plastic model '55 Corvette and man, I wanted that *so* bad but it was a buck twenty and I only had sixty-six cents, you know, and I don't know what stopped me because I sure wanted it and I had this shopping bag and it woulda been so easy to put it in there, no one was around – and I coulda just slipped it in – "

"And ya didn't."

"Nope."

" 'Fraid your father would beat you up?"

Roy sighed. "Oh, yeah," he said and he stuck a blade of grass between his teeth, "well – " then he thought, "naw, he wouldn't beat me up or break my arms or anything like that – but I think he would have been real disappointed in me and I couldn't handle that – hurting him like that – I dunno. It's dumb. But I just couldn't. I sure wanted to, boy, let me tell you, because I wanted it so bad but I couldn't." After a minute, Roy said, "And you stole carrots. Gee, I can't believe you did that. Why? Why did you do that?"

Edward just sat there and shook his head. "I don't know," he said softly, "I really don't know." He ran his hand over the dry grass again. "Davis was in on it – one evening, we were in the backyard and Davis said, 'Mr. Jackner sure has a big garden,' and I said, 'Yeah, must be neat to have food like that right in your backyard,' and I don't remember if we said anything else except that the next thing I knew, we were climbing over the fence and pulling up carrots." Edward smiled. "They did taste good – dirt and all – sweet, you know? Real sweet. Gee, they were good – but we knew it was wrong – Davis' mom found the carrots a few days later in the rhododendron bush . . . "

"How'd she know you and Davis snitched them?"

Edward shrugged. "I dunno. But she knew. Maybe mothers are like that. Anyway, she made us go over and apologize to Mr. Jackner."

"What'd he do?"

"He looked real surprised – we were both crying – oh, we felt terrible about that – "

Roy laughed. "Really? Or were you upset that you got caught?"

Edward didn't say anything for a minute and then said, "I felt guilty for doing it and it was wrong – okay?"

Roy was quiet. "Okay," he said, "don't get sore. Don't get sore. But I wonder why people steal? I wonder why people do crummy things that hurt other people?"

Edward pointed. "Look."

Above the horizon, the vast moon rose, and soon Edward and Roy were bathed in yellow light.

"Wow," said Roy, "isn't that grand?"

"Yeah."

The moon continued to rise until it was big in the sky, and Roy said, "What do you suppose is on the other side?"

Edward smiled in the light. "The dark side."

"Yeah," said Roy. "What do you suppose it's like?"

"I don't know," said Edward. "I don't think anybody really knows."

"Boy," said Roy, "it's gonna be neat when they can finally see the dark side."

"Yeah," said Edward, "maybe."

"Maybe?" said Roy, staring at Edward in the light, "maybe? Why maybe? To know what the other side is really like – to know what's really there – wouldn't that be great?"

Edward, not looking at Roy, but looking into the jaundiced light of the moon, simply said, "Would it?"

Roy did not answer and neither spoke for a few minutes. Then, wordlessly, they rolled their sleeping bags out on the tarp, crawled in them and after a time, Roy said, "C'mon. What do you suppose is on the other side of the moon?"

Edward stared at the moon for a long time and finally said, "Gee, I don't know."

"Maybe there's an ocean on the other side – d'you suppose?"

"I dunno," said Edward again, "maybe there are a bunch of creatures there from another planet and they got bases all set up there and they're waiting to attack Earth. No, wait – it's an ancient civilization – no, no," and scooting up on one arm, he said, "we're from the moon. See, we came from a place way far away and our ancestors came to the moon first to see if the Earth was an okay place to land and take over – "

"G'wan," said Roy. "Boy, what you been eating these last few days – g'wan. So that means we're actually monsters from some other place – "

"I didn't say monsters," said Edward. "I just said we come from some other place, some place, way, way deep in space. That's all."

"Jeez," Roy said, "Jeez, that's enough. G'night. Hope the monsters from the moon don't land and take you 'way."

"Already landed," and Edward poked Roy in the ribs. And Roy poked him back.

"Monster!" he said. "Moonman!"

"Lunatic," said Edward and they poked, jostled and wrestled some more, then laughed and fell asleep –

– and Edward looked around and the sky was black with the sun shining high and the crater walls rose high above; ice on the rim gleamed and immense waterfalls tumbled down cliffs and the water flowed into a sea in the distance and all around him, lush vegetation, though not very high, but like broad-leafed blueberry bushes with huge blue-red fruit, and ferns, like bracken, lush on the crater floor. Roy was beside him.

"Jeez," Roy said. "D'you suppose this is the dark side of the moon?"

"Yeah," Edward said, "must be. Wow, it really is weird here." They had been sitting as though they had been tumbled there. Then they stood and began walking. "How is this possible?" said Roy. "Why is there air?"

Edward shook his head. "Maybe this crater is so deep and so big that somehow it trapped air – or maybe it's some gimmick of a civilization. Or maybe there is a huge clear glass dome overhead that we can't see – but this sure as heck has to be the other side of the moon."

"What makes you so sure about that?"

"Because that's the last thing we were talking about before we went to sleep."

"Oh," said Roy, like it somehow made perfect sense. "Wow," he breathed, "wow, it's so neat."

They began walking down a slope that was covered with a thick growth of blue green moss and in the moss, pale blue and red flowers like miniature hyacinths (which Edward's mother grew in rainbow profusion in Edward's backyard) and they kept on and came to a cliff and could overlook that sea and Roy said, "Look!"

And on that sea, graceful ships, long and narrow, each with gold sail, flew through the water on silent course, heading for – "A city!" whispered Edward, "Can you imagine that, a city here on the other side of the moon – " And the city was a collection of spires all yellow and blue and green in the light, like a fantasy of the most delicate kind and it sparkled, shimmered in the light of the sun and Edward and Roy sat on the edge of the cliff, looking out over the vast scene before them: the waterfalls pouring off the cliff faces, the vast crater, the blue sea stretching out before them and, looking carefully, they counted five more cities on the edges of the sea and Edward said, "Wow, the other side of the moon is such a grand place to be – "

– he opened his eyes. It was very dark. Clouds had moved in, covering the moon and the full night was there and Edward scrunched down in his bag and said to himself, "Oh, Jeez, oh, man – " He looked around in the dark and from somewhere he heard voices, but at first he couldn't tell whose or where they were from –

" . . . she's feeling upset – a bad dream is all – "

" – God damn it, I don't care! She needs to shut up – "

" . . . please – let me . . . "

" . . . after all the shit she's put us through – "

" . . . daddee – "

"Stanley – don't – !"

"Daddeee – DADDEE! DA – "

Smack!

A stunned silence, then, a sob and a woman's voice, "Oh, Margee, Margee – "

Then utter silence. And Edward huddled down, down, down into his bag, down, down as far as he could go – praying and hoping that dawn would come soon – hating to know the other side of the moon.

The Big Brown Satchel Of Mr. M.

MR. M. WALKED along the avenue with the apartment building on either side in the city of Es. He stopped, put his big brown satchel up on a low, brick wall, put his hand into it and . . .

. . . from the third floor, old and brittle Mr. Remalde, seventy-two with sparse gray hair, still dressed in his maroon bathrobe, poured himself a cup of coffee and peered out at Mr. M., who had his hand in the bag. Son of a bitch, Mr. Remalde thought, you got dirty pictures in there and you're gonna start handing them out to the little children who are walking by. I should call the cops on you, that's what I should do. I know your kind – I was once a cop – I've seen a guy do just what you're doing in the summer of '42 when I was working out of Cleveland, he did exactly what you are doing. And Mr. Remalde sipped his coffee and wondered what to do. Call the cops. That's what I should do, he thought, call the cops on the likes of you. Your good clothes are just a sham. What to do. What should I do with a scum like you, and he drank another gulp of coffee that slid down his throat like bitter juice and he wondered what his wife would have done if she were still alive, God rest her soul, she'd love him for calling up the police and protecting the citizens of this fair city of Es, Es by the mountains, by the sea . . .

. . . and Mrs. Volkran on the first floor of the same building pulled the faded drapes aside and said, "Oh, my, he's reaching in that briefcase for a gun, probably a very large one and then he's going to turn and come across the street, grab me, to rob and beat me just like what happened ten years ago in that city to the south in the shadow of That Mountain, yes, he looks just the same as the other one who pulled out a gun from a briefcase only that one was purple, I do believe, came right over and aimed the gun at my husband's head and killed him flat, just like that, oh, my, oh, my, what should I do? She quickly pulled down the shade, made sure the front door was locked, and put a chair beneath the handle and moved as quickly as her sixty-year-old body could, down the hallway, to the back door no, no, she couldn't stay there because that was how the other one had entered, he'd come through the back, oh, dear, oh, dear, what was she to do? And she finally decided that she'd hide near a window if she heard noise at the front or the back – she'd get out that way – no, no, don't rapists and burglars usually come through the window? Where was she to hide? She should call the police; this ax murderer should be stopped. But what if he had friends? She might be done in by three or four. She went back and forth and back and forth. Maybe two or three police couldn't handle ten or twelve would-be arsonists – she'd be burned out of house and home and then what would she do? Oh, dear, oh, dear. And if thirty of those Mafia appeared, they would tommy-gun her right there on the spot – oh, dear, oh, dear. . . .

. . . and from across the street, Mrs. Higgens and her husband John had just finished making love and he glanced out the window and said, "Now there's a queer sight if you will, a gentleman standing there with his hand in his briefcase – probably checking to see if he has his house keys."

"Oh," said Mary Ann, "wouldn't that be just so bad, to be locked out and not be able to get back in? Surely his landlord has extra keys."

"Well," said Mr. Higgens, studying this problem most thoroughly, "that's assuming his landlord lives in the same building."

Mrs. Higgens sat up on the bed and pulled a blanket about her shoulders and said, "That's right. If he weren't well what would he do? I wonder if he has money to make a phone call to his landlord?"

"I don't know. You know the way people are these days, plastic money and all and no ready change – maybe we should invite him in and give him some coffee until he can figure out what to do, poor chap. What a trap to be without one's apartment keys. That really is too bad."

His wife stood. "Maybe he'd like some breakfast too."

"Yes," her husband said, "he might like sausage and eggs over-easy."

"Yes," his wife said. "Sausage and eggs over-easy must be his favorite meal. He looks like such a handsome man for such an inconvenience to befall him. I wonder if he has a wife." She put on a pale green blouse.

"Doubt it," her husband said, looking out the window, "she probably died years ago in some fatal accident."

"No," his wife said, "of a disease."

"Cancer."

"Most likely. Maybe he's very sad."

"Could be," her husband said. "I'd be sad if you died of leukemia."

"Maybe we should see if he wants to get in touch with the local chapter of a support group for leukemia and polio survivors."

"Yes," her husband said now standing and putting on his trousers. "I've noticed him walk before, just like he once had polio . . . "

"A shame it affected him so badly, all alone, no friends and evicted from his apartment – " Mary Ann shook her head and began to put on a skirt.

"Still rummaging through his suitcase, maybe he's searching for an address of a friend . . . "

. . . and Missy Cole, a bright and blond young lady of twenty-three glanced down from her second story apartment at the same time and said, "Why, he just looks like Ken. He's got a little piece of jewelry in there that he's going to drop off to his girlfriend's on his way to work. How sweet. Yes, he just looks like Ken, and that's a pearl necklace he's got in there and his lady friend will wear it ah, with such pride, just like I did when Ken gave me that diamond necklace three years ago, oh, that was a lovely thing, Ken, Ken, why did you go? Oh, I remember when you proposed on the deck of the ship as it splashed up the Sound – oh, my world, it went round and round." She looked again and thought, that is Ken – no, no, it can't be Ken, can it now? And she quietly opened up the window and looked down at the man with his hand in the brown satchel and something sparkled in there – it must be a ring and yes, just maybe that is Ken and Missy began to feel real faint and made it back to her living room and just sat, simultaneously loving and hating Ken very much and not really knowing what to do – it had been five weeks since he said good-bye and if that truly was Ken down there, he might be waiting for her but she couldn't exactly see too well. Did she dare go down there? Let him know how much she cared and how much she hurt? She really didn't mean to back off like that – she was scared and maybe she should have said so, but she didn't know how to really say it, oh . . . golly, now she was beginning to sound like her mother . . .

. . . and Mr. Zwank in the upper apartment of The Eldorado Heights ("Mountain View" the outside come-on sign had said, "Two bathrooms and dining room with crystal chandelier, view facing south and east, soundproofed and guarded parking, covered, too.") He glanced down as he sipped his iced coffee and thought, Hm. Just like Howard in purchasing. Always spending his time looking for this or that. Honestly, that gentleman has probably left important papers on his desk. Probably an important deal hinges on his getting to work promptly at eight and look at that, it's now seven-thirty and most likely he will miss his bus. What a fool that man is to jeopardize his position at an important place. Why, he might be risking his position for second vice chairman at the Boeing Airplane Plant.

All that money he could get. Why, a salary of sixty-thousand could easily increase with proper planning. Eighty-thousand, imagine him risking a salary of eighty-thousand by being careless and leaving home the plans for some advanced airplane part. Probably has to do with the main jet. And he sipped his iced coffee very slowly, remembering back to those times when he had almost lost a promotion to the second vice chairmanship for Henrietta Pratney Dwight Airlines out of Arkansas and how lucky he was that he worked so hard with such discipline with a capital "D" because he was so forgetful in the past and had almost lost so many chances but he had learned to be careful, oh, so careful, indeed to be meticulous! And Spare! And Prompt to the second, yes, to the second! and he looked with scorn to the man with his hand in that brown satchel, searching for the plans that he had obviously left behind on his desk, just as he, Mr. Zwank, had almost done ten years before . . .

. . . and Mrs. Tilly, age thirty-six, who lived up the street in a house that stuck out a ways so she had a view up and down the block from her living room looked up from her program "As The Years Go By," looked up from Dr. Frederick Case wondering what would happen to his career if he got involved with the steamy Nurse Melinda Dear in ICU and Lord, he subvocalized on the television, I can't blow my career by risking this but Melinda is so irresistible and if I am careful, no, no! And melodramatically, his hand went to his brow, "I must study these reports, rounds are just a little while from now and I have to know these cases, these cases, Melinda why can't you get out of my mind – " and Mrs. Tilly looked up from this and took a sip of beer as she looked down the street to the man with his hand in the brown briefcase and she thought, "You son of a bitch, you're just like Rick, you stupid, moronic son of a bitch, you got your hands in that briefcase and you're arranging and rearranging everything just so, just like he did – I know you're doing it, God, it was a battle living with you those years, everything had to be in a certain place and we had to go there at a certain time, oh, it was awful, *awful* and I hoped I'd gotten away from my father but no, how was it I married someone just like him? Just as perfectionistic – and she glared at the man with his hand in the satchel and she said, I hate you Rick, I really do, you God damn shit, five years and a kid later and you ran off because she was so good with figures – oh, I hate you you God damn macho prick, oh, God how I *hate* you, and she pulled long again on the bottle, not tasting what was really there but always trying to dilute the brutal truth that kept breaking upon the horizon of her awareness that maybe it just wasn't all his fault and she drank the beer and finished it and opened another one and then there was a commercial on television about toilet paper and how soft it was that you could cuddle it on your face all night without abrading skin at all and Mrs. Tilly looked at the man and said, "Oh, Rick I hate you and I'll hate you for the rest of my life I'd like nothing more than to go out there and take that fucking briefcase and slam your hand in it all the way down to your little withered balls," and *slam* she threw down one bottle and then grabbed at another; *shlep* went the twist-off cap and she sucked long on that one and the television soap continued on, with Nurse Melinda coming to the door of Dr. Case's office, saying, "The patient has had a hard night, Doctor Case, he is very stiff and feverish." and he looked at her and you could tell how he was doing as he subvocalized an inward groan and dared not stand up and Melinda's breasts pushed much too hard against the fine fabric of her uniform, white and pretty as could be, and Doctor Frederick Case swallowed and said majestically, "Melinda, would you close the door behind you? I'd like to speak to you personally," and the camera focused on her face and a smile oozed about her full lips and then the focus was on the doctor, his eyes very wild and his lower lip quivering just a bit and the scene faded out and "Oh, shit, I hate you Rick!" sobbed Mrs. Tilly as she leaned forward, head in her hands with the music for a commercial extolling the qualities of a mountain of wash, that music filling the room with such expectations of a better life and Mrs. Tilly cried . . .

. . . and little Jeremy Zachary Jack age six-and-a-half happened to be walking nearby and stopped when he saw Mr. M. with his hand in the brown satchel and said, "Hi, Mister, what's in the bag?"

Mr. M. just grinned and said, "Well, looky here." And he pulled out a globe filled with galaxies and stars and said, "Care for one?"

"Why sure," said little Jeremy Zachary Jack.

Mr. M. laughed and gave it to him and took another one out for himself and closed the satchel just like that and then continued on his way on that delightful sunny day.

The Breath Amidst The Stones

"FOO-FRA!" SAYS the wall.

I look up from the sleeping desk. "I can't understand you. Take the plasterboard out of your mouth."

The wall sneers; the grain distorts. "I don't have plasterboard in my mouth," says the wall.

"Then what were you saying?"

"Foo-fra."

"Foo-fra?" I scratch my head. "What kind of word is that?"

"I don't know," says the wall. "I just invented it. Maybe – " and the wall stares at a picture by van Gogh – "maybe it's an expression that's halfway between 'fooey' and 'frampt.'"

"Fooey I understand, frampt I don't."

"Huh," replies the wall. "I just made up frampt. I suppose I should define it before I use it in other words."

I nod. "It would really help."

"Skidge," says the rug.

I stare down. The blue-green rug smiles pleasantly.

"Skidge?" I say.

"Skidge. I like that word. I thought it up."

I rub my eyes. "What does it mean?"

"It's a combination of skid and edge. I'm sure it has applications to rugs in general, but I'm not sure how."

"Maybe," says the wall, "it can mean a rug that has a tendency to skid near the edge."

"Spain," says the big picture window.

"Sorry," I say, "Spain is taken. It's a country."

The glass warps in embarrassment. "Damn. I meant it to mean a soapy pane of glass. No good, huh?"

"No," I reply, "no good."

I look about me, amused and angered. Amused because all those things which we used to consider as having no life – well, now they do, and how they wrestle with their special conditions of existence is amusing. Yet, I'm angered . . .

"Sputz," says my pencil.

"Sputz," I repeat. "It sounds like a mispronunciation of spuds, which means potatoes. Is that what you mean?"

"No," says my pencil. "I meant it to mean the act of spelling incorrectly."

"Oh."

The pencil crawls across the desk and, in the border of my income tax form, it begins a game of tic-tack-toe with my pen. The pen suddenly makes a big black pool of ink. It whispers, "Have you any Kaopectate? I think I'm getting the runs."

I shake my head. "No." The letters on the paper run from the engulfing black tide; then the tax form stands and tries to shake the ink from itself. Then the paper lies back down, the letters rearrange themselves, and what once read "If you do not itemize deductions and line 15 is under $15,000, find tax in tables" comes out

$Ji dtə 00ɟ yoiʕɟ51zeit Q
f
d0
i
x

And the letters know they are in the wrong positions, but since they never learned how to spell, nor learned anything about word order, they give up and lie around, babbling incoherently. A *t* jumps up and down. A capital *A* tackles a small *z*, and they tumble across the page.

I sigh.

In the background, I hear a slopping. The water is climbing out of the fish tank again. And the fish inside dart about, always very frantic when the water does this. This time I don't bother trying to put the water back in the tank. Every time I tried before, there was nothing really to grab onto. I watch the water. It is still experimenting with mobility. First it lengthens itself out like a snake and tries to inch forward. Then it rolls. As it tries new forms, it mutters, "Maybe? How do I . . . ? No . . . no, that won't work." It rolls up into a moist ball and tries to roll. "Better," it says. It rolls over to the cat, which stands with stiff fur. The animal always stares at the water with a look that must be incredulity. The water mimics the cat's form – even the tail, which it switches about as a cat might. A pregnant guppy stops its mad swimming long enough to look out from the water in the place where a cat's eye would be. The form then looks at itself and the fish inside. "Most amazing," it says.

"You're getting better," I say.

"Thank you," says the water. "Finding a convenient form is most difficult."

"Well, at the risk of making a bad pun, your options for form are indeed fluid."

"Hm! Fluid indeed. Aren't we funny." And, like a cat, the water sits on the rug, ears back.

"Move!" says the rug. "You're getting me wet."

I shake my head. "You really should be more careful. You risk being soaked up."

"True," says the water, pacing about. "Also, since more surface area of me is exposed, I guess I risk rapid evaporation."

It walks back to the fish tank, which is trying to scrub algae off its inside surfaces. It mutters, "Can't see a God damn thing."

"Crap," says the water. "I don't really want to go back into the tank and sit there. I feel like a kitty stuck on a potty box."

I shrug. The water crawls back into the tank.

I hear whispering. I look around. The books are talking among themselves. Suddenly there is a paper-thin scream. *Tropic of Cancer* has just opened its pages and exposed itself to *Jane Eyre*. Portnoy is complaining again. My abnormal psychology text is shouting theories that either drastically conflict with theories in other texts or simply do not make any sense. I sigh. Let them shout. The theories have little to do with reality, anyway. The *I Ching* is tossing yarrow sticks, and the Bible is screaming, "Pagan! Heathen!" The dictionary is looking into itself and shouts words that it finds amusing: "Foregut!" Rustle of pages. "Galago!" Then, "Macronutrient!"

A wastebasket sneezes, and papers fly up.

"Willbillet, woorbillet, woobillet." The wall frowns. It looks to me. "Not all words have to make sense, do they?"

I shrug. "I don't know. It helps if they do."

"Isn't there such a thing as poetic license? Woorbillet?"

"Words are supposed to mean something," I say.

"Scoobie-doobie-do? Twenty-three skiddoo? Ya-hoo? Don't give me that crap."

"I don't want to argue. Maybe you are right."

"Yippee-skippee. Wait! Where are you going? Are you angry at me?"

"No," I say. "I want to go for a walk. Ever since The Change, it's been awfully noisy in here."

"Ah," sighs the rug, "was not The Change wonderful? Isn't it magic to be aware? To be sentient?"

"For you," I say. "Me, I'm not so sure. Right now I guess I'm really pissed at the Valaslavians."

"Maybe you're pissed," says the water. "We're not."

I get my coat. "I'm glad for you. I mean, I really am. But don't forget how hard it is for us people to deal with The Change."

"You're angry," says my pencil, "because we won't be exploited any longer. We now have minds of our own. We won't be controlled by you any more."

As the pencil talks, it makes an exclamation point on the paper.

"Think what you will," I say. I limp out the door. My inner agitation keeps me, thankfully, from remembering why I limp. As the door closes, it wishes me a nice walk. The sidewalk looks at me. I smile.

"Tread lightly, stranger," the walk says.

"Since I hurt my foot, I don't have much choice."

The walk still looks at me with wariness. I stop walking to let two rocks cross in front of me. Following behind them are seven little stones. I walk past brush and hear gasps. Looking down, I see two beer cans making love. I shrug.

"Stop!" says a stop sign. "No parking within thirty feet!"

"I'm not going to park," I reply. "I'm just out for a walk."

I continue on. And I'm angry. The Change. The God damn Change. If we had only been more careful; Valaslavia looked so wonderful. We certainly studied the planet, the culture, and it certainly seemed that it would be a very nice addition to our Empire. And so we set our ship down near a city. The inhabitants came out. People. They looked just like people. We had our IBM Translator, and I read the speech – a very nice speech, really, although somewhat standardized. "Greetings," I read, "in the name of Earth, you are now a subject of our Empire."

I was just about ready to continue with our list of expectations and various kindnesses when I heard: "Go plitz yourself."

I did not have to know the meaning of the word to know that I'd been insulted.

I glowered at the Valaslavian. The Valaslavian smiled meekly and pointed down. There was a large rock by my foot. A very large, squarish rock.

I looked around to my crew members. They shrugged. Lieutenant Arko shook his head. "The jerk doesn't understand. Try again."

"In the name – "

"*Plitz* you!"

I guess I got angry and grabbed the Valaslavian by his tunic, and then pain! Pain! Pain! I looked down. The rock was sitting on my foot. The rock moved in a grinding motion, and I felt the bones in my foot turn to mush. I screamed. Once. Twice.

"Respect," said the rock, "respect, respect, respect! Even though these life forms be inferior to us, respect!"

My foot was beyond hurting; it was also beyond repair. I squeezed my eyes shut and behind my eyelids saw yellow and blue and purple lights.

Lieutenant Arko looked very pale. "I think we made a mistake," he whispered.

"Uh," I replied. The rock backed off my foot.

With Lieutenant Arko and Communications Engineer Toshiba helping me, we began to back away to the ship. The rock jumped toward us. We scrambled into the great white ship. And from all over, rocks began to leap toward the ship; rocks of all shapes, sizes, colors. And we heard the message: "All has life. And as the Great Ones from Trixpoxya made us aware, so we make you aware!"

"But," I called down from the hatchway of the ship, "we are already aware!"

"Yes, yes," said Communications Engineer Toshiba. "See?" He wiggled his thumb. "Notice how aware I am of my thumb! See? I can touch all five fingers with my thumb! Isn't that neat? I'm aware I can do that – "

"Awake!"

"But we are awake!" said Lieutenant Arko. "See? My eyes are open. I am aware of my awareness!"

"*Awake*! And we give you the power to give others what we give you!"

Our minds were filled with something – I don't know what. But I felt a presence. Or my mind – not my head – ached. Somewhere within me, a thin wail; something reaching forward, something reaching back, and then – then – touching.

The whole ship shuddered.

"Kabort?" I looked around. A mouth had formed in the wall. "Ka-plut?"

"Pootz!" The floor shifted.

Then a deep growl. I swallowed. We all looked at each other. I still had the translator in my hand; it self-activated, and I stared at it with astonishment. "The stars! The stars! They are mine! No longer am I controlled by sweaty, soiled fingers of the inferior flesh! I shall go where I wish to go! I shall go where no machine has gone before!" The hatch sealed itself. The growl came again; once more the ship shook, and our minds were filled with immense power and an incredible sense of destiny!

"Hang on!" I yelled.

The ship leaped skyward at I don't know how many g's. The ship bounced around the universe like a ping-pong ball for I don't know how long. It was obvious that the ship was enjoying sentiency.

We all knew what we had to do. We did not dare let the ship get back to Earth. We jammed the controls. We pulled wires. We stuck chewing gum in tape heads. We blew fuses. We kicked and hit and destroyed as much of the navigational/communications systems as possible.

But the ship had a mind of its own.

And Earth appeared on the viewscreen.

And in our minds we heard the command: "Awake!"

We all looked at each other hopelessly.

I remember. I remember it well. I sigh. My jacket snuggles around me for more warmth. Such the memory. Now the reality. I shrug. My foot hurts. I want to return home, but in order to do so, I have to cross a drawbridge. The span is up; the bridge is yawning. I look to my watch, but the little hands are folded. "Sorry," it says, "but I'm taking my rest break."

The First, Last And Only Painting Of Pablo Caso

THIS IS THE story of Pablo Caso – a strange story about his ambition, his accomplishment and his disappearance.

Pablo was born in Southern California to parents who had grown extraordinarily wealthy as grape growers and wine producers. And nothing, nothing was too good for little Pablo. He got the finest education and, very early, he showed a profound interest in art. Parents, friends and teachers were overjoyed: the depth of his interest was certainly a measure of immense talent. Yes, yes, another Picasso in the making here (a teacher once said that Pablo even looked a little like Picasso but another teacher said, "No, I think he looks a bit more like a happy Van Gogh.") and Mr. and Mrs. Caso began saying, "Pablo! How nice to see you so interested in art. Would you like to try painting? Canvas for your birthday? Paints? Here is one hundred dollars, Pablo, why don't we go down to the art store and you can buy whatever you wish. If you need more, there is two thousand dollars for you, whenever you want it, at the bank."

But Pablo said, "No, but thank you. For now, I just wish to study."

At first, everyone was disappointed, but then the realization: of course! Don't pressure Pablo into painting! If he wants to study the great masters, then that is the way to motivate and encourage; bring the great masters to him or take him to the masters.

And so, Pablo, accompanied by his parents and often his close friend, Mickey, who was bright, big and diligent, went to museums everywhere. Pablo met and talked to artists. At every new gallery opening, or art show, there was Pablo.

By age seventeen, there was little that Pablo did not know about art. In his bedroom, bookshelves sagged under the weight of art books. Artists stopped by to see if Pablo had begun to do anything with the talent that simply had to be present, but needed, you know, a little push – talent and interest – they must be nurtured, encouraged, not demanded or controlled; no unreal expectations should be set. But still, Pablo did not paint.

Mickey (who was trying his hand at art and doing very well, much to the chagrin of Pablo's parents and teachers) said to Pablo one August afternoon, "Hey, hey, Pablo, old friend, are you ever gonna paint?"

Pablo did not answer. He stood looking out the French windows that opened out to a balcony. The late afternoon sunlight flooded in; Pablo was a silhouette in the light. Mickey sat in a chair on the other side of Pablo's bedroom. As Mickey waited for Pablo to reply, he looked around, vaguely wishing that he could be as neat as Pablo (he always wore good clothes, kept his bed made, his room clean although, oddly, he never did anything about the sagging bookshelves).

Finally, Mickey looked back to Pablo who continued to stand in the sunlight, hands behind his back. Mickey sighed. "We've known each other since we were five years old. Since you turned eight, you've immersed yourself in art. Nine years you've been visiting galleries, reading, talking to artists. Are you ever going to paint? Or is it just a nine year hobby that you've enjoyed but are not going to do anything with?"

More silence. Then Pablo turned and, though he faced Mickey, Mickey could only see an outline of him. At last Pablo said, "You know why I don't paint? I don't have to. If I were to paint, my work would far, far outshine Picasso, Michelangelo, Rembrandt, Van Gogh. I don't have to justify my existence by painting. I don't have to paint to prove I'm an artist. I'm not that insecure that I have to produce."

Incredulous, Mickey stared. Regaining his composure, he leaned forward. " – ah – maybe it's not a question of – as you say – 'justification' or 'insecurity' leading to production. If you're such a great artist, why don't you share your art, your soul? Why keep it locked away in your fingertips?"

Pablo walked away from the windows, sat on the bed and looked at Mickey. Mickey saw something in Pablo's eyes that he had never seen before – an intense sadness, yet determination. "Believe me, my friend," said Pablo softly, "I want to paint. I want to paint more than anything in the world – but I cannot do it right now. If I paint, it will be only when I am ready to die and that won't be for quite some time. Because when I do paint, I will paint only one picture. It will be the best, the most perfect picture ever painted. If I were to live after I painted such a painting, I would forever feel that I could somehow improve upon it – I would be competing with myself to the end of my life – "

Mickey waved his hand. "You talk nonsense! Do you realize how long it takes before an artist can turn out something excellent? My God! I've heard it said that a good writer takes ten years to develop. What you are saying – if applied to writing – is that someone who has never written a word could sit down and write a book that would be the ultimate book! What nonsense!"

Pablo shrugged. "I simply know that when I paint, it will be an exquisite painting and I don't – can't – paint it until I am ready to die."

"So what are you going to do between now and the day you die? And how do you know you won't walk out in the street tomorrow and be hit by a truck? Then you will die having never painted what you call the perfect painting. You'll die in a distortion, in self-hatred – for never taking the time to make something of your life as you sit around waiting until you feel it's time to die! Pablo! What incredible trash! I don't believe it! I don't think you have a single gram of talent in you! I think you are fooling yourself. If you are really an artist, you would be painting and sketching like crazy because life is so short and there is so much that you must do!"

Again, Pablo said nothing. But his gaze at Mickey was, as before, that mixture of sadness and determination. He looked away from Mickey. "I hear what you say. All I will say in return is that we will see who is right," then, looking directly at Mickey, "and who is wrong."

Exasperated, Mickey shook his head, then suddenly stood. "But don't you see, Pablo? Don't you see? Words are so cheap! It's the action, always the action that makes the difference between dream and reality. Don't you understand? I'm trying to spare you humiliation, Pablo! You talk of being better than anyone, yet you've nothing to show! You're a dreamer! You're fooling yourself!"

Pablo drove his fist down on the bed. "And you! You are a fool! You are asking me to prove myself and I say I don't have to! I know I am good!"

"Pablo!" said Mickey, spreading his hands, "where is your mind? What if Beethoven said those words? He might have created one symphony, not nine! Or what if he had died before he created any? Or what if he went around whistling his symphonies but never bothering to put them to paper. Don't you see how painful it is to see someone seemingly gifted – not using their gift? To see potential simply remaining potential?"

Pablo shrugged.

Finally Mickey said, "Maybe you have no gift. Maybe you've had us all fooled for years." Then, with an air of decision, resignation, "When I see your art, then, to me, you'll be an artist. Not until then. Until then, you are a close friend, who, while interested in art, is hardly an artist." Mickey shook his head again and left.

Pablo glowered.

That night, Pablo disappeared. He left a short note: "I have studied long enough. Now I must go to work."

The note was open to any number of interpretations. Mr. Caso had several feelings about Pablo's leaving: "That's how generosity is repaid. That's love for you. You give them everything and that's how they treat you." Sometimes when saying this, he might be sitting in his big, leather reclining chair with a wine glass in his left hand, gesturing with his right; the wine would slip up and around the side of the glass.

Or, if not resentment, then: "My boy has spunk. Takes after his father – goes right out and tangles with the world – just like I did only I did it when I was fifteen. Best education is to go out and step into the bull ring." Sighing with pride, he'd look at the wine in the glass as though noticing how sweet, rich, dark the wine and how still, so very still.

And Mrs. Caso? At times she paced about, wringing her hands, saying, "What did we do? What did we do? We gave him everything! How can he just up and leave? Only seventeen! A boy! Did we give him too much? Did he lack love? Should we have made him work for everything?"

Sometimes, she might be sitting in a chair by the window, watching the sun set: where is my boy? Where is he now? What is he doing? Back east? On a ship in the Pacific? In Australia? Greece? Where? Where is my boy? And she would continue to sit, with eyes dark as though drawing darkness from shadows as shadows drew darkness from night. Sitting, sitting, black silhouettes of trees dissolve in the night, sitting, sitting, will something emerge from the darkness? A hope? A prayer? A sparkle? A shining kernel of truth, of understanding? Something? Anything? But nothing would come and eventually, like a shadow herself, she would move through the room to go to bed only to lay on it until the weight of silence, of night, forced her eyes closed.

It was like this for ten years. Every couple of months or so there might appear in the mailbox a letter, a postcard with rare and strange stamp or picture: Spain, Belgrade, Leningrad, Athens, Cairo, South Africa, Madagascar, Rio de Janeiro, Chile – sometimes he would stay in one place, work for a year, other times he would go through three countries in a week; but whatever he did, where ever he was, it was obvious he was having a great time, yet also there was something else: he was studying – no matter what his postcards, his letters said, somehow there was a thread of something – everything was described in such a way that showed Pablo to be watching, looking, as though he was avidly participating, yet also a spectator.

Whenever Mickey was in town he visited the Casos, to see if, by some strange act of coincidence, God, synchronicity or whatever, Pablo had returned home. For ten years he was disappointed, but he would stay to read the latest letter or postcard. He was not around too much; he and his art had become well known with showings in Los Angeles, San Francisco, Seattle, Vancouver and after he turned twenty-six, he had even been contacted by galleries in Chicago and New York.

His success was of some discomfort to the Casos; however, they were always glad to see Mickey and seemed happy for him. Mickey always down-played his success; once he told the Casos, "Yes, I'm pleased to have done well, but I wish Pablo could be a part of it with me."

Mr. and Mrs. Caso loved Mickey for his sensitivity to their feelings.

And whenever Mickey dropped by, Mr. and Mrs. Caso might say, "Have we been deluding ourselves? Did we do him an injustice? Maybe he left because he felt we expected something extraordinary . . . "

Mr. Caso might shake his head, sigh and sip his wine.

And Mickey, at a loss for words too, might simply say, "I don't know. Do you have any idea when he'll return?"

Mr. Caso would likely say to his wife, "Where'd you put the last letter?"

Mrs. Caso would get up, find a recent letter and they would discuss, dissect, speculate about, question the letter: why that word? What did that mean? That's an odd note to end on. He sounds happy, don't you think? I wonder what he's doing there! Maybe he's getting ready to come home. Isn't there a big art museum there? Do you suppose he's going to start painting now? I think he's sad. Listen to the way this reads – doesn't he sound sad there? I think he's lost. A poor lost soul wandering the ends of the Earth.

It was on such an evening, ten years almost to the day after Pablo had left, that Mickey and Mr. and Mrs. Caso sat around the table, drinking wine; August Venus was a burning pearl in the darkening shadow of sky. Mr. Caso was refilling empty glasses. A knock on the door.

Mr. Caso looked puzzled. "We weren't expecting anyone, were we?"

"No," Mrs. Caso said. She got up, turned on the porch light, opened the door – a shriek of delight, "Pablo!"

In the dusk, Mickey and Mr. Caso started at each other for a second – then, screech! chairs shoved against stone floor; everyone gathered about Pablo; lights went on in the house and Pablo, standing in the doorway, looked embarrassed; his hair was down to his shoulders, he was bearded, tanned, muscular, wearing a blue denim jacket, blue jeans and had a pack on his back. He then grinned, looked sheepish, and finally said, "Hello." He walked in, shrugged off his pack and sat at the table. Pointing to a glass of wine, he said, "This one mine?"

Suddenly, everyone was talking at once – and the talking continued far into the night. You'd think that by the time everyone got to bed – about three Sunday morning, that no one would be getting up too early. Mickey stayed the night but, about five a.m., he awoke with a very odd feeling. He shook his head; what is that? He concentrated. A sense of joy and sorrow, wonder and despair, sunlight and darkness. Mickey, somewhat beside himself and not quite knowing why, climbed out of bed and, as quiet as a shadow, opened the door, crept down the hallway – the door to Pablo's room was open. Pablo was not there. Puzzled, Mickey continued. Hearing something, he dropped to his knees to look through the keyhole into an empty spare bedroom. He stared for quite some time, not quite knowing what to think. There, in front of open, east-facing French doors stood Pablo – naked. It was just before sunrise. Pablo stretched his arms out as though being crucified; the rising sun suddenly bathed him in the light. Mickey distinctly heard, "I am ready." Then, a pause, then, "I am life, crucifying itself on the awareness of itself. Mortality need not forgive itself for being mortal and being afraid. I know what I do. And I am ready."

Abruptly the sunlight coming into the room became brilliant. Pablo exploded in color – every color imaginable filled the empty room – and it occurred in utter silence. Quickly, the light faded. After some minutes, Mickey, caught between being spellbound and at a loss as to what to do, slowly stood, then opened the door.

Pablo was gone. Or – was he? For the room was filled with him; every square centimeter of ceiling, wall and floor was a fine detail of Pablo's twenty-seven years. Upon looking closely at the floor, Mickey saw flowers of such detail as painted with a single human hair. The walls were landscapes, cities, scenes in rooms and public places – all so perfectly captured that it seemed they were painted with the scene right before the artist. It was as though Pablo knew every second of his life and accounted for it. There was even a scene in the lower left north wall where, by squinting, Mickey saw himself and that evening when Pablo left, there was Pablo, a silhouette in the light of the setting sun, and Mickey sitting on the bed – the copper color of the bedspread was perfect as was Mickey's green plaid shirt. Amazed, Mickey looked up. The ceiling faded from blue around the edges to black in the middle. Present were constellations from the northern and southern hemispheres.

Dazed, Mickey kept turning around. Involuntarily, he whispered, "Pablo! Oh, God, Pablo! How right you were! It is like I am walking about in your heart! Forgive me – "

He heard a whisper. "Thank you, Mickey." The voice came from a little sparkle, a miniature sun, suspended in mid-air. "God bless you, Mickey, and take care."

The little sparkle drifted to the wall, toward an image of Pablo, at age five, dressed in a red and blue striped short sleeve shirt and short blue pants. His face was turned, looking back to an unseen observer. Mickey had the uncanny sense that anyone looking at Pablo would feel that Pablo was looking directly at them. Pablo's mouth was open as though joyously shouting; his expression was eager. In the sky above him, the sun and the moon. The scene was that of Pablo running, one arm outstretched, his finger pointing to – the horizon? Mickey simply shook his head in wonder, disbelief; spellbound, he watched the little sparkle, that minute star, drift toward Pablo, settle on Pablo's finger and glow, glow, so very, very, brightly.

PERFECT DISGUISES

EDWARD LOVED HALLOWEEN. It was a time to let his imagination run wild. At age ten, he had a pretty good imagination. He could look into a mirror and instead of seeing a brown-haired, befreckled and green-eyed kid, he would see a ghost, a goblin, a Hollywood movie star – anything else but Edward, age ten.

But Halloween was best of all. Halloween. Ah, yes. Cowboys and spacemen and queens and clowns.

Edward had several friends he'd trick-or-treated with for the last couple of years. There was Roy, who either liked crew cuts all year around or who always got them, whether he liked them or not. He also had a tendency to wear plaid shirts and was kind of pudgy. Whenever Edward went over to his place to visit, inevitably Roy's dad – a rather pudgy man himself with a crew cut and fondness for plaid shirts – was either watching the news or was downstairs putting together or taking apart a transmission or a carburetor or a master cylinder, or something like that. The only people in Roy's family who didn't have crew cuts were his mother and his sister Roxanne. Though Roxanne was also a bit overweight and liked to keep her hair short. Just like her mother.

Another of Edward's friends was Vincent. He was the same age as Edward and Roy, but he looked older. Vincent had always enjoyed Halloween too. In fact, Vincent sometimes looked like a symbol of Halloween – he was scruffy as a scarecrow, gaunt as death, and grim as the Reaper.

Oddly enough, Vincent usually dressed as a clown on Halloween. Roy went in for cowboy themes – his favorite TV character was The Lone Ranger.

When Edward and Vincent visited Roy, they usually sat around the Philco with big mugs of hot cocoa and watched *The Lone Ranger*. When they went to Vincent's, they sat around with Cokes and watched Vincent's favorite cartoon character – Bugs Bunny. At Edward's house, they sat around with all sorts of snacks, but didn't eat any of them while the TV was on because they were usually too busy watching Edward's favorite shows, science fiction films and monster movies – the scarier the better. After the shows, they would eat. When you're having so much fun being scared out of your wits, who wants to be distracted munching Cheese-Its? Or Hi-Ho Crackers?

When Halloween came around each year, Edward always found plenty of ideas from the movies that he could use for costumes, from the Metaluna Mutant of *This Island Earth* to the Creature from the Black Lagoon. Name the creature and there was Edward, trying to figure out a costume for Halloween.

"So what are you going as this year?" whispered Roy one day in Social Studies class. He sat in back of Edward and had a habit of whispering things to Edward. And Edward was always chagrined because he had to lean back to hear Roy and sometimes Mr. Jackson caught Edward leaning and once wondered out loud if Edward was stretching. (Edward had once answered "Yes," to which Mr. Jackson suggested that maybe he should work on stretching his ears so he could hear better, so that he wouldn't look so ridiculous. At that moment Edward couldn't tell who he hated more, Mr. Jackson or Roy.)

But this day Mr. Jackson was absorbed at the blackboard explaining why Communism was dangerous to the American ideals, and so when Roy asked the question about Halloween, Edward wrote down on a slip of paper, "Haven't decided yet."

"Better decide," whispered Roy. "It's Friday night. You got three days."

Edward nodded. He wrote a note. "What are you going as?"

"Lone Ranger," whispered Roy.

Another note: "Go as his horse."

"Why?" whispered Roy.

"You won't need a costume," wrote Edward.

Pause. *Punch.* A fist in Edward's back. "OOOOO!" said Edward.

"What's going on?" said Mr. Jackson.

"Oh, farts!" whispered Roy.

That evening, after staying late and each writing one hundred times, "I will not talk out of turn," Roy and Edward walked home together in the early evening dusk. Roy kicked at yellow maple leaves as he walked. There was the smell of burning leaves and Edward said, "Something's eating you."

"Nah," he said, avoiding Edward's eyes.

"You sure?"

Shrug. Kick at leaves.

"Did I do something? You mad about having to stay after?"

"Nah."

Edward shrugged. "If you wanna tell me. I'll listen."

Long pause. "Did you get an invite to Jan Matthew's birthday party?"

Edward had to think for a minute. "Yeah. Didn't you?"

"Did Vincent get an invite?"

"Yeah," said Edward.

Roy didn't say anything.

"I don't get it." Edward said. "She wouldn't invite Vincent and me and not invite you. Maybe your invitation got lost in the mail."

"Maybe," said Roy. He abruptly turned. "See you tomorrow."

"Hey!" said Edward, "Call her up – ask what happened – "

"Yeah," said Roy. "Catchya later."

He walked, head down, kicking at leaves.

Edward stood there, not knowing exactly what to do – knowing that both Vincent and Roy really liked Jan Matthew, but as far as Edward knew, she didn't really show much interest in anyone else except for Mark McCleary who, as near as Edward could tell, thought she did not exist.

When Vincent came over to see him that evening, Edward told him what Roy had said. He sat on Edward's bed and said, "Sure, I like Jan Matthew. So does everybody else. But if Roy didn't get an invite – I dunno. He should know she doesn't really care – but it sure is crappy, anyway." Vincent scratched his head.

"Well," said Edward, "if she doesn't invite Roy, I'm not going."

"But you don't particularly like her."

"Yeah."

"I do."

"Yeah. So you'll probably go?"

Vincent sighed and looked more gaunt, more grim, and more serious. "I don't know. It's really nutty that she'd invite you and me and not him. I know he likes her and I do, too. And I want to go real bad –" He shook his head. "I dunno." He sighed. "What time you want to get together to go trick or treating?"

"We can leave my place at seven-thirty," said Edward. "What are you going as?"

Vincent lay back on Edward's bed and put his hands behind his head. "I'll probably go as Clarabelle," he said. "Like always."

"Hey," said Edward. "Roy could go as Howdy Doody and I could go like Buffalo Bob!"

"Eh," said Vincent. "I dunno. I thought you always liked to go as some sort of monster."

"Wow," laughed Edward. "I could go as you!"

"Funny," said Vincent, smiling a little. "Funnee."

Then it was Halloween night. Edward dressed up as the Creature from the Black Lagoon – a Creature made of dyed burlap and a lot of imaginative sewing by Edward's mother who really couldn't understand why Edward would want to dress like that when there were so many other costumes and disguises that seemed equally good. Why didn't he choose a costume like Roy's, she wondered, a nice white cowboy outfit with a white hat and a black mask that required much less work?

Vincent showed up as Clarabelle.

And just as Clarabelle and the Lone Ranger probably wouldn't have much to say to each other, neither did Roy and Vincent, hiding behind the usual Halloween chatter. "What did you get?" – "Oh, Mr. McConnely always gives out apples." – "Wow, popcorn balls!"

And they talked about who was dressed as what. And they saw Mr. and Mrs. McDowell carrying a pumpkin, walking with four-year-old Lisa (a witch) and five-year-old Stanley (a ghost) and standing behind them as Lisa would say, "Twick-er-Tweat!" and hold out her bag and grin at the cascade of chewing gum, Butterfingers, cookies, and so on.

Oh, yes, oh, yes, it was a perfect Halloween evening, what with the clouds moving across the moon and Clarabelle and the Lone Ranger and the Creature from the Black Lagoon walking together in moonlight, then shadow, walking down a street of houses with fire-toothed pumpkins, fat and wonderfully baleful, sitting on porches, grinning out windows. Oh, yes, oh, yes, with bags fat with candy, goblins and witches and ghosts and spirits moving down and about the street and crossing it, and there was even a wind to move the trees and make the candlelight flutter and wave in pumpkin faces. And in this spooky pageantry, Clarabelle, the Lone Ranger, and the Creature moved and talked of everything except what really mattered. But when you're having fun, who talks of what matters?

And they were all trying very hard to have fun and yet Edward knew something was missing. Something had changed. Forever. Somehow things were not as fun as they should have been. Something was wrong. Something was gone.

And then it was time for Jan Matthew's party, and Vincent went. Alone.

After that, Roy and Edward didn't see too much of Vincent. The party was never brought up, the mystery never solved. But that night, Edward made a wish – and dreamed.

It was Halloween night and he, Vincent, and Roy were walking together down the street. But this time they weren't in costume – they just looked like they usually did – Roy with his crew cut and plaid shirt, Vincent gaunt as the Grim Reaper. They had their trick-or-treat bags with them and every house they went to they were greeted with exclamations of delight. The Johnsons said, "What wonderful costumes! Oh, how frightening! Oh, we're terribly frightened of you!" And each of them got a Milky Way candy bar.

The Elliots clapped their hands to see how Vincent and Edward and Roy were dressed. "Wonderful," they said, "excellent costumes!" They each got an apple and their choice of fresh taffy or Life-Savers.

Jack and Susan Thompson laughed. "Well, look at the adults! What perfect disguises! Here's a Coke for you, a Seven-Up for you, and a Nesbits for you."

With bags finally filled, the three friends stopped. They looked at each other. The wish was the same. So much to say, how do you begin? They stood there on that Halloween night, looking at each other – and did the only thing they could do.

Vincent tugged at a zipper in his scalp – and it continued to zip right down his face, neck, chest, crotch, and out stepped Clarabelle from the Vincent suit.

Roy did the same – and from the Roy suit, out stepped the Lone Ranger.

Edward did the same – and from the Edward suit, out stepped the Creature from the Black Lagoon. And, picking up their bags and costumes, Clarabelle, the Lone Ranger, and the Creature from the Black Lagoon stepped together from the moonlight – into the shadows.

Popcorn

JAMES, AT THE ripe old age of twenty-five, was absolutely convinced that he knew what his problems were, that they were manageable and that they were meager. He saw himself as handsome (tall, blonde, blue-eyed and muscular and healthy and so forth and so on), confident – ran a flower shop and was something of an explorer – two months in South America, three months wandering through Europe. He also knew he had an impulsive side which, for some incomprehensible reason, got him into trouble at times: okay, he wouldn't see Judy again; the hostile bitch didn't like the fact he was in bed with someone else when she dropped over unexpectedly – I mean, he thought, so what's the deal? I told her I might do that. God, women just want to bust your balls. What a hassle women are. I know she was in bed with someone else anyway – of course she denied it, but what do you expect? Women are like that. Or, when he bought that car that he really couldn't afford: so what's the deal? I deserve nice things. I deserve the best there is. I'll just put my landlord off and tell Jeremy that it'll be a few months more before I can pay back the thousand. He'll understand. And the business is going great; I'll make it all back before too long. Or, when Sally kept hassling him?

"I'm so angry at you I could scream!" she said, not too long ago.

"Oh God, here we go again."

"How do you think I felt at the party when you kept eyeing every woman? How do you think I felt?"

James looked at Sally. Beautiful woman, he thought, that long, blonde hair, those green eyes and what an ass and oh, those tits are yummy.

"Well," she said, "answer me!"

"Huh?" said James dreamily.

"You don't really give a shit, do you?"

"Well, of course I do."

"So why don't you answer my question?"

"What question?"

"Remember the party?"

"Yeah, so what?"

"Remember how you kept looking at the women there? It was like you were mentally undressing them."

"No harm in looking."

"But how do you think I felt?"

"I dunno."

"I felt hurt," she said. "I felt cheapened. I felt like you didn't care. I felt insulted."

Innocently, James shrugged his shoulders. "So?"

Sally shook her head. "So you don't really care how I feel. That's what you're saying."

"Of course I care how you feel."

"You don't sound like it."

"Maybe you're mistaken."

Sally just stared. "You son of a bitch. Somehow it's my problem and you don't have anything to do with it."

"Well," said James with much exasperation, "exactly what *is* your problem?"

Sally grabbed her coat, her purse and said, "I think my problem is you. Goodbye. You're not worth it."

She stomped out the door.

Jesus Christ, thought James, must be her period. If she has all those problems, then good riddance. Who needs her? Plenty of women in my life. He smiled to himself. One of the pleasures of owning a flower shop: all the beautiful snatch that walked in.

And so, James at age twenty-five, was well content with his world, except for, of course, some impulsiveness and women problems, but everyone has problems with women. You can't live with 'em and you can't live without 'em.

Now, we all have birthdays and James is no exception. On a hot summer day, James turned twenty-six. Customers stopped by to wish him well.

Little Johnny Mathews stopped by and presented him with a homemade card: on the outside, a crayon drawing image of James' flower shop. On it, the lettering spelled "May your business – " and James opened the card " – always flower."

"Aw," said James, "that's real neat. 'Blossom' would have been a better word though – "

Johnny wilted a bit.

"But it is certainly a nice card. Here." James gave Johnny a rose that he was going to throw away anyway. Johnny went away smiling.

Melinda Jackson, a real cute number from the local high school, dropped in. She was sixteen, had long brown hair, big brown eyes and a habit which James liked of leaning over the counter so her large but very covered breasts rested on the counter and of course, James knew without asking, that the look of innocence was anything but that. Most likely she was trying to get him in bed and then cry "rape." Yeah, thought James, I know your number, kiddo. But he was nice to her and admired her body because he knew that's what she wanted him to do, even though she tried to make conversation with him and tried to come across as though she actually liked him.

Others walked in, bought flowers, went on their way and James profited well that day and just a few minutes before closing (James was glad to be going home; God, it was a hot day: skinny dipping with Jenny in her pool was going to be fun and what they would most likely do later would be even more fun), an old man walked in. An old man, stooped, needing a shave, walked in. An old man, wearing a dark cap and a dark overcoat, walked in and with infinitely sad eyes said, in a voice heavy with ache, "You're James Clark."

Question? Statement? James wasn't sure. "We're closing now, sir. I'll be open tomorrow at eight."

The old man looked at James. He nodded. "Yes," he sighed. "You are James Clark."

"If you have some business – " began James, getting angry.

"Indeed I do," said the old man, reaching in his coat. "Indeed I do." He brought out a package and put it on the counter. "Happy Birthday," he whispered. He softly closed the door behind him.

James stood there, surrounded by roses, marigolds, orchids and ferns. James stood there, surrounded by lush greenery, immersed in fragrance, and looked at the brown wrapped package. A little nervous and angry, he ripped off the brown wrapper. Inside was a little baby food jar filled with –

"Popcorn!" grinned James. "Popcorn! Now how in the hell did that old buzzard know that my special love in the whole wide world was popcorn!"

Popcorn! He could eat bushels of it. He loved popcorn smothered in butter and rich in salt. He loved taverns where he could devour a bowl of it with his Budweiser. He was hopelessly addicted to popcorn. He looked at the bottle. Why so little, he wondered? Damn skinflint – this will only make a couple of bowls.

Eagerly, however, he left the shop, went to his apartment, put on a steak, played the stereo (loved the Stones) and hummed along with the music. "Under my thumb. . . ta-ta-te-ta-dum-de-dedum," brought out the popcorn popper, the butter, the salt, got out a beer and pulled long on it went to the balcony, set up the TV tray next to the lounge chair. He went back in, turned the steak over (oh, smelled *so* good) and then put on the popcorn and he hummed to the music, sucked on a beer and stared over the lake to the mountains beyond and was glad as hell for the eastern exposure.

By the time he finished the steak, the popcorn had finished popping. He got a bowl, filled it with popcorn, poured on salt and butter, and sat, soaking up the view, munching popcorn which turned out to be the best he'd ever had. "Maybe the old jerk will stop by tomorrow and I can find out where he got it. Christ. Where would an old fart like that find this stuff? Maybe he ripped it off from a Safeway."

Then he just sat there, listening to the Stones, drinking his beer –

And dreamed. He was walking in what appeared to be a vast arena. He knelt. Steel. It became warm to the touch. He was surrounded by brown, shiny objects about half his height. They're like huge popcorn kernels, he thought.

The floor became hotter, but for some reason, he didn't feel the heat through his shoes; it was nonetheless hot. He noticed something else; he was getting smaller and smaller and his clothes shed off him like skin, fell to the floor and burned. My God, he thought, what is happening to me? He looked down; his body hair had vanished and he guessed he was what, five or six?

Nearby, a kernel began to swell and suddenly exploded and the face of his mother lorded over him: "You little bastard," she screamed at him. "You little bastard! If it weren't for you, I could have left – "

"Mommy," whimpered James, "please don't, Mommy – I'll be good – "

"Just get out of my sight! God, why did I get married? You'll turn out just like your father, chasing after women, putting his God damn dick into everything that walks – "

"Mommy – " cried James, arms outstretched. "Please, Mommy – "

"Leave me alone."

Another kernel exploded nearby. The face of James's father looked down. He was drunk again. He looked at James blearily. "Jimmy boy."

"Daddy," said Jimmy, "Mommy doesn't love me."

James' father made a noise that was halfway between a sob and a laugh. "The old whore don't love nobody. She's what's all wrong in the marriage. Don't ever get married. Women just fuck you over. Hadn't been fer her, why I'd be a happy man – "

"Daddy," cried James miserably, "what'd I do wrong? Why does Mommy hate me? I'll be good."

His father laughed a bleary laugh. "Hey, c'mere and give your old man a hug – "

James did.

James' dad became angry. "You only did that 'cause I told ya to. Nah. You don't really love me. No one loves me. Shit – "

"But Daddy – "

"G'wan. Beat it."

Stumbling, James went on and another kernel exploded and his Aunt Mabel puffed high above him. "You're a wicked little boy. You're wicked. You are never to get angry at me. Nice boys don't have those feelings. If you ever want love, you can't be angry. Now because you spoke angry to me, I'm not going to say a word to you for the rest of the day. I'm really mad at you and you hurt my feelings and you're a bad little boy."

Another kernel went off then and Uncle Dwight glared down at James. "You be good. You be good or we'll send you back to your mother and father and God knows how much grief you've given them."

"But I didn't mean to – " sobbed James.

"You should go and tell your parents how much you love them. If it weren't for them, you wouldn't be here. You owe them a great deal."

Another kernel exploded; it was his Grandmother Lisa. Her kernel did not pop so high. She said to James, "Come here."

Fearfully, James did.

With two white and puffy arms, she held James and said, "I know you're miserable. And I'll try to have you spend the summers with me. Just think of all of this as a bad dream."

"I hate my mother. I hate everybody – "

"I know – because you've been hurt – before long, you'll be on your own. Try to forget all this. You'll be happy someday, and you won't remember any of this – "

James woke up with a start. Stunned and angry, he just sat in his lounge chair. Son of a bitch, he whispered. Fuck. What a weird dream. He shook his head. God damn it – that old geezer musta put some LSD in my popcorn. That son of a bitch – he shook his head again. Shit. What was all that bullshit? He began to think back on the dream, then got up and killed a quart of wine in minutes and fell asleep.

He awoke the next morning with a murderous hangover. He remembered little about the evening before. When he found himself beginning to think about it, he turned on the stereo. Loud. And he kept the music loud all the way to work.

He got to his shop fifteen minutes late; once there, he took some Tylenol and followed it by Alka-Seltzer.

A few minutes later, the door opened. And there stood the old man.

There stood a stooped old man in baggy black pants and heavy, dark and stained coat with the saddest eyes in the world.

"What the fuck do you want, you God damn wino?" sneered James.

The old man said nothing but walked toward the counter.

"I said, what do you want? You a pervert or what?" James backed away from the counter a few inches.

The old man looked at James. He shook his head sadly. "You learned nothing?" he asked. "You learned nothing at all?"

"I don't know what you're talking about."

"You learned nothing?"

"Do you want to buy something? IF you do, then buy it. If you don't, get out of my store. Seeing you in here is bad for my business."

The old man shook his head, tears welled up in his eyes and spilled over. He sniffed.

Oh, God, thought James. Just like a woman; gonna make me feel shitty with crying. Oh, Christ. Why me? Why this morning of all mornings? Oh, shit.

"Look," said James. "I've got work to do. I haven't got time to babysit lonely old men – I don't know what – "

The old man sighed heavily and fumbled with his coat, paying no attention to James. He pulled out a frame and fumbled with a stand on the back. Puzzled and somewhat mesmerized in spite of his anger, James watched. "Look," said the old man with infinite sadness, "for God's sake, look." He stood the frame on the counter, then turned it around. It was a mirror.

James looked. He saw himself and as he looked, he saw something curious happen: it was as though his shirt became invisible; then his skin became transparent, as did the musculature, and finally James saw his heart. Then he was looking into his heart and there was a scene of bleak, gray sky, dark denuded trees and a lightly falling snow.

Stunned, James looked up. The old man was gone. James looked in the mirror again and the old man was peering at him from the scene in his heart. "Now do you understand?" the old man whispered. "Now do you understand? God, it's *so* lonely in here." And the old man turned and walked away through the softly falling snow.

One Short Dreamtime Ago

I DO NOT recall if this was a dream or not and it really makes no difference. It all began when I moved into an apartment on the side of the city known for its clouds and endless nights. Now I can't say why I decided to move there, especially when the rest of the city had more moderating climates: the clean and most elegant buildings occupied the zone of Joy north of 52nd Street; the Love district was on the west side, of course, with the climate best suited for wonderful sunsets, tranquil evenings and low, delightful, ever warm, romantic buildings for lovers. But the other part of town, yes, I had to investigate that.

Mr. Emu was my landlord. Now he actually looked like his name—but that did not tip me off. Yes, he did look like an emu—big of body, thin of neck with bulging eyes and a nervous alertness. He took my check in his delicate, almost feathery hands and tried to smile.

"You look like you're from the wealthy sun belt," he said. "Land of high towers soaring into the rarefied air. Why do you come here to live? Everyone else tries to get into the romantic zone with the endless sunsets and everybody sighing all the time from love. Why are you here?"

I shrugged. "Life is experience. I want to experience this climate, this city."

"Ha," said Mr. Emu, blinking rapidly. "Ha. Everybody wants to move out of here. You move in; well, that's for you to decide why, I suppose." He stuffed the check in a pocket of his goose down gray suit. "I'm sure you'll find this place most interesting." He nodded quickly. "Yes. *Most* interesting."

Before I could say anything, Mr. Emu turned abruptly and left. I sat down on my wooden box filled with many editions and reprints of Dostoevsky's works and looked out the door. Through a break in the clouds, several moons could be seen in this phase or that. Not too many stars in this part of the city. The light was always like twilight. Then I wondered. Why did I move to this side of the city? Was the air too rarefied for me in the wealthy zone? Yes, it was a pleasure living so high and looking down on everything. And the sky was so wonderfully blue all the time and often when you looked down you could not see the rest of the city at all – just layers of fog, so we didn't really have to look at anything except the sky and think status quo conservative thoughts about this and that, and go around readjusting our mirrors. But one day looking out over the vast expanse of the city that, on that day, you really could see, I saw the dark side of the city, the dark clouds, and decided that I wanted to live there – what was it like? So, here I am, I thought, and I decided I was hungry then. From a dark blue paper sack, I pulled out a black orange and began to suck on its gray interior. At the door appeared a gentleman.

"Hiss," he said. "I'm Mr. Spider."

"Hello," I said. "I'd shake hands but I'm not sure which arm you use for greeting."

"Makes no difference," said Mr. Spider. "I weave my greetings elegantly and in many ways. What brings you to this area of the city?"

What little light there was in this area, particularly in the room, shone off Mr. Spider's many eyes.

"Got tired of living way up in the sky. Wanted to come down to earth – eventually want to make it to the romantic side of town."

"Ah," said Mr. Spider, "a searcher. Gotta know pain before you can really know love? Is that it?"

"I don't understand," I said, finishing my orange.

"Ah," said Mr. Spider. "The webs we weave. It all makes no difference, really. I must be going. I have dinner yet to drain and I'm supposed to entertain some widow tonight. If she doesn't gobble me down, I might be back . . . farewell."

"Goodbye," I said.

I wondered about all of this. Looking out the door, I saw a gray comet move across the sky and somewhere a sad tune played. Then clouds moved across the heavens again. And I wondered, yes, why did I move here? Idle curiosity or something else? What else? I looked about the room. The walls were done in black and gray imprints of hands and the sink, not working too well, had a spigot that sounded like someone snoring. I fished about in the dark blue bag and brought out a large, quite dark banana and as I ate it, a memory of dear sweet Arieal came back to me. "You're leaving?" she said vacantly, her gowns flowing like strands of cirrus. Her eyes were very blue and translucent and at times, I fancied I could look right in them and see the other side of her skull. We made love like little rabbits, but to really talk was somewhat exasperating since we never really had that much to say.

"Why are you moving?" she asked.

"I don't know," I said. "Time for a change."

"What?" she said.

"I just told you."

"Oh. I'm sorry. I was busy admiring my emptiness. Well, I hope you enjoy it down there." She smiled vacantly. "I can't believe we've been making love all these years and we still forget each other's names."

"Think nothing of it. It was fun in a vacuous sort of way."

"Yes," she said. "Well, I must be going. I must take some time to space out and look at the sky."

"Goodbye," I said.

I finished the banana and threw it at the ceiling where it adhered and turned into a stalactite. Apparently that is what other occupants did as well. Many hanging stalactites formed the ceiling.

I then decided, after putting the books of Dostoevsky on the table and deciding to do nothing about them, that I really should wander about this side of the city. I walked out, left the door open behind me, and was promptly assaulted by the smell of ammonia boiling up through cracks in the street. A man stood nearby, smiling. "Good evening," I said.

The man said nothing.

"It is evening?" I said. "I know regular seasons don't exist in this part of town. Nor does time actually – so I was just being civil. You know, trying to talk – "

The man pointed to a badge that, printed at the top, read, "Hello, my name is:" and in the space where there should have been a name, was a rectangular square. I looked and discovered I could look right through the man. And then he just drifted away and another man appeared – smiling – and the same thing happened.

"Spirits," said a familiar voice.

"Mr. Emu." I said. "I didn't know spirits were made of ammonia."

Mr. Emu shrugged. "Very earthly spirits, undecided about what they wanted to be and, having not decided, never became real – existential swamp gas, will-o'-the-wisps. Every name the same: Zero."

"Sad?" I said.

"No," said Mr. Emu matter-of-factly though nervously. "Just the way it is on this side of town."

The sky had cleared away once more – stars arranged themselves in a constellation which then promptly disbanded.

"Have you discovered exactly what you are looking for yet?" asked Mr. Emu.

"No," I said. "Any suggestions?"

"You could meet our mayor."

"Of the city?"

"Not the entire city. Just this part of it."

"I guess that'd be nice. What's his name?"

"You'll know when you meet him."

"Oh," I said, "this must be him now."

A dull black hearse pulled up and a figure in a dark, pinstriped suit got out.

He had no face. He wore a very nice top hat, black gloves, and looked very nice, but where his head was – nothing.

"Well," I said, "I'd like to talk to you, but offhand it seems that might be difficult to do."

As I suspected – no voice.

Mr. Emu nodded in an abrupt fashion. "Our mayor is a man of few words." He paused. "None, actually; however," said Mr. Emu, "that *is* our mayor."

The mayor went to the back of the hearse, opened it and motioned me to get in.

"Why?" I asked.

Mr. Emu looked faintly amused. "Well, in order to live in this part of town, there is a small ceremony you must go through."

"What?" I asked. "I didn't know of this."

Mr. Emu shook his head. "Every neighborhood has its customs: if you go live in the romantic section, it's customary to have a loud and rapidly beating heart and large pupils. To live in the sky, you always have to be rich and looking down your nose. To live in the Dance Zone you have to know three hundred sixty-five dances and dance on command before the Tap Dance Commission. Here, you have to – "

"Oh," I said. "I see. Well, I guess I got too much life in me right now to give *that* up – "

The mayor slammed the back of the hearse and got in and drove away.

"You'd best be moving on," said Mr. Emu, returning my rent check. "Are you going to take your stuff from the apartment?"

"No, I think not." I had noticed the dried out carcass of Mr. Spider was blocking the door to the apartment and I simply didn't want to hassle with anything. "Nope, Mr. Emu, I think I'll just be moseying on. Which way is out?"

Mr. Emu smiled. "Any way is out. Just start walking."

I shook Mr. Emu's down-soft hands, admiring the delicate bone structure and being careful. "You seemed so alive," I said.

"Thank you," said Mr. Emu. "I'll take that as a compliment."

"Goodbye," I said.

"Yes. And when you are ready, do return."

I waved. And walked. From the shadows there came a small child who took my hand. He looked up at me and in his face, stars, galaxies and I had a hunch that the part of town where we were heading to was going to be delightful indeed.

The Baker

SAM, THE BAKER, was well known in the city for his obvious skill and expertise when it came to pastry – in particular, rolls. His rolls were always well done. They were perfect in shape, rigidity, taste and class. No one ever questioned Sam's rolls. They were perfect.

Sam knew how well his rolls were done. And he did not step beyond his particular area of expertise. He was a proud individual; his clothes were white as flour, stiff as starch. He kept his shirt sleeves rolled up, but not beyond the elbow. On his left forearm, a small, heart-shaped tattoo. It reminded him that he was a good son and how much he loved his mother and respected his father and that was only right and the way it should be.

Sam was a large man. He was overweight, but not by much. He got the proper amount of exercise that the doctor recommended. He got enough sleep, ate the right foods, dressed well, washed his socks and worshipped God. He was a baker, and proud of that, and that he functioned so well in that capacity. And every day he looked in a mirror and admired himself; his large puffy face like gently risen dough and his cheeks, red as though lightly tinted by rose food coloring. The baker was a happy man and when he stretched he felt expansive as though he could reach from sea to shining sea.

He was proud of himself. He was a fine baker and could afford to use only the finest ingredients. And things were going well for the baker. He had many friends. He did business with only the best people in the city. Virtually every day, someone with a wide tie and diamond stick pin and a dark pin-striped suit would walk in and say, "Samuel, my good man, I'll take a dozen of the usual rolls. Not too spicy now. At my age, I cannot handle heartburn."

Sam agreed. "Why, of course," he would say, "I just got through baking a batch. They are still warm." And while he went over to the numerous racks in the shop to find the rolls, the very important person might sniff the air of the bakery. The person's eyes might water at nostalgic memories of mother's home cooking that the odors evoked. And the person would realize then how good a bakery it was; it was the best bakery in the world. It was Sam's Bakery, best of bakeries, and Sam would return (interrupting the rich man's fantasy) with a brown paper bag filled with rolls and the very important person would smile and nod and pay then say, "Thank you, Sam, for these wonderful rolls."

"And thank you," Sam might reply, "for being such a fine and genteel customer."

Good feeling would flow between the men and the very important person would leave and the baker might sit by the vast and whining ovens and think of the good feelings that his work could evoke in people. Then he might get philosophical and think, "Ah, what joy it is to take the common flour and turn it into delicacies for the stomach. What joy to take soft dough and mold it into rolls. How wonderful that is." Then he might sigh and get on with his work.

Before too long, Sam had such a business going that people were waiting in line to buy his pastry, in particular the rolls. While he was enjoying the business and the money, he knew that the work load was getting to be a little much for him. He needed three or four assistants, but the thought of paying out so much money to workers to help him out bothered him. He was mentioning the problem to a very rich banker one afternoon.

"You know what you need?" asked the banker.

Sam nodded. "I need someone to help me."

"Yes. You need a robot."

Sam spanked the top of the counter with his broad, flat hand and flour dust billowed up. "Of course! Of course!"

The banker continued. "We use many robots in my textile mills. And are they good! They require no maintenance. They are guaranteed a lifetime."

"Yes," said Sam, "that is just what I need! Where can I get one?"

"Well," said the banker, "I just happen to be a partner in a company that manufactures them. Due to the scarcity of some of the materials used in manufacture, the robots are rather expensive . . ." The banker then shook his head. "No, no, maybe you would do better to hire someone to work with you."

"No," said Sam, "the idea of a robot really sounds like what I need. The bad thing is that I may need more than one. There's an awful lot of work to be done here."

"No need to worry," said the banker, his diamond stick pin glittering like light off a spider's eyes, "one robot does the work of fifty men."

"I must have one," said the baker, "that's just all there is to it. I must have one."

The banker munched a roll and thought. "Tell you what. Make me a partner in your business and you can have a robot – free."

Sam thought. He clearly recognized he was in a fix – he needed help but couldn't possibly afford a robot. But what he could do was take the banker up on his proposal and when he, Sam, had made enough money, purchase the robot and buy back the banker's share. Sam nodded and smiled and he and the banker shook hands. In a week, a robot was delivered to the bakery.

Sam was delighted. It was a beautiful robot. It stood as tall as a man, had two arms that came out opposite of each other, half way up the cylindrical body. And from the bottom of the barrel-like body, two legs and feet. The light bulb shaped head had no features. The robot itself was dark gray in color. There were no instructions. Sam shrugged. He pointed to a sack of flour.

The head turned. Sam said, "Bring that sack to the table."

The robot did just that.

Sam nodded. At first slowly, then eagerly; yes, yes, this was going to be just fine.

Business boomed. Sam was overjoyed. Soon he had to expand his business to keep up with the demand. Not only could he afford to expand, but he had just about enough money to buy the robot. There were times, however, that Sam wondered about the robot. It was quiet. It did the work with efficiency, but it was quiet, so very, very quiet. Finally, one day the robot spoke. "Master," it said, "I need cleaning. Flour has filtered in through my joints. I need servicing."

At once Sam was irritated. "You aren't supposed to need servicing!"

"Master," the robot said, "that is true. However, the flour is causing damage and I must be modified for these unforeseen diff – "

Sam waved his hands. "Get back to work!"

To himself, Sam smiled. The robot was guaranteed for a lifetime against defects or breakdown. And in his mind he ran through a conversation he was sure he was going to have with the banker: "Mr. banker, you gave me a defective robot. It won't move. It doesn't work. You can have your robot back and I want my shares back." Sam smiled at his genius. A fair trade. Later, he would buy another – but modified – robot and be out only the cost of the robot, not the cost also of buying back the shares as well.

And Sam smiled again. He had a case. He could win. And he went home that night feeling good. He assumed that the robot would simply stop functioning. It did indeed stop functioning, but in doing so, it exploded. When Sam came to work the next day, the storeroom and work room was a place of strange fumes. Sacks of pure, white flour were ripped open by jagged metal. Into some sacks, black oil dripped off metal parts.

Sam was infuriated. He called the banker who came down immediately and wrung his hands, saying that he did not have any idea how this could have happened. Sam told him what he was going to do and the banker replied, "Well, I don't blame you, I don't blame you; we'll get this worked out . . ." The banker left and Sam began to clean up the mess, more irritated at the chaos and waste than actually losing the robot.

By mid-morning, Sam had most of the storeroom straightened up. He was fairly certain that the spoiled flour had been discarded, although he vaguely wondered about the effects of fumes and gas from the robot. But then, he could not very well dump all the flour and besides, cooking in the oven would most likely take care of any possible foreign substances which might be in that pure and white flour, and hence subvert the taste of his pastry and rolls.

At a very much reduced rate, Sam made more rolls. He really missed the help of the robot; he hoped things could be settled quickly with the banker. He could not afford to go on too long without the help of a robot.

Of course, business remained good, although the supply was certainly meager. Very important people with diamond stick pins and pearl necklaces waited in line for more of those wonderful pastries and rolls that Sam made. He had pretty well set aside the idea that the explosion of the robot had harmed or altered his ingredients. And that evening, when he finally closed down, he had actually managed to put a few pastries and rolls away for the morning. He was very tired and he fervently hoped something could be worked out with the banker in the morning. He could not go on like this. Just as he was walking out the door, he thought he heard something. It was a very faint and distant voice and what it said made Sam very uneasy: "Help! I'm trapped in a roll! I want out!"

Sam shook his head. He was tired, that was all; just very, *very* tired. He closed the door.

When he came to work the next day, there was a long line of people waiting for him. A general, face flushed with rage, shoved an open sack at Sam and demanded, "What the hell kind of rolls are you giving me! Just listen!"

Sam listened to his rolls which he had made the day before. "Well, frankly," said one roll, "I don't care what Brucie thinks. I think that mean old general is a cutie and I'd like to get him in bed!"

Another gentleman rushed forward and opened up his sack and said in a thick German accent, "Ach! These are not the rolls I want!"

Warily, Sam listened. "Id, Ego, Superego. Who gives a shit? I may play the role of psychiatrist, but I don't have to believe all that crap. All psychiatry can do is help you like yourself."

A housewife rushed forward. "And just look at what you sold me!"

Again Sam listened. This time, it was the voices of two girls. "I don't want to be a housewife-baby machine. I want a career! I got other things to do!"

A very distinguished gentleman, one of Sam's best customers, strode up, indignant, and opened up his sack. "Just listen to this tommy-rot!"

Sam did. "Yeah, my old man wanted me to take over this business, but fuck, man, I'm gonna join a commune!"

Sam waved the man away. He saw a tremulous old Negro who shyly opened up his bag. "Listen, baby, Negro is a white man's word. The word is Black, baby, *Black*. And we got as much right to what we want as any one else!"

Sam put his hand to his forehead and walked into the bakery. The crowd jeered and scolded and threatened him. They threw back the bags filled with rolls until there was a pyramid of brown paper sacks in the middle of the floor. God, he thought, oh God, how the rolls have changed. Now what do I do?

Soon after, he left and simply went home. And sometime during the night, the bakery was bombed. A fire resulted, but no fire engines responded because the fire department was also very unhappy with Sam's rolls. The bakery burned and burned and the fires spread and soon the entire city was engulfed in flames.

Sam watched the city burning. All night long, the city burned. By morning, all that remained were black concrete walls; the hard, charred bones of the city. And Sam, the baker, thought, "No bakery. Guess I'm no longer a baker." He suddenly felt chilled at the thought. "If I'm not a baker, what am I?" Panic seized him. He got up and began pacing. "Without pastry, without rolls, what is my life?" He swallowed. Then he looked around. The grass on which he was standing was very green. He stopped pacing. The distant mountains were blue and snow covered. He looked up. The sky was very blue and the sun was rising. He laughed. He felt his heart beat. He laughed again. He felt something in his pocket. He looked. A roll. He took a bit of it, then spit it out. It was stale and hard. Sam shook his head. He turned his back to the smoldering ruins, tossed the roll over his shoulder and, walking away, he whistled a tune that carried high and far in the clear and still morning air.

ALTAIR II

NOW YOU SEE it's like this: everybody's got their something that they just gotta show other people. Maybe it's a secret, maybe it's a record, maybe it's a picture . . . but everyone has got something that they just gotta show. And so it is with Edward when at age twelve, he discovers how to build a world. Yes, that's right, you heard me right, a world; a world made of a round balloon, covered with Elmer's Glue-All and torn newspaper, and glue and paper pushed and smoothed and ridged and valed then painted over into a world that is Edward's dream of what a world might look like way out there, circling some little star we always take for granted in the great night sky – yes, perhaps it's the fourth planet or maybe the third – little difference it really makes but Edward discovered how to make his dream planet something real and frankly down to earth and he did it right in his bedroom one rainy Saturday in March and his mother said, "Just what are you doing?"

And Edward said as he put on the last paint, "I've made me a world. I'm calling it 'Altair Two,'" and he wrote it out, smiling as he did, "The 'II' also means 'also.'"

His mother, she sort of looked for a minute and finally said, "Where did you get a name like that?"

And Edward, painting a sea a bit more blue, said, "Roy and I saw *Forbidden Planet* and that was the planet's name only in the movie it was called Altair Four." And scenes of the movie came to his mind though he still didn't really understand the part about "monsters from the Id."

And his mother sighed. "Well, don't forget you got other work to do – you hear? Have you done that book report?"

And Edward looked up, just a bit of disappointment in his face and said, "Nope. But I'll do it. I wanna finish this."

"Okay," his mother said, "are you ready for lunch?"

"Yes, ma'am," Edward said and he put the world on a pencil axis to finish drying and had a lunch of hamburger and soup and cantaloupe too and when he went back upstairs, Altair II was dry as the American Southwest and Edward sighed and simply said, "Neat," and then proceeded to admire his handiwork: in the southern half, was the great crescent of impact crater partially submerged by acrylic blue of deep blue sea. And along the equator, another land like two vast misshapen Italian boots dangling down from the north and it was a splendid world of water, rock, of crater pushing up a sprawl of land with two immense volcanoes there, high and white and at top and bottom of this world, polar ice gleamed and stretched and Edward went into a waking dream of climbing those high mountains there and looking out over lands brown and green, or imagining himself at a lake beneath the range of mountains that made the Andes look as low as the Adirondacks and Edward sighed and later that afternoon (after making sure the paint was really dry) he put the world into a paper bag and went out, yes, yes, to show his world and yes, the rain had ceased its tap dance and was that some blue sky that was showing through and maybe even a little sun that made drops of water on leaves dance like little transparent pearls? And into the afternoon, he took his world, first to Mr. Jackson who lived next door and who was out changing a tire on his car and having such a bad time of it but he still looked up and said to Edward, "Ho, how are you today? Edward, and how are you? Boy let me tell you, cars, they is a bitch but don't say I told you that to your mom, she might think I'm corruptin' you. Oh, why won't this damn lug come off?" Jackson was a burly man, with black-gray hair that was receding from his forehead like an army retreating from a front that was advancing from life's perplexions and he worked and said, "Boy if I ever thought I'd be where I am today – you know," and he looked up with his gray eyes, "when I was twenty-five, I was gonna have bucks galore – " he snorted, "so much for dreams." He tried to turn the tire iron again, "Oh, this friggin' car, please 'scuse my French." Then he looked up again. "Whatcha got in the bag?"

And proudly Edward brought out the world.

"Oh," said Jackson, "that's kinda nice. Buy it at the store up there? They get the damnedest things – "

"Made it," said Edward grinning wide.

"Really?" And Jackson maybe looked at it an inch closer as if somehow that might make a difference. "Huh," he said, "pretty good. Ain't you the clever one?" And after a few seconds more of measured interest, he turned again to the car and said, "Wish I had time for such things; dang, wish I did. Time goes fast when you're forty; be glad you got the time." Then sucking in breath, he finally stood up, then pushed on the tire iron with booted foot, and still nothing happened. Jackson sighed and leaned against the car and simply said, "Gawd, wish I were twenty-five I'd do it different all over again and this car would be in the garage and someone else would be doing this. Whatta mess."

Edward, smiling a little less, put the world back in the bag and simply said, "Just wanted to show you what I done."

"Yeah," said Jackson. "That's pretty good. Well, I got work to do. You tell your folks hello."

"Ok," said Edward, "bye for now."

And he went on his way and ran into Mrs. Coster coming up the street, pulling back behind her that vertical wire contraption in which she hauled her groceries from the local A & P. And she always dressed in a limp brown coat with dull brown buttons up the front and always a couple of frays dangling like strings from a kite and *rattlescrattelwattle* the cart, like some strange airy robot following her down the street; following this lady Mrs. Coster, who was maybe seventy with gray hair done in curls as fragile as thin spun silver and she looked out through glasses that had smudge marks near each side where seemingly she lifted them off and put them back on and she looked as meek as a dispirited mouse but she managed to smile just a bit and was in voice as wind sighing through a mausoleum, "Hello, Edward, I haven't seen you for a while," and *scrattlerattlewattle* went the cart containing a large brown bag filled with a big sack of sugar and prunes and marmalade and a big avocado of unripe hue plus a bag of pet food for her Siamese cat ("Muffy," who looked at you with two blue cross-eyed pools that looked into your soul and then beyond) and Edward said, "Look what I made – I just finished it this afternoon!"

And out of the bag came Altair II.

"Well isn't that nice."

"Yeah," said Edward, "I think it's neat."

"And this is what," said Mrs. Coster, "Africa? And I don't see Australia there." *Scrattlerattlewaddle.*

Edward frowned just a bit and said, "Oh, no, you got it wrong, this isn't supposed to be the earth. This is another planet around another star."

Scrattlerattlewaddle.

"It's not meant to be the earth at all."

"Oh, I see. How's your mother been these days? Did she get over her operation?"

Edward put the world back in its bag. "Yeah, she's fine."

"Well, that's good. You know I've known her for years. Oh, my! My husband and your father used to go fishing a long time ago. Oh, my, those were fun days. Yes, that was a long time ago." And she nodded, "Yes, time goes by very fast young man. It goes by so very fast. If we'd have stayed in Arizona like we should have – "

And Edward said, "You have a nice day now, Mrs. Coster."

"Oh, yes, I will, yes, I will."

"I'll tell mom you said hello."

"You do that dear, you do that now."

"Goodbye."

Scraddlerattelwaddle.

Edward went on and thought about going to see if Roy was at home, for Roy was his best friend and they liked doing things together and Edward thought sure he might like Altair II, and on the way, he ran into Sally Jean McKenzie who lived in this real nice home with the Cadillac out front and the yacht in the backyard that never seemed to make it into water very much, and there were always fights going on in that elegant and wondrous house and Edward went up to Sally Jean McKenzie, age sixteen and said, "Hey, you wanna see what I just did?"

Sally Jean, lovely girl with long brown hair, eyes as dark as endless hurt and with lips turned to a forever frown and sometimes sneer, looked and Edward smiled very wide as he pulled out his world and she looked and nodded just a bit.

"Ain't it neat?"

Sally said, "Uh, huh."

"See?" said Edward, "when this meteor hit, it made this ring and shoved all the land way, up there – "

Sally nodded just a bit and said, "Uh-huh."

"And these two volcanoes here, they're eighty thousand feet – "

Sally Jean nodded just a bit and said, "Uh-huh," and there came from her house, not far away, this yell, "You son of a bitch!" and *crash.*

Sally Jean just kept looking at the world Edward held in his hand and said, "Uh, huh," and nodded her head just a bit and *wham* "Get your hands off me you fucking pig!"

And Sally Jean she wandered onward, and nodded her head just a bit. And Edward sighed and put the world back in his bag and headed on up to Roy's place and Mr. Scrupner was in his yard getting ready to mow the lawn even though it was still wet and he was an older man, fifty-four, bald and wearing blue tee shirt and jeans and with a belly that looked like a sack of flour and he said, "Well, hello there Elton; how are you?"

"Great," said Edward, "but my name is Edward."

"Sorry, but what the heck, what's in a name?"

Edward paused, not knowing Mr. Scrupner all that well but he smiled and said anyway, "Can I show you what I just did?"

"Sure," said Scrupner, "Whatcha got?"

Edward brought out his world ah, slowly, like a magician pulling a rainbow from a hat. And he held Altair II as though it was a strange and wonderful fragile gem. "Whatcha think?"

Mr. Scrupner looked at it. "Well," he finally said, "whatever it is you did a real good job. It's not the earth now is it?" And he grabbed Altair II from Edward's hands and held it aloft, "No, don't look like it. Now this part here, that looks like Japan. That world war was really something; oh, them slanteyes were bastards to the end. I mean right to the end. Oh, we should have nuked them all. We should have invaded Russia too. Honest to God no wonder we're in the mess we're in. I should have stayed in Army intelligence, yes, that's what I should have done. Now this part, this looks like southern California here yes, that was a good time, why, I was manager of a restaurant chain but I didn't pick my employees right . . . caught one colored pulling change right out the register – well I didn't actually *see* him but someone said that he did, oh, you can't trust them at all – now Hitler, he was a bit extreme, but you know he did have some good ideas – "

"I have to go now," said Edward and he held up his hands ashamed and mortified that he had let Scrupner touch Altair II.

"Oh, certainly Elton, here you – oops!"

And in handling the world, Mr. Scrupner's hands slipped and Altair II fell through the air and *crack* split in half when it hit the concrete at Mr. Scrupner's feet. "Aw," he said, "God, I'm sorry about that." He bent over and picked up the pieces and placed them into Edward's still outstretched hands. "Next time make it tougher so people like me can't blow it up." He reached into his back pocket for his wallet and produced a dollar bill. "Here you go, Elton, buy yourself a sundae, it's on me."

But Edward just looked at the pieces of Altair II in his hands and without saying anything, just turned and walked on until he came to a park and sat on a bench and the tears splashed on the big blue seas and vast brown lands.

"Wow, what's that?"

Little Troy, perhaps age eight, stood there looking at the broken world in Edward's hands.

"It was Altair II," Edward said, "until Mr. Scrupner dropped it."

And little Troy continued to stare and he was always such a sight with hair always this way and that, and his eyes were that wonderful clear and honest blue like you find at dawn and he had on this cowboy shirt with pearl buttons except that the middle one was gone and he wore jeans with holes in the knees and black Keds tennis shoes and he looked at the world and said, "Aw, gee and you must be sad. What a neat world! Aw, gee, that's too bad."

Edward said not another word.

And Troy ran away but in a few minutes returned with six-year-old Mary Lynn, and nine-year-old Daniel Smith and they all had scotch tape, paper, crayons, glue – and they all helped Edward fix the broken world of Altair II.

ALTERNATE REALITY 578.5

I AM IN a bathtub and I look up to the blue tiled walls with the clouds floating in it and out from it, looking a bit like white shelf fungi that you find on trees in the Great Damp Northwest. I am in my clothes and my cat, Alleymanderous, is sitting on the side of the bathtub with a giant black tarantula in its mouth. I do not like this. The water is beginning to harden like it's Jell-o. I cannot move. I look up at Alleymanderous and I say, "Don't. Please don't."

In the background, Beethoven's *Eroica* is playing and when the music nears its crescendo, Alleymanderous drops the spider; it scrambles up my stomach, my chest, my chin, up to my nose then up to my eyes. I want to close my eyes but I cannot. "No!" I scream, "No! Please!" The tarantula comes closer and –

. . . darkness. I am aware that it is growing light again. This time I am aware that I am covered by sand. I look around. The sky is pink and everything is covered by a light frost. "Mars?" I whisper. What am I doing on Mars?

I also notice that my penis is exposed and I see a little point of light above. A minute later, a little spidery craft lands right near my penis. For a long minute, it is quiet, still. Then movement – a mechanical hand with a strange fixture at the end of it approaches my penis – to take a sample, I assume. I imagine the machine thinking, "Is it alive? Is there life in that strange, thick log?" I close my eyes. This is a dream. This just must be a dream. I want to wake up. Any minute I will wake up. I hope. And –

. . . darkness. The light. And I am sitting in the bathtub and am sitting in what appears to be red wine or strawberry juice or something. Alleymanderous sits on the edge of the tub with a book that has no title. He sits up like a rabbit and says, "Life is but a dream – "

I smile. " '. . . filled with sound and fury . . .' "

"Signifying everything," says Alleymanderous.

"Nothing," I reply.

" ' 'S tale told by idiots.' "

"Well," I finally say, "have it your way. Just what is this dream trying to say?"

"That this is life," says Alleymanderous.

"Is it?"

Alleymanderous nods. "The bathtub. The constancy."

"How do I wake up?" I ask.

But Alleymanderous turns the page and does not answer.

"Maybe all these dreams are incarnations," I say. "I have to go through all these life dreams until I come back to the dream that is reality. Is that it?"

"Out, out brief candle," says Alleymanderous.

"So what am I to do?" I ask.

Alleymanderous hands me a straw. "Eat, drink, and be merry."

Dumbly, I look at the straw, then bending forward, I drink and become drowsy, sleepy, and dimly hope that maybe next time . . . darkness.

. . . and slowly, the darkness becomes lighter and I finally realize that I am still in the bathtub and I feel a sense of relief – either I am still in the dream or I have awaken from the dream and am, in reality, in a bathtub where I must have fallen asleep. But I notice Alleymanderous dressed in flippers and an ingeniously designed face mask. Alleymanderous points with a paw to the water in my bathtub. I stare. "How'd the floor get tilted?" I ask, noticing that the water level dips down in the direction of Alleymanderous. Alleymanderous shakes his head and points up with his paw. High above, on what I thought was the wall, is an overflow. "What?" I say. "What? I'm in a bathtub in a bathtub?" Alleymanderous nods and manages to get the cleverly designed snorkel out of his mouth. "A bathtub in a bathtub, a dream within a dream. Boy, you can't help but get clean. Awesome, no?"

"No. No, not awesome at all. How do I waken from a dream and back to reality and not into another dream?"

Alleymanderous flips water up from outside the tub that I am in and says, "Some things are not known. Or knowable. Yet."

With dismay, I now indeed recognize the vastness of the tub that surrounds my tub. I even notice the bathtub ring high above. I vaguely wonder about the size of the creature that must bathe in this tub. Suddenly feeling very modest, I put my hand over my privates and say to Alleymanderous, "Aren't you concerned about any of this? How can you be so calm?"

"Because," says Alleymanderous, "it's not my dream. Besides," he adds, as if all of this makes perfect sense, "I'm not the one taking a bath although I don't mind snorkeling nor scuba diving."

"Then why the hell do you raise such a fit whenever I try to bathe you?"

"Simple," says Alleymanderous, "I can't stand baths." With that, he somehow manages to get the snorkel back in his mouth and flips over backwards into the water outside my tub. "Alleymanderous," I yell, "how do I get out of this?" But he doesn't answer and I close my eyes really tight, hoping that when I open them again, things will be different and when I do open them again, even though I don't notice any difference in physical sensation – I rejoice. I am not in the bathtub. I am outside of it, sitting in a chair reading a book and I rejoice. I look out the bathroom window and my heart freezes. Mars is impossibly huge in the sky. I look to the book I am reading. "Nope" is printed on the page. I flip the pages. "No," "Nyet," "Uh-uh," I read. I sigh. This does not look good. Then Alleymanderous walks in wearing Adidas running shoes, purple running shorts and a pale purple towel over his shoulders. He looks like he has been jogging with his fur wet and dripping and I don't think cats can sweat so I then assume he ran through a lawn sprinkler. I look at Alleymanderous. "Now what?" I say.

Alleymanderous looks up. "Care to join me in a fifty yard sprint?"

"This is insane," I say.

"Maybe it's life." Alleymanderous shrugs.

"Life is insane?"

"Life is a dream."

"Is dreaming insane?"

"Maybe it's life."

"This isn't helpful."

Alleymanderous takes off a front shoe and licks his paw. He then puts it back in the running shoe and yanks the Velcro strip over with his teeth and anchors it. "Interesting," he says, "how strangely logical dreams are. That you would even think of a detail like the Velcro strip to give credence to something like a cat wearing running shoes. Clever. Cunning."

"Diabolical," I say, "very diabolical."

"Oh," says Alleymanderous, "you don't know how diabolical it *truly* is."

Suddenly, and with great foreboding, I turn and look into the bathtub. There is a large version of myself, floating in the bathtub. On the head of that image, with one eye gone, withered, sucked out like an egg, sits the tarantula. "Get me out of here!" screams the version of myself. "Get this fucking dream over with! This is crazy!"

"I'm trying," I say, "I'm trying. I don't like this any more than you do, but it's like I can't get out of it. It's like I have to go through this damn thing to get past it!"

"Do something!" yells the me in the bathtub, "this is fucking *dreadful*!"

I look at Alleymanderous. "So what do I do?" I ask.

"Like I said," says Alleymanderous, toweling himself off, "fifty-yard dash?"

"Maybe we can dash out of this dream?"

"I don't know."

"I don't care what you do," says the me in the bathtub, "but for God's sake, do something before my visitor gets hungry again."

So I stand, take a step and –

. . . darkness. And slowly light returns and I am in another bathtub, but it is filled with steaming water. And that's good because the sky is real black, the stars are bright and there is a very bright point of light and I look around to a snowy landscape. Alleymanderous leaps up on the side of that bathtub. He is dressed in a space suit.

"Uh, you know," I say, "this doesn't look like Earth. Pluto, a moon of Uranus maybe, but not Earth."

Alleymanderous lifts his face visor. "True," he says, "away from the bathtub, the air is a mite thin."

"When does this end?" I say.

"Are you sure you want it to end? How do you know that, if it ends, it won't be worse than before? Maybe this dream is better than what your real life really is."

I shake my head. "I can't believe that my life is, in reality, any worse than what my life now appears to be. Besides, I have to be dreaming all of this . . . I just have to be."

"Oh?" says Alleymanderous.

"What do you know about all of this?" I say. "Do you dream?"

"Of chasing mice, yes."

"Doesn't help me much," I reply, sulking, looking around to the bleak landscape. "I just want to go back to where I was before."

Alleymanderous laughs. "Don't we all? Oh, don't we all? Oh, don't we all have memories of those good times?" And he laughs again and pulls his faceshield down, secures it, and with that, Alleymanderous leaps from the side of the bathtub and I watch him walk away – soon to vanish in the vast snows and unending silent shadows.

The Journey Of Mr. M.

MR. M. ON this fair day in the city of Es was in a hurry; he was late for work, he missed his bus, and he was harassed indeed. He jostled by people, his brown briefcase swinging this way and that, as he hurried through the streets of Es by the sea. And as he rushed, he heard bits of disembodied conversations, "Well, I don't care if he does get blue balls, I'm not ready, and that's the way it is – " and, "Yes, the new office tower can go right over there; fifty stories will provide ample vertical space," and "Mommee, momee, I haveta pee – " and oblivious, Mr. M. went hurrying on, with an "Excuse me," here and a "Pardon me," there, and he heard the toot of taxies and the rumble and grumble of a plane overhead, and all the while he was thinking, "Late, late, of all the days to be late, it has to be this day – and I have that report to give at nine o'clock and it's after eight now, oh, damn, why me – that bus was two minutes early that son of a bitch – " and he opened the door and stomped up the stairs only to abruptly realize – "Oh, damn, wrong door," and he turned to go back down the steps only to find – "God damn it – it's locked!" And he pushed, and he shoved, but the door was locked. "Oh, damn it!" he yelled, and very angry, he stomped up the stairs, and came to a landing, and another gray door. He opened it, and with exasperation said, "Another flight of stairs! Oh, Christ, just what I need." And he started up that flight of steps and came to yet another door – and opening that – "My God," he whispered, "why me? Another set of stairs – " And by the time he was at the eighth floor, he was beside himself. "This can't be happening to me," he whispered. "It just can't be happening to me. Please God, why me?" He looked at his watch: 8:05. He sighed again and unconsciously looked about; the door through which he had come was dark gray. The steps on which he sat were concrete gray. The walls were pale brown, the handrails a deeper brown and the light above was a bulb encased in a frosted cup; Mr. M. listened – quiet, quiet, so very quiet. *Snap-snap*; he opened his briefcase and looked at the title of the report that he was to give at nine o'clock: "Potential Gross Revenues Via Raising Car Insurance Rates Five Percent." And there was another report he had given last week, "Monies Saved by Discontinuing Discounts to Motorists Without Accidents." And there was a Snickers candy bar, a roll of Wintergreen Lifesavers, a blue tie from yesterday, some large paperclips, a Papermate pen (silver top, blue barrel) and a catalog from a sporting goods store. He sighed and closed his briefcase. Yes, he thought, yes that helps. I'm simply in the wrong building. The Peterson Building must just be right next door. He closed his eyes for a minute. Was there a tall building next to the Peterson Building? He thought and thought. He tried to remember, but for the life of him, he could not remember what was on either side of the building much less how high the buildings were. How could it be, he wondered, that I've worked in the same building for ten years and honest to God cannot remember what is on either side of the Peterson Building? He thought and he thought but it was impossible to remember – for all that he could recall, it might as well have been the Sahara on the left and the North Pole on the right. "Shit," he muttered, "damn, why did this have to happen to me!" He closed his briefcase; yes, yes, that did help. One thing he knew was that somewhere, there had to be a way out. And that no building in the city was over sixty stories. Even if the way out was at the top – "Okay, he said, "so be it, so be it. Maybe I am in the highest building – so it goes – " and he thought for a bit – at least fifty-two more flights to go. Somewhere there had to be a way out. Just to be sure, he turned and tried the door once more – it did not open. He sighed again, and began climbing the steps. He climbed. And he climbed. His rage and dismay at simply finding more stairs beyond the next door, was occasionally tempered by memories – the soothing memory of his wife, Alice, in their backyard the other day, grilling hamburgers over the outside grill; ah, the sweet smell of woodsmoke. His daughter, Shawn, thirty-five, coming over last week with her fifteen-year-old daughter, Ann. Yes, she just had her braces taken off and wasn't that a happy grin she had? Radiant! And that blond hair down to her neck, and all those freckles and she must have had the greenest eyes anywhere, *clickwhoosh* of door opening, *click*, closing, locking, and then there was the time they all went to that national park, what was that park – the boat ride and the mountains rising on each side like vertical wedges *clickwhooshclick* and was that the time and that his wife got ill as they drove down those winding roads that went down forever? *Clickwooshclick* and there was the time – yes, yes, he and his brother – yes, he was seventeen and his brother was twenty and they were going down the coast – yes, the west coast and it was four a.m. and they were on motorcycles and the moon was full and the waves of the ocean were silver and went forever *clickwhooshclick* oh, God, this is so bizarre – this is so incredibly bizarre, how many flights have I come? I must be nearing the top, I would have to be nearing some sort of way out – he glanced at his watch and it still read 8:05 and he kept going up those stairs, one flight after another, one door after another and then his mind just drifted and finally, he sat, *click-click*, opened his briefcase again, and took a bite of the Snickers and just closed his eyes, and he thought, "Somehow, some way, this just can't go on forever, it just can't." Then, leaning forward, he began weeping uncontrollably – "How," he thought, "how is this happening to me? How? If I hadn't missed that bus, if I hadn't been in a hurry, I would have been here on time and opened the right door . . . oh, God, this is so bizarre." He had a silly thought, these tears are not good for this gray suit, I know they will stain it, I just know it. He sighed again, took another bite of the Snickers bar and ate a Wintergreen. He took a deep breath, straightened his tie and said. "No building in the city of Es is over sixty stories, I know I must be near the top." He stood, picked up the briefcase, opened the door, *clickwhooshclickwhooshclickwhoosh-clickwooshclick* and after a time, he sat again and not even thinking, simply looked about him. He studied the door through which he had just come. He looked to the walls, the light burning, the brown handrails. He opened the briefcase, ate the rest of the candy bar, the Wintergreens, and then left his briefcase sitting there and then looked up to the next flight of stairs, the gray door and beyond that . . . beyond that . . . more stairs and how many beyond that? He looked at the briefcase. No point in taking that, he thought, I don't know where this is going, but I don't think I'll be needing that. Refreshed by the candy bar, he said, "Maybe it's all attitude; being upset won't help. I need to just relax, I need to just go on," and he laughed to himself, what choice is there? As he walked up the steps, a memory of when he was child came to him, a memory of playing in the grass, of being amazed at the color of it, of looking to the sun burning in the sky and seeing the world for the first time and how grand it was coming into it all, how beautiful, how terrifying, how strange and he laughed and shook his head; a long time ago, a long, long time ago. He opened the next door, and stopped. And gasped. Before him, a mighty galaxy spread its swirling arms across the sky and near by, suns burned and comets slashed the heavens, "Oh, God," whispered Mr. M., "Oh, holy God." Amazed and spellbound he looked about him and abruptly became aware of the door – closing behind him, pushing against him, pushing, pushing and for a brief moment Mr. M. closed his eyes, sobbed – and then the door closed and vanished forever – behind Mr. M.

The Little Black Box Of Brundool

IN THE MARKET square of the city of Pantyan on the planet Prandor, you can find just about anything to suit your fancy – be your fancy exotic, pleasureful, esoteric – or painful. But before you go to the market square, you had better know just what your fancy is because you might run into Brundool.

Brundool is neither cynic nor saint. From a distance, he looks like a rather tall, leathery male who is also bald, has a dark beard streaked with gray, and clear green eyes that have a very penetrating quality. He carries a satchel over his arm. In the satchel are fifteen to twenty glass cubes that he sells for 4.5 Imperiums apiece. The cubes are made on Opayknon – Brundool's home planet. The Opayknons are not particularly interested in how many of the boxes Brundool sells – they find the idea of achievement and profit pathological and alienating. What the Opayknons do find fascinating is self-acceptance and how it makes living become magic. So, in a sense, Opayknons – as well as Brundool – are magicians. And the little glass cubes, perhaps as big around as a human fist, with all edges held fast by gold-colored metal, are a trademark of their magic. And Brundool wanders about the square politely inquiring about a person's health and even politely asking if they might be interested in a little glass box. Usually, the question people ask is, "What do they do?"

Brundool answers, "They help one find peace with oneself through self knowledge." Some of the wiser species will eagerly pay. Many turn away with a look of profound discomfort like the last thing they want to do on Prandor is, oh, Gods, getting to know yourself. Perish the thought!

And so, one day Brundool is wandering about the market, looking at the vast displays of items, goods, materials from Prandor and other worlds as well. He goes to a booth and the seller is selling fruit. The seller is a blocky sort of Prandorian; a fellow with small, dark and sunken eyes and black hair. He has an abrupt, unpredictable quality about him as though he listens to what you have to say but has his mind also on something else; business at hand or unfinished business in his mind. Compulsively, he arranges the displays of fruit over and over again. He looks up to Brundool.

"Ha," he says, keeping still long enough to make contact with Brundool, "the magician; the carrier of magic in clear boxes." He smiles. "What great truths have you today?" With round and bright yellow Rantaya fruit, he begins to make a pyramid.

"The only truth I have today," murmurs Brundool, "is that you're willing to give less but charge more."

The seller doesn't pause. "Do you wish to buy something or not, Brundool?"

Brundool smiles. "No. My only wish is to make you uncomfortable."

"You're succeeding."

"Are you going to buy one of my cubes today? I'll even do as you do: charge more so that I can delude myself into thinking that more money means more self-worth."

The Prandorian stops what he is doing and bares his teeth. "There's no magic in what you do, Opayknon, only snideness and no, I don't want to buy a box."

"What *are* you selling?"

Brundool turns and sees a young man, perhaps just a short time into adulthood, standing next to him. He looks into the man's dark eyes and is almost overwhelmed by the pain. He realizes immediately that this person is one who should not have the box. Brundool smiles. "I sell nothing. Excuse me. I have to leave."

"What are you selling, mister!"

Brundool sighs. "For those who wish to explore themselves, I sell a way to do it. For those who fear themselves, I sell nothing."

Again, Brundool turns, tries to walk away but the man grabs him by the arm. "I want what you sell!"

"And I choose not to sell to you. If I were not concerned about you, I would sell-but it is not to your benefit and it would violate my – "

Before he can finish, the young man pushes Brundool. Brundool flails, his shoulder bag falls – the young man grabs it, takes a cube and throws the satchel down. Remarkably, none of the cubes break.

Someone shouts, "Get him!" and "Thief!" Some of the people begin to give chase but Brundool yells, "No! I will find him soon enough! No harm done." He gets to his feet, and dusts off his maroon suit.

The seller of the fruits is outraged and his cheek muscles are tight with anger. "But he must be stopped! Surely he will do harm to someone else! This must be reported!"

Again, Brundool waves his hand in irritation. "No, no, I tell you. He will not be harming anyone else. Believe me."

Reluctantly and muttering, the vendor goes back to his stall. Others drift away. One tall Prandorian boy with great, wide and dark eyes and dressed in the pale yellow robe of nobility, respectfully and somewhat fearfully hands Brnndool his satchel. Brundool shakes his head and ruffles the boy's hair. "You're a wise one." He reaches into his satchel and gives the boy a cube. "I think you'll use this correctly. May it help you stay gentle and wise."

"Ogra ta, magisi," murmurs the boy in his native language, "pa tonso magisi Opayknon ska." ("Thank you, magician, great is the magic of Opayknon.")

"Bru kra pa tonso skeel grutna," ("And great is the wisdom of nobility.") The boy grins and runs off with his treasure. So young and wise, thinks Brundool. How fortunate. He then makes his way through the crowds, through the warming morning, through the calls of sellers, buyers, past the booths full of goods and voice and flesh and movement and color and moods; he makes it to a small restaurant just on the outside of the market square. He sits at a table near the wall. The waiter, Nyan, comes over and places his hand on Brundool's shoulder, "Are you all right? I hear that you were assaulted and robbed."

Brundool smiles. "It's true. But I shall get the cube back soon enough." The waiter looks at Brundool with a very knowing look. "Oh," says the waiter, "one of those."

Brundool nods. "One of those," he shrugs. "Fortunate for me. Most unfortunate for him."

"Indeed," says Nyan. His round face expresses sadness; his gray eyes look down. "I take it you wish to watch the process and not be disturbed."

Brundool nods. "I would like some wine. I'll be here for a while – please seat no one at my table. I fear a most unhappy experience."

Nyan nods, leaves and returns with a glass of deep amber wine. "I'll make sure no one disturbs you, Brundool."

"Thank you."

Brundool sips the wine, then closes his eyes and searches for the presence of the cube; he flinches when he finds it and thinks, oh, yes, though I do not know where it is now, it is indeed performing well and there is event number one: his name is Joseph Granit. He is twenty-one E-years old, born on Mars, 2364. His mother and father constantly argue over him: Why did you get pregnant! This ruins everything. God damn you. Listen, buster, you son of a bitch, you wanted a child, I gave you one. Yeah, well I changed my mind, bitch. Is he really my son or were you making it with Sungren in the 'ponics room? Oh, God damn you, you macho prick! You whore! Son of a bitch! Just hit me one more time and I'll have the authority – Fuck you, cunt! I'm leaving!

A wee, small voice: I'm responsible for what happened between my parents. It's my fault.

Internally, Brundool sighs. Oh, fates, he thinks, do I want to see more? And yet, I have to. Only five more events and Joseph will be totally blocked from any escape. How can these truths set Joseph free? If only he hadn't taken the cube and suddenly Brundool gets new impressions. Ah, yes. Event number two.

At age four, Joseph Granit is taken to the hospital with severe burns. Joseph is barely conscious; he hears his mother saying, "He fell into a tub of hot water." Joseph wants to scream, "She threw me in!" The doctors, upon examining Joseph, find evidence of bruises, scars, cigarette burns. They hold Joseph at the hospital; the mother is detained under suspicion of child abuse, then sent to an evaluation/rehabilitation center. Joseph will never see or hear from her again. And once more, Brundool hears the small voice: What have I done to deserve this? Am I so awful for my mother to hate me? Pause. I must be.

Brundool opens his eyes and stares at the wine. Distantly he hears the crowd in the square; he catches Nyan looking concerned. Brundool looks down. I've seen this before, he thinks, I know how this will end and I try to be so careful – Brundool catches himself-no, no, I'll not feel guilty over this; I tried to stop Joseph; I cannot protect people against themselves. This man brought it on himself. The only thing I can do is find the man, the cube and help him make the best of a bad situation. Brundool takes another sip of wine, closes his eyes, opens his mind and there it is again, Joseph Granit, in a foster home somewhere on Mars. The mother, truly a kind and gentle person, a person with very large blue eyes and face, lined from many years of life, its sorrows, joys, and the people one involves oneself with while living. Her face shows concern, her eyes are sad. "Joseph," the mother says, "you've been with us for three years. We've done all we can do to try to be loving to you and hoping you'll be trusting of us – but it's not working. We are exhausted. We know what your behavior says: 'Stay away, stay away. I'm a bad person and I'll prove it to you.' The last fire you set was the last one; your father – my husband – will not walk again. No more, Joseph, no more." She draws Joseph to her and weeps. "I'm sorry, Joseph. Maybe some one else will help you learn to love and help you see that you are truly lovable. We have tried. I wish it could have been otherwise."

Brundool again hears Joseph: I knew they would reject me. I was almost trusting them. The fire is nothing – they would have rejected me anyway. The fire is just an excuse to get rid of me. No one loves me.

Brundool thinks to himself: well, that's number three. He drinks his wine. Someone laughs not far from him. The day is getting warmer. He raises his hand, Nyan deftly weaves through the crowded restaurant like an unimpeded impulse, like a surge of water flowing about, between obstacles. Brundool points to the empty glass. Nyan nods; when he returns, Brundool has already closed his eyes and yes, it is a courtroom scene. Behind the Justice a vast expanse of glass; an immense volcano rises in the distance. Brundool has to back away from the memory; it is particularly profound – either because it is a more recent trace or because it has had a particularly "hard" imprint. The memory is very clear and sharp and Brundool has the sense that he is actually *in* the courtroom. The Justice, a woman with small rolls of fat beneath her eyes which are profoundly sad but stern, leans over a desk, holding papers before her. Her hair is white and thick and she speaks in a low voice, a voice weighed with seriousness and regret. " . . . third foster home in three years, Joseph. Ten years old and caught stealing money from the people who live next to your foster parents; before that, it was stealing clothes from a store, and before *that* it was severely beating a child because the child wanted his soft drink back – because you took it from him."

Muffled sobbing. Brundool sees what he guesses to be the foster parents in the room, sitting in chairs not far from the Justice. The woman is in her forties; her hair still dark. She wears a blue velvet-like robe with a bright yellow sash. The husband sits, his arm around his wife; he looks very much offended and angry; the muscles in the neck are tight, his face is red. His gray eyes radiate contempt for Joseph.

"Do you have anything to say, Joseph?" asks the Justice. "Anything to say at all?"

Joseph looks about the room. Then he sullenly looks to the floor.

The Justice drops the papers to the desk and folds her hands. "I'm well familiar with your case," she says, "I know the medical records. I know how much you must hurt. But can't you – but don't you understand that people are trying to care for you – are you going to try to hurt everyone for the rest of your life – because you've been hurt – "

Joseph looks up. The Justice simply stares, then pales and draws back. She shakes her head. "I understand that look very well, Joseph. And it hurts." The Justice looks down to her desk. "I have no choice but to send you for three years detention at the Kressal Institute on Prandor. After you are released from there, you will be on a four year probation." The Justice looks at her hands. "I don't want to send you there, but clearly you cannot be in the community here-you need help beyond what we have here – and the Kressal Institute is well known for –" Without warning, Joseph Granit screams and leaps to the desk. Two guards rush over and tackle Joseph before he can make contact.

Brundool puts his hands to his eyes. Oh, Gods, he thinks, that these things happen. How is it possible for such a small human being to carry such immense, endless darkness so devoid of any positive substance, any nuclei about which hope may condense, ignite, burn? How is it possible that, even when memories of pain are replaced with kindness and loving, still the pain persists, like an immense pit in the universe which takes all galaxies, stars, planets and funnels then, atomizes them and empties them into even a darker universe?

Brundool holds the wine in his hands. It is very dark, very lovely. To give love to Joseph, he thinks, would be the same as pouring this wine on the ground.

Nyan comes over. "Are you all right, Brundool? How goes it?"

Brundool slumps in his chair. "It is sad, my friend. Very sad."

"Are you finished?"

"Almost," says Brundool. "It won't be long. Our friend is up to four. Two more. Then I shall seek him. It will be easy then."

"It always is, isn't it?" asked Nyan.

Brundool smiles. "Most certainly. That is the nice thing about selling my wares; it can liberate and, thankfully, it can do the opposite. And when that happens, location is indeed easy."

"This one looks particularly hard on you."

Brundool nods. "From a moral standpoint than an empathetic one-I can distance myself as all this hits our friend – but once it hits – then I have to do something. And *that* is not always easy." He then makes a gesture with his hand; palm facing down, then up – a signal that the *way* of this moment is to proceed as before the interruption; please be not offended, for it must be done. Nyan nods. "By all means," he says. He gets up to look for empty glasses, empty plates and searching looks that ask, "Service, please."

Brundool sips the wine, folds his hands across his stomach and, yes, here's number five. It is a meeting room; there is the administrator of the Kressal Institute, Dru Tloros. He stands before Joseph Granit. Dru has a blank expression, neither punishing, nor judging. Just matter-of-fact. "Joseph Granit, you have been with us for two Earth years. During those years, your behavior has improved only slightly. And today, while on guarded pass, you attempted escape. What do you feel should be the consequences?"

Joseph, dressed in the red uniform of Inpatient of Kressal, looks stiffly at Dru Tloros. "Set me free. I cannot benefit from this place."

Dru listens; his gray eyes focus on Joseph in a very penetrating way. "We have been through this before, Joseph. It is not that you cannot benefit, it is that you *will* not. You have us in a peculiar position; we try to help, you reject us; we do nothing and you do something that forces us to respond-inevitably, you try to set us up to punish you – "

"You've told me," says Joseph.

"Many times," comes the reply, "many times." Dru puts his hands behind his back. "Joseph, if you had your way, how would things be for you?"

"I'd be free."

Dru smiles. "How can we set you free when not even the people who work with you can really trust you?"

Joseph shrugs. "I don't trust them, they don't trust me. So what's the difference?"

Dru Tloros crosses his arms and regards Joseph. "For one so young, you are clever. You consistently generate rage, get punished which feeds right back into your rage. Do you think any community anywhere would feel comfortable with you out free and roaming about?"

"You're supposed to cure me," says Joseph.

"Cure only comes with cooperation, Joseph, you know that. I consider you ill and dangerous."

"You've told me that before, too," says Joseph.

"I hereby order you to remain here, in detention, for three more Earth years. And I will keep you here, by the power invested in me by the Kressal Institute and by the Government of the Territory of Sur Tasslanska; when you decide to cooperate, that will change things. Until then, you remain here."

Joseph glowers. He is a strong boy now, tall, with sandy colored hair and bright, malicious blue eyes and sly demeanor. "Go ahead," he mutters, "try to lock me away forever. See what I care. I'll just keep escaping until I get away – for good."

Dru Tloros simply shrugs. "You have no idea, apparently, what you continue to do to yourself."

Joseph sneers.

"You may go back to your quarters," says Dru Tloros.

Joseph turns and exits out a side door. Brundool watches this and thinks, one more, all he needs is one more and at his age – so young – there are many, many more. Brundool keeps his mind open. Another scene focuses. Dru Tloros again. Joseph stands with guards on either side of him, holding his arms. Joseph is dirty, disheveled. Dru Tloros sits at a desk; his look remains impassive though Brundool senses a resignation. Finally Dru speaks. "You escaped and managed to elude us for several days."

Joseph says nothing. But Brundool picks up the constant, never ending hate, hate, hate.

"You also tried escaping some time ago."

Joseph does not reply.

Dru Tloros leans forward. He puts his hands out in front of himself and examines his hands as he talks. He does not look directly at Joseph. "I am suspending *all* privileges. You will be escorted at *all* times."

Joseph's hands clench. "I knew you would do that."

Dru Tloros sighs. "You did it to yourself. Perhaps someday you might see the connection between your behavior and the consequences of it. Perhaps someday you'll stop using people to punish you. Perhaps someday you'll understand. But I see that that day will be a long time from now." Dru stands and gestures with his hands. "Take him away."

Joseph spits at Dru. Dru Tloros walks away as though nothing has happened.

But to Brundool, listening and watching, something has indeed happened. He nods and sips his wine. "Number six," he says quietly to himself. He puts the wine down and waits. And in seconds it hits: a scream, a piercing, howling scream fills his mind; Brundool grips the table and tries to distance himself. His mind fills with images; a flood of pain, pain, pain – a rape, battery, violence, violence, escape, beatings, hot, intense, searing rage, rage, rage, medication, attempts at mind-transference with a Clomobian to try to yank from Joseph the root of the sickness but the root has grown so deep for so long that it has fused with Joseph's identity: *feel* bad, *am* bad, *been* hurt, *must* hurt, *will* hurt back, *feel* guilty, *am* guilty, *feel* worthless, *am* worthless, *need* punishment, *must* be punished, *hate* self, others *hate* me and more escapes, attempted arson, child abuse, assault and on and on and on and interspersed with screaming, a tortured, mindless insect rage, rage, rage that never stops, *I hurt, must hurt back,* and on and on and Brandon struggles to his feet and puts his hands on the table and stares ahead; patrons turn to see him; they look startled; some begin to stand to help him, but he shakes his head, no, no, it's all right, I can control this.

Nyan comes over. "You are ill, Brundool. Let me find a physician."

"No," Brundool whispers, "no, the only thing that needs finding is that box, and I know where it is now. All I have to do is follow the screaming I hear in my mind." Brundool stands erect.

"Are you . . . " asks Nyan.

"Thank you, but I am all right." He moves from the table, through curious upturned faces, through the market plaza, through town. The screaming intensifies; it takes all his energy to keep enough emotional distance so that he is not overwhelmed by it. He walks, perhaps five kilometers down an ancient, well used road. The screaming is constant in his mind now; he grits his teeth with the effort of keeping enough control of the screaming so that *he* doesn't lose control. He begins to slow his pace; fields of bright, red flowers wave in gentle wind on both sides of the road. Brundool stops. The screaming, the howl is maximum; somewhere nearby . . . he takes a few steps, looks this way, that way – there. An area not too far away – all the flowers, grasses, bushes trampled, as though something had thrashed about, rolling, clawing at the earth. Brundool looks and for an instant, the scene has an abstract, a transparent quality, a sense of depth and reality as though a film of something had been pulled away, as though time had abruptly focused on the moment. Everything is incredibly and brutally real and honest and present. And though Brundool hears only the wind, his mind, however, is filled with images and screaming and howling. "All right," Brundool says to himself, "all right." He walks to the trampled, flattened area. Right in the middle of it – the little glass box. And it is filled with blackness. Brundool lifts it and is not surprised at its weight. He holds it up to the brighter of the two suns, but no light shines through. Brundool sits on the ground with the box in his lap. He closes his eyes and with all his will, pushes, pushes and pushes the screaming, the images from his mind, out, out, back, back into the box and with his mind seals the cube over and over again, making sure that *nothing* escapes, not even a whisper.

The cube grows steadily heavier. Brundool shakes his head, glad to be freed of the pain; he sighs from relief, then looks at the box in his lap. "Joseph Granit," he says, "I don't know if you can put your misery aside long enough to hear it, but I'm going to try to say something to you. What has happened to you was inevitable – that, at some point, you would run into yourself and not escape – and that has happened. This cube has not sealed you off from the world, you have done that and the cube has merely shown to you just *how* you have done that. And you have sealed yourself off so well in the name of your protection that there is utterly no hope of you ever being reached. What everyone has been trying to teach you is as strange to you as you are to me."

Brundool stops. Is Joseph understanding this at all? he wonders. How do you help someone understand something if they've never been exposed to it? If someone has only seen black, how do you tell them about color? Or worse, how do you get to someone who doesn't even want to know?

Brundool shakes his head at the cube. "All everyone wanted to do was love you, Joseph Granit. That's all. And how many times have you heard this?" Again, Brundool falls silent. He looks to the flowers around him, then to the sky, the suns, and he feels the wind blowing. How is it, he wonders, that there are those who do not find living magic? How is it so? He then looks back down to the trampled area, the crushed flowers, the scarred earth. How is it so, he wonders. The cube continues to grow heavier. "I'm called a magician, Joseph," says Brundool, "yet, there is some magic that even I can't perform. The desire, the motivation to change is wondrous magic, but it's a magic that *only* exists if *you* believe it exists within you. Ah, Joseph, how I wish you had that magic." Brundool sighs and places the cube back on the trampled earth. "And yet," muses Brundool, "there is a place for you, too, for I've run into this before. In spite of your obvious misery, you, as well as everything else, do have purpose and function and I'm going to send you to a place where you'll do the most good."

From his satchel, he brings out another cube and, instead of using it to project his fantasies to the inside of the cube, he turns it in a way that it becomes a device for mind-linking. Once done, the message to his home planet is simple: friends, I have a cube that must be placed elsewhere where it will do no harm. I need your energy to do this. A pause. Then Brundool feels a gentle warmth of agreement, support.

An instant later, the cube which contains Joseph Granit, in spite of its immense weight, lifts as though made of paper. "Good-bye, Joseph; like it or not, you are to have a job that you will perform well; like it or not, you will have a responsible position where you will perform in line with your talents. Farewell and good luck."

The cube rises slowly, then faster, faster and – *bink* – is gone from sight.

It is several days later. Again, Brundool sits at a table; Nyan brings him his favorite wine. Brundool watches the people around him, watches the people in the square, buying, bartering. Idly, he listens to a conversation held by a couple of obviously well-learned gentlemen at the table next to his. They talk of a phenomenon that many have talked of for the last several days: off in a remote part of the galaxy, where no stars exist, routine scans by instrumentation indicate that something – with the characteristics of a black hole-has abruptly come into being. How strange! How odd!

Brundool sighs, sips his wine, and looks away.

OH, THEM DANCING SHOES

YOU KNOW HOW it is, oh, you know how it is when you gotta have something so damn bad that you'll do just about anything to get it 'cause you know how it is, oh, sure you do: that red coat you just gotta have. It doesn't make any difference really what it is: a car, a boat, a Coca-Cola float – all you know is that right then and there, for whatever reason, whatever care, you just have to – you just gotta have what you gotta have right then and there and no bones about it no way.

So it was one day when slim and slender Jackie Hutton, age thirteen and a half with the curliest red hair and the most awesome bunch of freckles in the whole seventh grade class of Morgan Junior High School, saw them ankle-high, zipper-up-the-side, shiny black boots in the neighborhood Thom McAn store.

Oh, my God, his eyes went wide and yes, indeed, in his size! And he looked in his wallet – seven dollars and fifty-three cents plus a fifty cent bus pass and Vickie Herman's phone number which, while not translatable to hard currency, sure the heck was valuable anyway.

Jackie Hutton, trying to look calm and composed but with thumping heart, went up to a tall and somewhat bored-looking salesman in a dull brown coat and dull black tie and with dull dark eyes. He looked at Jackie Hutton like he was looking over a cliff at something mildly interesting a billion billion feet below. "Yes," he said distantly.

"Uh," gulped Jackie Hutton, "um – those boots in the window, on display – "

"Which boots?" said the salesman looking even more bored.

"The black ones with the zipper up the sides."

The salesman looked mildly amused which made Jackie Hutton look even more determined which simply made the salesman more amused. "What *about* those black boots with the zipper up the sides?" A little smile slithered like a viper across his thin little lips.

"How much are they?" asked Jackie, absolutely sure that he had enough money and could probably buy a strawberry sundae at the Newberry's with the money he'd have left over.

The salesman smiled like this was the most wonderful fun he had had in a good long time, perhaps, maybe, even his life.

"Those boots," he said, readying his tongue and lips for the strike, "are forty-two fifty."

Jackie Hutton swallowed, managed to say, "Oh."

The salesman, not satisfied with one strike, had fun with another. "A bit out of your price range?" Ah, the smile of satisfaction, of knowing how deep those fangs went and how much poison from one's own deep well one can extract to inject/infect another.

But Jackie was smart and, feeling the poison, decided not to give the salesman the satisfaction of struggle against obvious defeat. Instead, he smiled and said, "Thank you."

The salesman, having the fun of the day and knowing that the dullness in his own eyes had, at least temporarily, gone away, said, "Shall I put them aside for you?"

Jackie smiled. "Yes, please do."

"The name?"

"Jackie. Jackie Hutton."

"Very good. And when will you pick them up?"

"In two days."

"Very well." Slowly the dullness returned to his eyes and he was vaguely disturbed and surprised that this little befreckled jerk played the game better than he. For he knew it was just a game and he certainly had no intention of putting the shoes aside. No, not at all. No way could this kid, Jackie Hutton, no matter how thrifty, possibly come up with forty-two dollars, forty-two fifty to be exact. The salesman had his last strike for the day and Jackie, he left and walked on toward home.

Those boots, he thought, those boots. Gotta, just gotta have those black boots. And the school dance next Friday and Vickie Herman, yes, she'd be there and she'd think him so cool with those new boots.

He stopped at the Newberry's anyway and ordered a strawberry sundae and simply thought – what was he to do? What could he do? And he had to pick up those boots in just two days. Two days! What was he to do? He savored the sundae and simply thought – forty-two fifty – how can I – forty-two fifty . . . maybe Mom –

When he got home, Mom simply said, "I know how much you'd like those boots, but forty-two fifty – " and she shook her head, "that's one week of groceries and Lord knows where that goes – and don't forget that the money you have – your allowance – has to last you for another week."

"Yes'm," said Jackie, looking down at the floor and inside feeling like things were suddenly bleak.

"You know," his mother then said, in her gentle way, "those oxfords you have – if they were polished, they – "

But Jackie just sighed. "But they aren't the boots. They aren't ankle high and no zipper up the sides and they aren't shiny and new – "

"Well," his mother replied, "can't say I didn't try. Don't forget that dinner is in another hour now – "

Jackie just nodded and went out the door to take a walk and you know how it goes when you want something so bad – sometimes things happen that you'd never expect and it was just like Jackie's feet knew where to go and before he knew it, he was in front of a store, on the window of which read, "Shoes." That was all, simply "Shoes." And what was in the window? A black pair of boots, just ankle high with zippers up the sides and Jackie gulped. Even if they were used, they were probably still too much, but you never know – you just never know – and he went inside and an old gentleman with a thin face, white hair and very pale eyes glanced up from where he was sitting and smiled and said, "You'd like those boots."

Jackie, surprised, simply nodded, but then sighed and said, "But I've only got six-fifty and those boots sell at the Thom McAn store for thirty-five more – my allowance has to last clear into next week – " and he stopped and again sighed.

The old man laughed and sat back in the chair. "Uh-huh," he said. "And I just bet there's a dance next week and a young lady there who you'd love to impress."

Jackie turned a little red and his freckles did not stand out as much, but he nodded.

The gentleman got up and said, "Those boots, ah, those are special to me – I danced in those boots – yes, those very same ones and though they look new, like just today made – ah, but they're old – oh, yes, very old and so very special – "

"Well," said Jackie, "if they are so special, they're probably more than I'll ever have – "

"Let me finish," said the man, "so special they are – so special to me – that anyone who wants them so badly – you may have them – for free."

Jackie opened his mouth once, closed it, opened it again and closed it again and was finally able to whisper, "F-free? Why free?"

"You're objecting?"

"No – no, oh, not at all – but – but free?"

"Free."

"For me?"

"For you."

"Free?"

"Free."

"Why me?"

"Stop asking so much of divine intervention. Just put them on – and I warn you – they are special – are you willing to treat them nicely?"

"Oh, yes, yes, indeed yes."

"Polish them up every day?"

"Oh, yes, certainly yes."

"Wear them only on bright sunny days so the sunlight will sparkle and starburst in the polish?"

"Oh, yes," Jackie said, grinning and nodding and hoping and praying that yes, this was as it seemed and was as it looked and was no joke. But the man appeared to be very sincere and his blue eyes were honest as the blue sky of dawn and the man smiled and simply said, "You'll like these boots. You'll like them very much." He went over to the display case and picked out the boots. "Yes," he said, "sometimes it's amazing what a good pair of shoes can do; opens up possibilities that you've never seen; takes you places where you've never been – " and he looked at Jackie and smiled, "but need to go."

Jackie smiled and nodded and right then and there, put on the boots and zip-zip – up the zippers went and they looked just grand! "So comfortable – yes, so comfortable they are – are you sure – ?"

The man shook his head no. He then said, "Begone now. I've got to close shop – enjoy your shoes."

"Well," said Jackie, "thank you again."

He waved as he walked out the door and, in one hand, in a paper bag, carried his old oxfords and he began walking and as he walked, he felt like he was riding the wave, dancing the crest of good fortune – yes, yes, it is true, he thought, when you really want something, it has a way – and abruptly his thoughts stopped. He had meant to cross the street, but it was as though his feet had something else in mind. He tried to stop, but his feet kept going.

He walked and it seemed that he walked for hours, then days, but when he looked at his watch, not all that much time passed – until he looked again – his watch had stopped and still he kept walking; he walked out of the city, he walked out of the country, he walked and he walked – he walked to the horizon – and then walked beyond, walked past a sunset, and walked through a dawn and walked until stars thinned and then *they* were gone and still he walked on and finally, from being alone and scared and dismayed, he wept and wiped his eyes on his sleeves yet still he walked and walked – how much time?

A thought came to mind – he'd be late for dinner – but then, since his watch had stopped – maybe just a few seconds had passed – maybe time was going backwards – maybe there was no time at all – maybe all this was timeless – timeless? He thought, timeless? And as if at some sort of cue, he saw something distant and as he drew near –

"A tree!" he whispered, "an immense tree!" And then his pace slowed. And then, before the tree, he stopped. "Oh," he said, "but such a tree!"

It was like an immense apple tree, but without leaves and the apples gave off such a soft glow. By intuition? By instinct? He touched a near fruit. The glow resolved and Jackie looked upon a scene inside – of a dinosaur slopping about some ancient swamp. He touched another fruit; inside was a view of what Jackie guessed to be Earth – but molten and hot with a moon rising near. Another apple and Jackie looked upon pyramids being built. Yet another fruit and two spiders scrambled in an intricate web. Another fruit: an atom bomb flashing. Another fruit: a man and woman making love. Yet another fruit and the scene of a majestic mountain range.

Jackie touched fruit upon fruit and was spellbound by all that he saw; world upon world yet all of one world; life upon life but all of one life. History upon history – but all of one history – and then something curious. He touched one apple – and there was an image of a boy who looked very much like Jackie Hutton, only the background was caves and tropical rain forest. Another apple showed but another close image and this time – Eskimo. Another apple and the boy looked Aztec and finally one apple and Jackie Hutton looked upon Jackie Hutton staring back with the same intent gaze as the others.

Jackie then stood back and realized that all that he'd touched was a very small part of what was a very immense tree that towered over him and seemingly reached to the heavens, and he stood back and was amazed, overwhelmed, but then strangely at peace and he did not know quite why.

Then he began dancing, dancing about the tree, touching apple after apple, and then he was grinning and laughing and shouting as he danced about that tree and then he knowingly touched another apple – there was a brilliant flash – and when he opened his eyes, before him was an empty lot, grass and broken bricks between two buildings. His boots, those wonderful, special boots by themselves, went *zip-zip*. Gently, gently, Jackie Hutton stepped out of them, put on his old oxfords and – by intuition? By instinct? He stepped back and flash!

When the light faded, the shop with the window that read "Shoes" on the front had reappeared in the lot and in the front window, those boots, those boots, those wonderful, wonderful boots, and Jackie smiled and simply said, "Somehow these shoes I now have are quite good enough," and he let out a long contented sigh. "What's important here – " and he laughed at the thought of finishing what he had to say; he simply began walking toward home at a most leisurely pace, loving the sunlight so warm on his face.

Gift Of The Rings

WE'VE ALL HAD days like that, ah, yes, where the morning air feels as magic as a dream and the sun burns bright like brilliant hope in a sky serene and endless blue and yes, yes! It was this day, this dream of perfection summery day that Edward perhaps age twelve finished his breakfast and then yelling "Bye!" to his mother was on his way to explore that ah, yes! excellent day and stepping outside, he looked up to that elegant statement of sky and remembered a picture he saw in a book – a picture painted as though standing on silent snowscaped surface of Saturn's moon Titan with Saturn as crescent with rings seen edgewise in a blue black sky and Edward thought, God, wouldn't Saturn be neat to see in this sky? Wow! And then Edward, he looked around and thought, what'll I do today? Go see Roy? Maybe a movie? And so wondering this and pondering that and thinking about that silver crescent of a ringed planet he went to the back yard to find his bike and who should he meet on this journey into the day but the neighbor, Mrs. Grildy, who was working her garden and touching each plant with loving caress. She looked up and said, "Ah, good morning, my good friend, out to explore this day, I see."

Edward nodded, as he begin to climb on his bike, and Mrs. Grildy pointed to a flower. "Tulip," she said, in her old and loving way, "And a rose is here and there a pansy. Oh, my, goodness," she sighed and carefully pressed the dark soil around a proud daisy bobbing in a playful breeze, "My husband, ah, he was before your time, he loved flowers, yes, he did, Roses, oh, how he loved his roses. And I, and I, oh, how I love chrysanthemums. And you Edward, now tell me your favorite flower here."

"I dunno. I like 'em all."

Mrs. Grildy, she looked at Edward through those round glasses, past the strands of gray hair over lined forehead and she said, "Yes, yes, I suppose you do but some day you will find a flower, yes, you will, yes, you will – that will be a flower just for you. Now you begone and if you get back soon enough I just might have some ice cream for you, you just never know." She grinned and gave a little laugh. "My husband, oh, he used to love ice cream. Yes. And roses too." And who knows why, but she raised her hand perhaps to shield her face from light or from a breeze but the sunlight caught the ruby of the ring and it glowed and flashed. "You come back now; don't forget the ice cream. Strawberries too?"

"Oh, yeah."

"Now you be careful."

"Thanks Mrs. Grildy."

Edward was on his way, down those streets of his neighborhood, on that day, that Saturday, when the air was cool and so glass clear where everything was as sharp, distinct and bright as though etched by the perfect knife of God and on rode Edward and splashflash of spray and Edward heard the playful bray of the hyena laugh of Mr. Abrath, tall and huge like a mighty tree, but unlike a tree with crown of leaves, Mr. Abrath's crown was rather bald, and he watered his lawn in long broad strokes and he said, "Well, young fellow, got your morning bath, you did, you did, haw, haw, haw."

"Hey, Mr. Abrath, you cut that out!"

Mr. Abrath splashed him again. "Whoa-ho there boy, mistook you for the lawn!" He laughed again, "Now where you goin' so early this bright morn?"

"Well, I – " said Edward stopping his bike.

"Don't tell me son, why, if you're like me, you're like to wander here and dabble there. Now ain't that right?"

"Well, I – "

"Yes, sir," said Mr. Abrath, "just as I thought, probably going to get with your friend Roy – "

"Yeah, and – "

"Yes, indeed," said Mr. Abrath, and he turned the nozzle on his hose to a bubbling surge and slopped water about thick base of camellia, blossoming red, "Probably goin' down to the stables and horse around – wo-ho-ho-ho don't stirrup no trouble now – wo – ho – ho – ho – ," and the water burbled, slopped and babbled forth splashing here and splooshing there and Mr. Abrath continued, "You're just like me, I do believe; why, when I was back, let's see, forty-three – why yes, Pittsburgh, Pen-syl-vain-e-ah, yes, sir, we wandered down this old road with trees on either side oh, such a lovely sight that was – " Who knows why but as he spoke he held his hand in such a way that again Edward saw a ring, a large ring filled with deep blue stone and at length he said, "But here, now, friend, you should get going, you have a long day of play ahead and I, oh, God, back taxes to do – putting them off as long as I can – oh, God, don't grow up it's just too taxing on the spirit wo-ho-ho-ho – "

Edward pushed a pedal down, caught the other with practiced foot and yelled, "Good-bye!" and was on his way to explore that splendid day –

"You son of a bitch!" And *crash* and *wham*!

Edward slowed his bicycle down and saw Sally Jean McKenzie, leaning against the 1957 family Ford and in the house, that expensive, lovely red brick house, *Crash*! and "I'll call the cops!"

"I dare you, you shovel-butted – !"

"Stay away from me with that chair – "

Crash and *thud* and then thin wail, "Sally Jean, come save me . . . "

Sally Jean ignored the plea; she just leaned against the car and took a ring off her finger, put it on, took it off, then she threw it on the ground, stepped on it, ground it with her heel, picked it up, put it on, took it off, threw it down and then looked at Edward slowly pedaling by and he looked away and continued on, on past the house where Mr. Wolverton had recently died and Edward sighed as he remembered the old man, dressed always in blue coveralls, with a gray, wide brimmed hat with a small brown feather stuck in the band and how he used to talk, "Ouuuuu," he'd always say, "ouuuuu, yes, I remember the day when that lot was filled in and the store was built – ouuuu, yes, that was a bit before your time – ouuuuu, yes, quite a bit before your time." Mr. Wolverton, thin as straw, bent by seasons of the years, looked to Edward, and then beyond as though looking at a time way back when – which suddenly was happening right now and he'd say, "ouuuuu, yes, and where you stand right now used to be nothing but forest, my friend, I cut trees right here, where you stand, ouuuuu, but that was a time ago. Yes, yes, that was a time ago. When I was twenty, I took a train into the mountains, ouuuu, to Monte Cristo, yes, it was a big town way back then, ouuuu, yes, it was a big town way back then – " He used to lean on his cane as he talked and Edward always loved the ring that he wore. "Alaska black diamond," Mr. Wolverton said. "Ouuuu, got it in Juneau in 1910, I was twenty-five. Ouuuuu, what a grand time I had up there!"

Edward stopped his bike and stared at that now empty house and still could not believe that Mr. Wolverton was really gone. And he sighed and went on, on past Samuel, the lazy German Shepherd in Ericson's front yard whose sleep was louder than his bark. Then past the house of the teacher McKlee who was a large lady with curly brown hair and who taught elementary school not far away and who seemingly had an unbounded love for everyone and she always wore this gold ring with a diamond so bright that it seemed to make the very sun pale and she had this wonderful laugh, "Oh, Edward, how is your mother why I have known her for years for just years my she's such a nice woman oh, you are ever so lucky to have a mother like her oh, yes you are, oh, ho, ho, ho, I should say you are – " and how was it that she always seemed to stand in the light just right such that her diamond always sparkled but perhaps it was just Edward's imagination that this was so.

And through the morning, Edward pedaled on and finally came to Roy's home, "But," his mother said, "he has the flu and must stay in bed."

"Aw," said Edward, "on such a great day? To be sick? In summer? Ah, geez, well, tell him I stopped by and to get well."

Roy's mom smiled and said, "I'll tell him that. Why don't you call back later on?"

"I will," Edward said.

So he hopped on his bike and . . . who knows why or how these things occur? But sometimes when the very plans that we want don't seem to work, another plan, unexpected, falls into place and he rode onward on that lovely day and why this happened, even he could not say but he stopped his bike: there on the ground – the band of a ring but there was no stone. The band itself was as silver as crescent of a moon, as lovely as polished ice, as bright as promise. Edward picked it up and looked at it this way, looked at it that and wondered out loud, just what kind of stone did this once have? And after a minute, what kind of stone will this have? He put the ring without stone in his pocket and for some motivation that he could not understand, went down this street and came to the library. And once inside, went to the astronomy books. And once there, found the book that he loved, a book of paintings of the planets and stars and opening the book, there was a picture of the thin crescent of Saturn, as seen from Titan. Edward breathed out very slowly; the crescent of the ringed planet was done in white and the sky was a deep blue black and around the planet the rings sliced about and around to the night side and Edward stared a very long time and sighed, that such a scene was so beautiful yet, he knew, so cold and so deadly. After a time, he walked back outside and sat on the lawn, back against a tree and looked out over the world and conversations from the parking lot behind the library drifted to him like strange scents on odd wind and he listened as he studied the empty ring, "You knew that book was due two weeks ago. So stupid you are for forgetting – "

" . . . but I didn't mean to, Mommy – I'm sorry – "

" – such a careless little girl – "

". . . and I told him if he laid one hand on me I'd bust him in the chops the son of a bitch . . . "

". . . well, we'll drop these books off and then go home and I'll get the barbecue going . . . but please don't say anything to mother about Phil's heart attack – "

"Oh, Christ, she's going to notice he looks like hell – what am I supposed to say, 'Oh, he just has an ingrown nail?'"

Finally, Edward put the ring back in his pocket and, standing up, went to his bike. On the way home, he stopped at the McKessons and bought himself a strawberry sundae and Diane, the clerk, maybe seventeen or so, looked at him rather blankly as she nibbled some cheese and had little to say except, "Here," when she served him, "a dollar-five please." And Edward noticed her ring had a very small setting and after he paid her, she went back to reading a magazine called *Secret Teen*.

After that, Edward rode his bike on toward home, the day now beginning to ebb and he slowly rode past Mr. Emerson's house and he slept in a lawn chair, a fifth of whiskey at his side and even from where Edward was, he could see a massive ring on his middle finger, a multifaceted face that caught the light of the late afternoon and ring and bottle both sparkled, like miniature stars had alighted or maybe strange brilliant insects and Edward moved on, riding, riding in the afternoon sun, past the house where the Steepledon's had lived – but they now were gone. Mr. Steepledon was a banker, brilliant and as chiseled as a freshly minted coin and he spoke very thinly about very few things and when he did talk to Edward, it was in a severely reprimanding style, "Always save money," and his dark eyes were hard and cold as black diamonds. "Be thrifty and frugal" and the muscles around his mouth were so very tight like they were ready to snap like bands twisted and pulled beyond manufacturer specifications and his suits were as pressed and neat as though made from steel. "Never waste money," he always said and Edward always noticed the five rings on his fingers and the light shone on them as light shone off chitin.

Just before home Edward saw Mrs. Grildy in her yard watering her plants and she waved and said, "Strawberries and ice cream or will that spoil your dinner?"

"Thank you," said Edward, "it'd be great."

He went into her house.

"My husband," she said, "he always loved his ice cream and the strawberries, oh, my, how he loved strawberries."

Edward sat down and said, "Gee, he must have been a real neat guy – "

Mrs. Grildy laughed and said, "Oh, oh, well, he had his problems – he sometimes drank a little much – " and she sat down with her ice cream and her strawberries and on her hand her ring was deep, deep red. "But yes," and she sighed, "I do miss him even now – oh, dear," she abruptly said, "oh, please excuse me for a minute – I don't suppose I should be telling you this . . . an old widow's memories, oh, forgive me I really should move on – and – oh, dear," she took off her glasses, "I'll be right back, now eat your ice cream and strawberries . . . " She got up to the bathroom and Edward pulled out the silver ring without stone and stared at it for a long, long time and then – who knows why – he looked out the window, and wanted to cry and for an instant saw Saturn – filling the sky.

Der Fuhrer As A Bad Kitchen Appliance

IT IS OBVIOUS to anyone with an even remote knowledge of kitchens that Hitler would have been a lousy appliance. It is one of those things that is very true. "But wait," you may say, "What proof have you that he would be unworthy of being an appliance? Or of being a bad appliance?"

"Simple," I respond. "Say he was a mix-master. Well, he most certainly was not. He was an un-mix master and, given that, he would be a gadget that would be always trying to unravel ingredients rather than trying to mix them. Always trying to unblend his perception of "bad ingredients." How destructive. What a waste."

"But surely," you may respond, "as an appliance, he must have some sort of redeeming function."

"How?" I respond. "What kind of can opener would he be if he opened up some cans but not others?"

"Maybe there is one can that he did open up."

"A can of worms?"

"You could say that."

"Hm." I respond. "He did indeed do that."

"Maybe he'd make a good dishwasher?"

"How?" I ask. "What kind of dishwasher have you that washes only certain dishes but spits the ancient, delicate china out on the floor because somehow their handles are shaped the wrong way. Now what kind of dishwasher is that, I ask you?"

"Well – " you say.

"You think he'd make a good washing machine – washing the white shirts but leaving the darker colors unwashed? Or you think he'd be a good dryer – but ending up drying only the pale clothes and letting the dark jeans and plaid shirts cold and damp? Would you accept such strange behavior in your appliance? I wouldn't. I would take it back to the dealer immediately and ask for a refund."

"Well," you might say, "I still think that he must have some sort of ability to be some sort of appliance."

"I should have been more general and included fixtures. A toilet would have immediately come to mind. But since I stated 'kitchen appliance,' well, I'll concede your tasteless point, but I really thought there was one appliance that better suited him," and I point.

"An osterizer? How would he make a good osterizer?"

"Because what an osterizer does to whatever is put in it – that's what der fuhrer would have done to the world. But that wouldn't make him really any different than a mix-master and we already agreed that he would have made a lousy mix-master."

"Indeed," you say. "Indeed. Any other possibilities?"

"After all that," I say, "What else is there?"

"I dunno," you say. "We missed something."

"Like what?"

"He'd make the perfect freezer . . . not a bad appliance at all, really. He really would make an excellent freezer."

"Why?"

"Cold, cold, cold. *Deathly* cold."

Friends

WILLIAM REMEMBERED WHAT the Others had said. "Go, William. Go to the City of Darkness and bargain. Bargain well, for if you do, you shall be amply rewarded."

"Bargain?" William said. "What do you mean?"

"Go to the City of Darkness," the Others whispered.

"But why?"

"For now it is your time."

William looked around to his world: the vast unending gray, to the fleeting dark shapes of the Others. "Where is the City of Darkness?"

"You will arrive when your feelings change."

"But I don't want to go."

"You must go. You must go to the City of Darkness. If you stay here, you shall be smothered. The grayness will crush you. Go."

Bravely, William went. As he moved, he began to feel lonely. The grayness became darker. He began to feel frightened and the grayness became black. He suddenly realized how alone he was. The stars and moon appeared in the sky. He was unique. And there was the City of Darkness. No streetlights. The windows were dark. The streets deserted. No wind. Even time seemed to stop and examine itself. A new crescent of moon illuminated the old buildings. William stopped. So this was the city. Somehow he was not surprised. It was as though he had an intuitive knowledge of what a street looked like, of what a building looked like. He wandered the streets, looking into the empty windows and as he wandered, he became more and more lonely; he became colder and the darkness was everywhere. So much darkness. He leaned against the cold brick wall of a building and swallowed.

"This is madness," he whispered. " 'Go to the city and bargain.' Bargain for what? Where do I bargain? With whom?"

William sighed. Uneasily, unhappily, he looked about. He was standing at an intersection. He looked up and down each street. In the thin light of the crescent moon, the streets, the buildings looked the same. "Damn it," he whispered, "which way do I go?" He shrugged. "What difference does it make?" He decided to go straight ahead, and just by chance looked to his left after he crossed the street. What was that? He stopped. A glow, a faint, faint glow, coming from one of the buildings down the street. William stared. Moonlight off a window? No, because that side of the street was in shadow.

Cautiously, he went down the street until he was right across from the shop. He stared. There was some sort of light in the window; a flickering yellow light. William crossed the street and slowly approached the window. There, in the wide display area behind the glass, a little flaming figurine danced. It was neither male nor female. Its body was blue, the surrounding flame yellow. It danced a graceful dance as though in a ballet. The figurine looked up and saw William looking in. The figure stopped dancing and simply looked at William. It smiled. And William finally said, "Oh, oh, I want you. Oh, I want you more than anything in the world. Oh, how I want you."

The little flaming figure appeared embarrassed and looked down.

William stepped back. To the right was a door. William turned the handle; the door opened. Inside, the room was filled with dancing, flaming figurines. William stood blinking in the light. The whole place was aglow in yellow, flickering light.

"May I help you, son?"

The voice seemed to come from everywhere in the vault-like room. William looked around the glass display cases on which and in which the flames danced their minute ballets.

"Over here."

William followed the voice. Leaning on a display case, leaning on crossed arms was a very large man with yellow hair and beard. He was dressed in a red plaid cowboy shirt which was open at the neck. His face was red, his teeth yellowed and, as William approached him, he saw that the man's eyes were dark and reflected many flames. "What can I do you for?"

"I – " William cleared his throat. "I want that flame in the display window."

The man scratched his beard. "It's costly."

William looked down to the scuffed wooden floor. "I haven't any money." Then he looked at the man. "But I'll do anything to have it."

"Will you now," said the man, slowly standing erect, "will you now."

"I will."

"Like I said, it's costly."

"How costly?"

The man looked at William. The man kept his hands against the glass and leaned forward. "Very costly." He looked down at William and his gaze became stern. "Are you willing to protect the fire?"

"Yes."

"Against water?"

"Yes."

"Against wind?"

"Yes."

"Against others who would steal the fire from you?"

"Yes."

"Are you willing to honor the fire?"

"Yes."

"Hold it? Love it?"

"Yes, yes."

The man sniffed. "Pah! You can't have it."

William looked abashed, then outraged and then suddenly beside himself, he reached over and grabbed the man by the shirt. "Damn it! I want it!"

The man smiled. "Ah, ah, that you do, that you do." Gently he reached up and removed William's hands from his shirt. "Ah," he said again, "you really do want the fire. That you do. I get all sorts of clowns who answer yes to my questions and as soon as they walk out the door, they do something stupid and extinguish the flame." He looked at William warningly. "It is your fire. For God's sake, treat it well." From a pants pocket, he pulled out a ring of keys and went over to the small door that opened to the display window which faced the street. As he unlocked the door, he muttered, ". . . tired of having young jackasses mistreat my fire. Can't be too careful . . . " He came back out of the display area and said to William, "All right, open your hands." William did. The man placed the flame in William's hands.

"It's mine?" William whispered, looking at the flaming figurine. It stood in his hand, looking at him intently; then, apparently satisfied, it sat in his hand and burned with an even flame.

"It's yours."

"But surely I must pay you something – " said William, looking very astonished.

"Respect is payment enough."

Abruptly, William looked troubled. "I don't think I should carry it around in my hands," he said. "Is there a safer place?"

The man pointed to his heart. "In here."

William was surprised, but lifted the flame up to his chest and from there, the fire crawled out of his hand and sat in his heart and William felt immediately warm and excited. "What a wonderful place to keep it," he said.

The man nodded. "Indeed. You know, I think you'll take good care of the fire."

"I plan to," said William. "Thank you ever so much." He opened the door of the shop and stood astonished. Had he been inside the shop that long? For outside it was daylight and the sun was bright and warm and people were walking about, all with flames in their hearts, and wonderingly William joined the crowd.

The city was alive. All the shop windows were full of goods and it was an exciting place. So many things to do. So many shops to see, so many people to meet. All morning, he was as a child, running about, and within his heart the figurine danced a quick and energetic dance, its flame so yellow and sharp and warm.

By noon, William was somewhat tired. He went to an open air cafe and sat eating a sandwich and drinking wine. Within him, the figurine burned with an even flame. The look on the face was gratitude. "Am I treating you well?" William asked.

The figure nodded, but whispered, "A little slower, please. And – " The figurine looked a little embarrassed.

William laughed. "Ah," he said, "I know. I know. Maybe you'd like the company of another flame?"

The figurine smiled and the flame became brighter. "Yes," said William, "that would be nice."

He nodded his head and ordered another sandwich. And while he was eating, lost in thought, he heard a voice. "May I join you?"

William looked up. A beautiful young lady with very blond hair stood near the table.

William nodded. She sat. Her flame stood and looked over to William's flame. William's flame waved. The other flame waved back. "What's your name?" asked William.

"Marie. And yours?"

"William."

Marie ordered a lunch, William ordered more wine and after some conversation, they decided to look about the city together. They walked leisurely together; they talked some, and once in a while argued about this or that, but always ended up laughing or smiling and grabbing each other's hands, and would continue to walk the streets of the city.

By mid-afternoon, they discovered a large park in the city. They strolled into it and found a secluded glen of grass and flowers. Marie came up behind him and put her arms around him. "Ah," William sighed, "ah, isn't it a beautiful, beautiful city?" Inside him, the figurine was smiling.

"Yes," said Marie. "It is indeed."

"And," said William, "is not the fire wonderful?"

Marie whispered, "Yes, yes, the fire is so warm and bright."

William turned in Marie's encircling arms. William kissed her. That afternoon, the fire of William and Marie touched many, many times. The burning figures within each would burn brightly, dance quickly, then slow, slow, and again, again, quickly, oh, quickly, then slow, slow, and again, again, quickly, oh, brightly, brightly, yes, yes, and then for a long time, they simply lay on the grass in each others arms, knowing of each others heat, welcoming and accepting each other's fire and within them, the flaming figures danced parallel to each other, nodding to each, smiling at each and at the end of each dance, bowing gracefully to each.

Finally, William said, "It is getting late. Why don't we go out for dinner?"

They dressed and, at the same cafe where they had met, seemingly just a short time ago, they had dinner. "My," Marie said, "the day has gone so quickly by."

"Indeed," said William, "and yet, our flames burn on. Thank you for sharing with me your fire."

"And thank you," she said and together they drank the wine. Together they ate their dinner slowly. Within each the flaming figurines danced a waltz graciously. The sun was setting and the windows of the higher buildings reflected back the yellow fire of the sun, and the early evening was so very warm. The crowds in the street thinned. The sun set, dusk came.

William and Marie finished their wine. "Well," said William, "shall we look about the city again?"

"Yes," Marie said, "yes, let's do."

They walked slowly now and William noticed that within each of them, the flaming figures did more resting than dancing. My, he thought, it has been a long day. How it rests on us. And he asked his fire, "Do I treat you well?"

The figure nodded, but whispered, "All this dancing has made me tired. So very tired."

"It is no wonder," said William, "you have danced long and well."

"Thank you," said the figure; the look on the blue face was of gratitude. "Thank you for treating me so well that I could dance so long."

Marie stopped; William did the same. Marie looked about the city. "Ah," she said, "the city is wonderful."

The city. It blazed with multicolored neon fire: reds, blues and greens. Everywhere the neon burned and the city was enchanting.

William sighed. "Yes, yes, even though the day weighs upon me, I nonetheless enjoy the city."

They came to an intersection and William stopped. "Look," he said, "this is the street on which the shop is located where I found my fire." He looked to Marie who looked sad. The figurine in her leaned to look. William looked: within himself, the flaming figurine lay on its side; the flame was uneven and flickering. "No!" William cried, "No!" He grabbed Marie's hand and they rushed to the shop.

The door was locked. "Damn!" swore William. He broke open the door and stepped into the shop. The shop was dark. "No," he whispered, "No. No." He stumbled back outside.

Marie, with her arms outstretched, was a fading shadow, then gone. The streets were deserted.

"Marie!" he yelled, clutching the air, "Marie! Marie!" He tried to run, but stumbled and fell. The lights in the city flickered out, one by one as though marking seconds. The flame within him sputtered. He reached into his heart and pulled the figurine out. "Why?" he asked. "Why are you doing this? Please, please don't go out."

He heard a very weak voice. "You treated me well. I wish I could burn forever, but I cannot."

"Where is the shop!" William cried, "Where can I find another flame?"

"For you, the shop is gone," came the faint voice, "and you can only have one flame."

"But – but – "

"Goodbye, William." The figure looked up at him with infinite sadness and tenderness. "You treated me so well. I don't want to go, but my energy is spent; I can no longer dance. But without your care, I could not have danced as long as I did. You treated me well, William, you treated me well."

The figure then leaned forward, kissed William's palm and collapsed. The flame went out. The figure turned to ash and a wind blew the ash from William's palm. And the last light in the city went out.

Edward And The Sphere

YOU KNOW HOW it is. You walk past a store or a place a thousand times and on the one-thousandth and first time, you are suddenly aware that the place exists – even though it always had. But it is as though it suddenly exists – for you – as if something about it says, "Now is the time for *you* to know *me*!"

And so, Edward is walking by this antique store he has been by so often that it seems to not exist – and he suddenly stops. "Huh?" he says to himself. He turns and suddenly all he knows is that he must go in. And does.

He looks around. Cluttered. On the wall, an advertisement from the twenties for Coca-Cola; a woman's face on a serving plaque, a tennis net in the background, and off to the left side, a bottle of Coke. On the shelf in front of the window, toys from the late forties and early fifties – genuine steel cars and trucks, comics – mid-fifties editions of *Little Lulu*, *Mickey Mouse* and *Bugs Bunny* (one issue has a cover showing Bugs with his feet jammed between pickets in a fence, while Porky Pig, looking to his right, is talking to someone and squirting Bugs with a hose that was meant to be aimed at a garden just in front of the fence).

Edward continues to look around; artifacts from Yesterday: a jukebox, a glass bubblegum dispenser, a wagon, clothes, an advertisement for Phillip Morris, tacked on the wall, showing the red suited bellboy paging and, somewhat mesmerized, Edward walks about until he comes to the display case and there, sitting on top of the case, a ball; a clear, solid glass ball, about the size of a large grapefruit. A woman at the far end of the counter, dressed in drapes of black, satin-like material, glances at Edward. She puts her nail file down and walks over. "Hi," she says; her dark eyes, like her lips, smile.

Edward lifts the glass ball. "How much?"

"Two dollars."

"Crystal ball?" he asks.

The woman shrugs. "Don't know. Just got it in today."

Without another word, Edward gets out his wallet, pays the money and places the ball into his lunch sack. Once home, he takes it to the kitchen, washes it and then dries it with Kleenex. He goes to the living room, puts it on the coffee table. It is late afternoon; the summer sunlight comes in through the large glass doors that lead to the balcony with a view of the city. He pours himself a drink of Scotch, sits down on the heavy sofa, relaxes and sips his drink, and watches the glass sphere. He takes another sip, watches how the sunlight sparkles off the glass, then how the glass seems to sparkle inside. He suddenly looks puzzled, leans forward – something sparkling in the glass, something very bright, then brilliant. Edward says, "Jesus Christ!", closes his eyes, then it is dark.

He opens his eyes.

It is mid-winter. There is no sphere on the table. Outside it is snowing so hard that the lights of the city look as though shining through fog. Edward groggily reaches forward to pour another drink; he has killed a fifth that evening.

Edward's pet spider sits on his lap. "Wonder who she's fucking tonight?" mumbles Edward. Edward feels the spider bite and inject poison into him. He scratches the spider's bulbous body appreciatively and feels the spider sap his blood. After a minute, the spider responds. "I don't know," it hisses. "Maybe your best friend? Or maybe the fellow you caught her kissing with at the party?"

"God," murmurs Edward, "why do I stay with her?"

"Because you love her," whispers the spider. It bites, injects and draws, draws again.

Laughter outside the door. Then someone says, "Hush" in a voice too deep and too loud to disguise the maleness. A few seconds of silence, a giggle, another pause, then the rattle of keys in the lock. The door opens; a large spider enters, followed by Brenda, Edward's wife. She turns on the light and, seeing him, says, "Oh!" She is instantly flustered; a look of guilt flashes across her face.

"Who was he?" asks Edward.

"Who was who?" Brenda asks airily, sitting down. Her spider jumps up on her lap like a pet cat.

"The fellow you were with outside. Whoever it was who whispered 'Hush' didn't sound like you."

"Oh," she says, "you been hitting the bottle again, darling? Does my little lush want to come to bed and try to get a hard on?" Her spider bites her; she smiles and pats her pet.

"Who was he?" whispers Edward.

"I'll tell you what." She leans forward; her spider sits in her lap, huddled like a tight little ball. "You tell me all about Sarah, you know, the one who answered the phone the night you were supposed to be working late by yourself. By the way," she smiles, "does her – ahem – 'office work' – improve when she's so drunk?" Again, her spider bites her and she smiles at the rush, then the draw. "You tell me about Sarah – and also about Susie and Martha and maybe – maybe I'll tell you about – hmmm – " she shrugs. "Maybe I'll tell a few things – " Then she smiles sweetly. "Then maybe I won't."

"There was nothing going on, I tell you." He finds his hands are fists. "She came back to the office because she left something there – I can't help it that she came in drunk – "

"Oh," says Brenda, "what was it she left at the office? You?" Her spider bites her; she smiles. The spider feeds; she pets it. "And of course, there was Susie . . . "

"Only to get back at you and that Sorenson kid. Didn't expect me back from the office so early, did you?"

She seeths. "You impotent prick. He raped me."

Edward smiles. "I'm sure he did. Was it one of the nicer rapes you've had recently?" His spider bites and draws and draws.

"You son of a bitch!" she hisses. Suddenly, her spider leaps from her lap and attacks his. Edward and Brenda become quiet, impassive as their spiders bite and hiss and scramble on the floor.

Dazed, Edward stares at the glass sphere. He still has his drink in his hand. It slips from his fingers and hits the floor with a soft *thump*. The sunlight still streams in through the window; he has the sense that just a few seconds have gone by. Numb, he looks around his apartment, knowing where he is but somehow uncomprehending of the reality of where he is.

Twinkle. Something in the sphere shines. Edward looks. He is walking with Brenda. His spider walks before him. Edward has it on a leash; the spider behaves very properly. Brenda's spider is on a leash also; it too behaves quite properly. Before him are two spiders dragging his mother and father behind them. They are enshrouded in sticky silk; Edward's mother is constantly belittling and berating his father. Edward is so intent on watching his parents struggle in their silk that he pays little attention to his spider. Even less to Brenda's.

He is vaguely aware of Brenda's parents, struggling in their silk, being led by their spiders. All he knows is that he likes Brenda's father for putting his wife in her place. He pays little attention to Brenda's angry looks at her father or her special affection for Edward's mother.

The procession proceeds. Edward continues to watch his parents struggle; he thinks, "This must be what love is; why else would they have stayed married?" He feels certain Brenda feels the same about her parents, but they never really discussed it. There were lots of things they did not discuss.

They walk a ways further, through forests of dense vegetation, then a clearing under the immense blue sky and massive sun. This marriage is happening on the planet Venus, the Goddess of Love. One thing Edward likes about Brenda is that she shares his idea of what Venus should be like and it is only natural that they would marry on Venus. It is the perfect place.

They reach the minister, who stands sweating. He has a spider on his shoulder. All through the ceremony, the spider gnaws on a cross made of bone. Not once does the minister's spider stop working and working the cross and the minister tries his best to ignore it, but it isn't just the sun that is making the minister sweat. At the end of the ceremony, the minister hands both Edward and Brenda a pair of scissors; Brenda cuts Edward's leash to his spider, Edward cuts Brenda's leash to her spider and both spiders turn and hiss at each other. The spider on the minister's shoulder snaps the bone cross in half and the minister sweats and screams. Edward's parents and their spiders, as well as Brenda's parents and their spiders begin to fight and bite and hiss and scream; the sky clouds over, the temperature soars to nine hundred twenty degrees Fahrenheit; the vegetation explods into flames and a sulfuric acid rain falls and again, Edward looks at the glass ball and thinks, "I am mad. I must be truly mad!" With resignation he stares at the sphere. "This is all crazy," he thinks, "yet, I know what it all means. As crazy as it all is – I yet understand it. I wish – in a way – I did not. But since Brenda, I've been afraid to really get involved with anyone – even Susie and I – inasmuch as we see each other – are simply friends – " He sighs with sadness and disenchantment. It is then that there is a knock on the door. "Edward?"

"Door's open, Susie," he says.

"What?"

A little louder. "Door's open!"

Susie comes in, a bright, dark-eyed, dark-haired woman of twenty-seven. She is dressed in a gay yellow dress with a belt of gold, interlocked rings. When she sees Edward, she becomes serious. "What's the matter?" He motions her over to sit next to him and look into the glass sphere. "If you wait long enough, you'll probably see something pretty horrible – I don't know how this thing works, but it seems to have an ability to show a person exactly as they are. I guess I have a lot of fear-hate of my mother that I transfer to all women – I bring out the worst in women and women bring out the worst in me. I was afraid of that. That's why I haven't gotten close to anyone after Brenda left – " Then he points to the ball. "See that shimmer in there?"

Susie leans. "Yes – "

"Now you're going to see what I mean."

Edward does not know where he is. His spider stands by his side. He watches Brenda walk away from him; her spider turns around once and gives a final "hiss." Edward sighs. To himself he says, "Well, at least it was mutual. Mutual hatred."

"Hiss," says his spider. "Women are like that. They beat you down. You can't trust them."

Edward snorts. "And I suppose her spider is telling her the same about men."

Edward then looks glumly about. He is naked, standing in snow on a world that is not Earth. The air smells of methane and ammonia. Mighty glaciers begin to advance; their fronts are high cliffs. The sky is white. "It's cold," says Edward. "It's cold and it's going to stay cold for a long, long time."

"Do you really believe that?"

Edward turns. Susie stands there with her spider. Edward points. "See? I've brought out your spider."

But Susie shakes her head. "No, it's always been with me. You and Brenda brought out each other's spiders so much that all you saw of each other were your spiders. Do you want to see what you bring out in me?"

Guiltily, Edward looks at her. "I'm almost afraid to look."

But Susie smiles. Her spider suddenly begind to shrink; as it shrinks, something on her shoulder begins to grow. It is a dove.

Edward stares, dumbfounded. "I bring that out in you? You feel that way around me?"

Susie nods very matter-of-factly. "Now, why don't you just relax and see what I bring out in you?"

Uneasily, uncertain, Edward takes a deep breath and relaxes. Amazed, he watches his spider shrink until it is very small; no, not gone, but very, very small. He picks it up; it is encased in glass. It disappears into his hand. Abruptly, he turns his head; a dove sits on his shoulder. It makes soft sounds, closes its eyes and seems very content to sit and snuggle on his shoulder. "But, but . . ." stammers Edward, " . . . how . . . how is that . . . "

"Because," says Susie, coming up to him and putting her arms around his waist, "we bring out the best in each other – it doesn't mean our spiders don't exist, it just means they don't get in the way. Of course," and she looks knowingly, "you have to know what your spiders are so you don't put yourself in a place where they *get* in the way."

Stunned, Edward looks up from the glass ball and stares at Susie. She smiles, kisses him lightly on the lips, then points back to the ball. The scene is of snow melting and being replaced by grass and flowers; the glaciers recede, while above the horizon rises the Earth. Edward and Susie stand, hand in hand, until the blue- and pearl-colored Earth fills the entire sky. And on their shoulders their doves sit, contented, and making not a sound.

The Strange Fate Of M. In The Odd Town Of X

M.WAS A lovely woman of fifty-some years who had graying hair and the bluest eyes set in the tannest skin that gave her face an almost bejeweled richness and indeed there was much about M. that was precious indeed. She enjoyed wearing blue dresses with the palest of flowers sewn in and it almost looked like the azure of the Caribbean dusted with flowers. And it must be said that M. seemed to live a rather mundane life; she was loved and respected and admired for her simply being herself which is why it caused her great alarm one morning to awaken and find that her watch – for the first time she could ever remember – had stopped. She rolled the covers back and went to her parakeet and discovered him with wing and foot outstretched – and perfectly still. She touched him with the eraser end of a pencil and it was as though she were touching glass. And she wondered out loud, "What has happened while I have been dreaming? Indeed something has changed." She went to the small radio which sat on the sill like a rectangular black bug and tried to turn it on – "click" went the switch, but the radio just yawned silence from its little speaker.

"How odd," thought M. And she went to the door and looked this way and that way up the dusty street between that hazeless blue sky that one frequently finds in the more southern lands. She looked to her watch; it was eight-fifteen and surely the plaza would be crowded with people, the market teeming with children and old ones whose sandals, like M's, would *slap-slap* against pavement but, as M. looked out, yes, yes, she saw people all right. There was S. from next door, a ragamuffin of a child, but today dressed in clean shorts and a brilliant white t-shirt and he was taking a stride, his eleven-year-old body full of purpose and guided by subtle internal will, but he was frozen in mid-stride. M. went up to him and touched him gently on the shoulder and again had the feeling that this person was glass; a bit yielding, but still a sense of fragility. She shook him gently, "S?" she asked, then fighting the panic she began to feel, she touched him again, just a little more. "S? S? Please talk to me."

But S. did not move. He looked straight ahead, his whole body an image of movement but now frozen amidst his apparently thoughtful purpose, wherever it was that he was going. And oh, how his t-shirt was brilliant in the light of the sun.

Oh, dear, wondered M., as she hurried up the street, what could have happened, why am I the only one who can move here? She almost tripped over one of the gray-and-white market tiger cats; it was sitting nobly in the cobbled street, frozen in mid-yawn, pink tongue curling in its mouth, eyes squinted shut.

She passed a potted, miniature birch, leaves turning in wind, glittering in sun – but again, the turning, the glittering, was all frozen movement.

She came to the market. Old Mr. K. was there, stacking his wonderful deep red tomatoes into a stable pyramid – and the action was stilled, the tomato almost in place. On Mr. K.'s dark, bewhiskered face, the cool concentration, of "Yes, this goes right here, yes, I must be careful – how I shall do this," his brown eyes focused on the action and M. established, or tried to, eye contact, but no matter how she looked at Mr. K., He only sees the tomato, thought M., he does not see me at all, no, no, not at all.

And there was Mrs. Q., the artist, painting the market scene with art so accomplished and practiced that it seemed to be art not at all, but a child's drawing of a house with a great smiling sun warming the world. Ah, Mrs. Q., her paintbrush to the canvas. M. admired the hue of red paint coming from that brush, the perfect color to describe the mangos on the table nearby that Mrs. Q. was painting along with the form of a man in a green shirt who was standing nearby looking at magazines at a newsstand and, he too, did not move.

"Oh, my," said Mrs. M., "everywhere I look, it is but the same. It is exactly the same. What could have happened? It's that country up north," she then thought bitterly, some new bomb must have dropped – or some new chemical they have used – but why is it only me who survived? She shook her head and moved on, trying to think of something to explain this, but as soon as one idea entered her mind, she saw something wrong with it almost as fast as she entertained it. She walked through the marketplace and, picking up an orange, discovered that it too had the feeling of glass. "So," she thought, "wherever it is that I am, it looks like I am to starve." In a sudden fury she threw the orange at a dog, leg still raised high, having just wet the stone of a wall. *Fump*, and the orange struck the animal, but made the sound of dead weight striking dead weight and the orange fell away from the dog, wobbling as it rolled, then stopped.

Mrs. M. kept walking and finally she came to the shimmering sea that washed against the town of X and the waves were perfectly still – some were stilled in mid-break, others stilled as they withdrew. A gentleman out a ways was frozen above the surface, ready to plunge into the water. A sailboat with a red-and-white striped mast dipped out toward the sea but the action was halted. M. stood at the seawall, knowing that normally in the gusty wind she'd have to keep pulling her skirt down to hold it against the wind, but, no, her dress hung languidly on her, as quiet as the day, and as still as the sea.

"Oh, my God, there is someone else here besides me!"

M. looked up. And then she stared. "Juan! It's you!"

"Marie," said Juan, "Marie, that is you – you are alive – " And she looked at the man, who was close by her again, who had those granite gray eyes and whose once-black hair was now gone and who nonetheless maintained a youthful appearance in body and spirit.

Juan sat on the seawall next to her. "It has been dreadful – I woke up this morning and the fish in the aquarium that I keep in my room – they had just frozen – then I looked out to my boat – no tossing, no creaking, no sound at all – did you know you can even walk on the water? It's like walking on spun glass – what has happened – "

But as Juan talked, Marie began to glower. "It is a shame you didn't sink – "

Juan's face became hard. "Thirty years hasn't erased all those old feelings – I can apologize only so much – "

Marie looked away.

"But don't forget that you owe me an apology too – you were flirting with Marteen down at the docks when I was going through that miserable bankruptcy – "

"I was hungry," she said. "What was I to do?"

"You weren't around when I needed you – " And Juan put his face in his hands, "Oh, no, oh, no, not again – has thirty years changed nothing? Here we are, just you and me – the only ones alive as far as I can see and here we are fighting – we should be rejoicing our good fortune at being alive – "

Marie sighed. "Some memories don't die easy deaths – I did not trust you then, can I trust you now?" She closed her eyes and said, "Oh, God, Juan, this is the time when we somehow need to make peace with each other – somehow we must forgive – "

Juan shook his head. "I know we need to do exactly that – but we've hurt each other so badly and the trust is so empty – you don't trust me and I don't trust you – what on earth are we to do – for now there is just me and only you."

She shook her head. "Oh, I know, oh, I know it's what we must do – but the feelings of ill will are such a wall between us, and the anger and resentment burn deep into our souls – "

They looked at each other, grief twisting their faces into tragic masks – and then Marie and Juan stood, and, shaking their heads, parted, each walking away into their own frozen worlds.

Gregory's Vision

IT IS OCTOBER 4, 1957. It is a day of panic, of wonderment, of surprise, concern, awe and disbelief. The Russians have put a satellite into space. No one understands how that happened; all anybody knows is that Something Has Happened. Something Is Changing. What Does It Mean?

To Gregory Bennet, it means nothing. He is an hour old, born of Martha Bennet, twenty-five years of age. Gregory Bennet lies in his mother's arms; she is in bed at the hospital. She and her husband, Jack, watch television. Sputnik, Sputnik, Sputnik swings around the world, singing its electronic song to a dazed, unready world.

Gregory Bennet stirs in his mother's arms, and cries.

Jack gets up and turns off the television. "God damn," is all he says.

Martha Bennet holds her son. "Gregory Bennet," she says. She smiles. "Gregory Bennet."

What is there to say about a child growing? Learning to crawl, learning to walk, learning, learning, learning. Learning that objects have names, that some objects are painful (sharp corners, beware, beware) or kitty gets mad if you pull its tail, kitty scratches! Mommy gets mad if you try to flush a towel down the toilet, mommy is happy when you eat all your food. Daddy gets angry if you change channels while he's watching the television, daddy is happy if you don't ask too many questions while he is driving. Learning, learning, learning. It's all learning, so much learning.

Or if it isn't learning, it is endless curiosity. Endless. Questions, questions. And the world is a fascinating place. And suddenly the world changes from being a place of objects with names to a place of why objects with names are what way in the first place: what is grass? Why? What is snow? Why? What is the sun? Why? What is the moon? Why? And finally, finally, the fenced in yard is intolerable to Gregory Bennet. He is now three and a half. It is 1961, April.

More and more, Gregory goes and peers out the locked gate. There is a little used street in front of the gate; across the street, a wooded lot. Oh, strange jungle of maples, firs, ferns and underbrush. Oregon Grape, grass, brambles. A place of sunlight, a place of shade, of spider webs hanging as if created by the weaving of air. A place of coolness, a place of the damp. Once before, with his mother, Gregory has been there. He wants to go again. By himself.

"All right," Mrs. Bennet says, "you can go to the woods, but only for a few minutes. You must return when I call you. If this goes well, you can stay a little longer next time." She doesn't tell him she'll be nearby, keeping him in sight.

Bravely, Gregory crosses the street (after looking both ways to check for cars). The family cat, Flak, a black and white critter, escorts Gregory to the woods. The cat's tail is high with pride; this escorting of Gregory he takes as serious stuff. The cat enters the woods first, finds a well used trail, meows, and Gregory follows.

And he is fascinated. Wordlessly he touches leaves unfolding from stickiness. He looks to the earth to see pale white shoots and curls breaking the soil. He hears the wind rushing through the trees, he sees the blue sky, the sunlight and stands transfixed in bewildered wonderment.

"Meow?" says the cat as though questioning. Then it comes over and rubs against Gregory's legs and purrs. Gregory sits on the ground and feels the dampness, the earth, and the cat places its paws on Gregory's knee and looks intently into Gregory's eyes. To this, Gregory can give no words. All he can do is reach forward and hold the animal close; the animal places soft, balled paws around Gregory's neck and licks his chin, then nuzzles him and many years later, Gregory will remember the strange beauty of that moment, when two totally alien-to-each-other life forms shared a special moment as though kindred. And in that moment of profound kindness and gentleness, the purring, the soft fur, the breathing, the shadows move, spiders weave the air, leaves uncurl, roots work down through soil and "Gregory! Gregory! Time to come home."

Gregory stands, a little dazed. The cat sedately and with dignity and the air of a Zen master, walks the pathway out of the forest and Gregory follows.

That evening, Gregory tells his father about going to the woods. His father listens and smiles. The news is on and the father suddenly says, "Sh!" to Gregory.

Major Yuri Gagarin, a Russian, goes into space. Mr. and Mrs. Bennet listen and watch the television.

Gregory picks at his peas. He wonders if he can get away without eating them and still have dessert.

In October, 1962, Gregory is five. And in kindergarten. He likes kindergarten and his teacher, Mrs. Auguston. She is tall, dark haired, slender and smiling. She enjoys children and shows enthusiasm. What Gregory likes most is drawing. He draws space ships, moons, stars. If he were asked why the names of Shepard, Grissom, Titov, Glenn, Carpenter, Nikolayev or Pipovich were important, he couldn't tell you. The only thing he knows is that this thing of space, of astronauts, is something that he has heard very frequently ever since he can remember.

As he draws pictures, he tells Mrs. Auguston (as well as his friends) that he wants to be an astronaut when he grows up. And he draws: he draws as he has seen it, but the lines aren't straight and it's frustrating to try to capture the mind image of that slender white needle ponderously pushing skyward. How many times has he seen it? The roar, and flames of yellow and red and orange; the smoke boiling out and Gregory remembers and draws; he does his best and the world is circular more by accident than plan; the continents don't look too awfully recognizable and the land is colored more in streaks than subtle shade. Perhaps it really doesn't make much difference if the rocket, so far away from the earth still has three stages and flames are still boiling out as though at lift off. Or if Saturn is improbably huge in the sky (and has a couple of rings too many). And what's that in the corner? A flying saucer? And – hm! – the aliens look a bit cat-like. But Gregory keeps the Crayola moving; the page, that finite universe of white space gets very, very crowded. Gregory smiles.

Oh, this thing of growing. Oh, God, this thing of growing and the names of growing: pleasure and hurt and Telstar and crying and Comsat and reaching! Growing. Growing! Of Mercury, of Vostok and going away to leave behind so that one may reach! Circling, circling, down the street, around the block, the circle ever widening, more complex, more sophisticated! Learning! Learning! Growing! Hey, Listen! Hey, Listen! Gregory and Gemini and Voskhod and Salyut! It's frightening and fearful and glorious and grand. Hey, Explorer! Hey, Vanguard and Pioneer and Mariner! It's lonely out there! Hey, fingers! Hey, thumb and hand and wrist and touch and grasp! Touch and touch and grasp again; hold onto, yet, let go. Hey, feet, walk quickly, yet with care; hey, legs, hey, Zond and Venera and Viking, Lunokhod and Molniya, carry us to new strangeness, the vast silences, the harsh sunlight and pink skies and blue skies and leaves and the rich damp of earth and the sunlight, blinking, off the metal skin of Apollo. ("Walk me, legs," says DNA, the captain of Gregory's Mission, to Ground Control, "oh, walk me, walk me, I shall report back, yes, the crayfish in the stream, salamander under log, spider building web and the earth below, the blue-white stone in the labyrinth of space.") At the picture in *Life*, Gregory stares with incomprehension at the scene of Earth rising over the moon's horizon; then he stares with profound wonder as the moon rises over tree tops, roofs, shouts of children, the bark of dog, the silence between people (who know about Telstar, but cannot speak) and Gregory grows, Gregory watches and wonders: the strangeness of space, of he, himself, the strangeness of others. Explore, Venera, explore, Mariner, the universe out there. Explore, Gregory, the universe inside, the darkness, the brilliance, the coldness, the heat, explore the distances, the universe without end, the endless pathways of ideas, of feelings; explore, Pioneer, explore, Zond, explore, Gregory, for the farther you reach out, the more you reach into yourself; remember, Gregory, remember the scene of Earthrise over the horizon of the moon; remember, Gregory and know yourself from the Earthrise . . .

Summer, 1963, Gregory, still learning, still learning; applying, what he has learned. Over to the wooded lot frequently. Making friends down the block, learning how to read, playing at others' homes and once in a while, the radio, the television broadcasts and news: ". . . L. Gordon Cooper, Jr. – longest Mercury flight . . . twenty-two orbits . . ." or, ". . . Valentina V. Tereshkova – first female cosmonaut . . ." And then it is time for dinner and Gregory must go home, down the streets and ever so often, he gazes skyward.

1964, Gregory, age seven. In science class, the teacher, Mr. Elven, asks if anyone knows what has happened today, October 12, 1964. Sally Larkspur raises her hand.

"Yes," Mr. Elven says. He likes Sally because she's bright and likes his class.

"Some men were put into space!"

"Who?" asks Mr. Elven. His face is impish; oh, he knows the answer; the question is, do you!

"Us!" says someone.

"No," says Gregory, "Russians."

"That's right!" says Mr. Elven. "Three men!"

"Wow!" Jeffrey says, "three!"

Gregory grins at Jeffrey; Gregory likes his enthusiasm and after class they talk about space and soon become fast friends.

Later, in the spring of 1965, everybody has a little better understanding of cosmonauts and astronauts. On March 18th the Russians go up (this time, a space walk of ten minutes and oh, the discussion that touches off in the science class and both Jeffrey and Gregory sit, utterly mesmerized, as Mr. Elven talks about the events in a non-technical way that students will understand).

When the Americans go up in their Gemini Space Craft on March 23rd and again June 3rd (America's first space walk), the class has a good understanding of all that is happening and everyone wants to discuss it endlessly and, of course, Gregory and Jeffrey talk and ask questions too, but Mr. Elven can't really go into the subject too much: it's the end of the school year; tests to give, report cards to be made out, and so on.

And then it's summer.

And playing. Gregory and Jeffrey are practically inseparable. They are as twins; they might as well be astronauts sharing the same capsule of interests, the same orbit of life as they go fishing down at the creek, or climbing trees, or staying over at each other's house.

The summer as quickly goes on by and suddenly the leaves of trees turn away from green; they turn away and become as the color of autumn sunsets, yellows and oranges and reds. Little flies crowd the cool air now, like minute satellites, flying and orbiting each other in trajectories and paths that would overload every bit of a computer's microcircuit, that would make a programmer ulcer in frustration and quit his job.

Autumn, autumn, autumn, yellow grass, felled by scythe of cold. The evenings creep early; the long days retreat and retreat, migrating southward. Your breath hangs in the air; you shiver and wonder where are your gloves, the heavy coat?

And so bundled, Gregory is in school once again. It is October 4th, 1965. Gregory's classmates throw him a party; a birthday party. From seven years to eight.

It is a surprise. Gregory is laughing and happy. The cake was made by Jeffrey's mother. It is a flat cake; on it, eight candles and there is a design of a rocket made out of pink cake frosting over chocolate frosting over chocolate cake and everybody crowds forward and stomachs rumble.

From Jeffrey, Gregory gets a plastic model kit of a Titan II rocket and the Gemini capsule with two small plastic figures of astronauts.

Gregory's classmates clap and say, "How neat!" and "Wow!" and "Oh, boy!" and "Need some help to put that together?"

It is a good day, a fun day and that night, Gregory dreams: he and Jeffrey aboard Gemini; below them, the Earth turns and turns, blue and white: the home-world, the point of origin. Down there, the back yard, sunny summer days, dandelions, the family cat, down there, down there, laying on your back, looking up to the blue sky with the sun crossing it as regularly as a heartbeat. (That sky: that sky with the moon floating serenely in it – "Maybe it's another world," said Gregory once, "wouldn't it be neat if there were people on it?" and suddenly the moon was no longer just the moon, no it was a magic place, a special planet. And whenever Gregory looked at the moon afterwards, it somehow seemed very different than before.)

And from up there in the capsule, Gregory and Jeffrey looked down. It was quiet. No transmissions came from the pearl of blue and white. Nor did Gregory and Jeffrey talk with each other. Both of them stared out at the world below them. And as they watched, the scene below became more and more covered by clouds and from the clouds, something came up to them; something shining and dark, something with brilliant flames boiling out from behind. Whatever it was drew closer, closer. Gregory and Jeffrey stared: it was a hand, a hand made of satellites and rockets. The hand was outstretched; the fingers were made of smaller space hardware, the hand, the wrist made of bulkier objects. Everything was there: the Saluts, Explorers, the Pioneers, Vostoks, Geminins, Apollos, OAO, Tiros, Transit, Cosmos, Landsat, Helios, Nimbus, Intercosmos, Venera, Polyot, Titan, Ranger – all of this fused into a human hand, reaching out, powered by massive rockets soundlessly firing, and in the palm of that hand, something shining, something brilliant, but the light so intense that neither Gregory nor Jeffrey could see what it was. The hand passed by and below, the Earth changed: the clouds became banded and it was Jupiter. The moon shattered and formed a ring and it was Saturn. The rings fell away; the clouds became blinding white: Venus. The clouds vanished and the planet was red; the landscape was strewn with craters and Mars turned. The color faded, craters increased: the moon; over the horizon rose Earth and Gregory and Jeffrey were on their way home. Gregory awoke in his bed. He hugged his knees. He pulled back the covers and, going to the window, looked out. It was early morning. Venus was bright in the sky and something shining and bright slowly crossed the sky. Sputnik? Tiros? Telstar? Gregory could not tell. He kept looking long after the satellite had vanished. He kept looking and wondering what it was that shone so brightly in that incredible hand.

He decided to tell Jeffrey about it when he saw him. He finally went back to bed, slept, and when he awoke, he remembered that he had wanted to tell Jeffrey about the dream but did not know how to put it into words.

1966. In science class, Gregory and Jeffrey choose to do a project on space. They look forward to the next launch of Gemini, March 16th of that year. They have worked to put together a display (with much help from parents and teachers) to show, in a very fundamental way, how rockets work. Part of the display is the Gemini-Titan model that Jeffrey had given Gregory. Other displays are model kits: Mercury Spacecraft, Atlas-Centaur; they would have liked to put together a Russian model, but finding no model kits, they rely on drawings and photographs.

When March 16th approaches, everyone in the class has a fair idea of what is involved. Sadly, after only 6.5 orbits, the Gemini flight must be cut short because of thruster difficulties.

Gregory and Jeffrey, nonetheless, get "A's" for their project and during the summer of 1966, with three missions occurring, both spend much time in front of the television.

And from thereon, no matter what the space mission, Gregory and Jeffrey sit before the television – watching, listening, and poring over pictures published in *Life*.

Both eagerly await every launch; they also discover a new friend, David, who, after his family moves into the neighborhood, finds, much to his delight, that Gregory and Jeffrey share his enthusiasm for space and space travel. And so, there are now three of them: Gregory, Jeffrey and David. At school, they rapidly earn the label of "scientists," a label which no one of the three does much to discourage.

Excitedly, the three of them look to 1967 as a great year. Each goes over with the other the plans, the new Apollo space capsule; each wondering what is going to happen, what will the Russians do?

It is a sad year.

In April, Vladimir M. Kamarov, in the first test of the Soyuz space craft, crashes after reentry.

A flash fire burns, kills three astronauts sitting in an Apollo capsule on a rocket at Cape Kennedy.

"Maybe this is it," says David, sadly. He is a year older, and prone to moodiness. He never combs his blond hair, which strikes Jeffrey as odd since David, otherwise, always seemed to try to look neat. He was not as spontaneous as Gregory or Jeffrey. He was quiet, but when he spoke, it was intelligent, well-thought out.

Gregory, on the other hand, was impatient. "No," he said, "it isn't over. People will keep going into space."

Jeffrey solemnly nodded.

All three sat in front of the television, listening to the latest news on the Apollo disaster. The capsule, blackened, melted inside, was shown.

Gregory shook his head. Later, he and Jeffrey had a listless game of Frisbee; David stood nearby, looking off into the distance, looking distracted, his hands in his pockets.

And October 4, 1967, Gregory's tenth birthday, he and Jeffrey and David get together at Gregory's house. Gregory's mother has baked a cake. It is, of course, a delightful cake. Everyone has fun. Gregory gets from his parents a telescope and, from David, a model of Apollo to assemble. From Jeffrey, a rocket launched by pumping air into a plastic rocket which is half filled with water. Eagerly they all go out and try it. The little rocket spurts faithfully up maybe sixty feet or so. All feel it's something of an informal tribute to the space age which began ten years ago, in 1957. But there is a depressing element – the death of astronauts and nothing major is launched by the U.S. or the U.S.S.R.

The tenth anniversary of The Incredible goes by quietly and sadly. And for the next year, the three study the latest advancements, sharing information and wondering what, when, the next triumph/tragedy will be.

Swing about little Sputnik; you're ten years old. Swing about a blue and silver gem; it's a struggle, Sputnik. It's a battle to grow. In 1967, four died. And add to the list, little singing companion of the Earth, three more in 1971: Dobrovolskiy, Volkov, Patsyev – all died before reentry when pressure was lost in the cabin (it was said that when the door was opened, the faces of the cosmonauts looked serene, untroubled) and a year before that – on Apollo 13 an explosion on board and God! God! The communications speak calm "technicalese" but just beneath, the happenstance, the hope, the danger of the loss of three more men: God! God! Almighty Tao of the galaxy, form and DNA, how much can Thou stretch a spider's silk? God! How intricate can Thou make a snowflake? How delicate the balance of the Yin of despair, the Yang of hope? God? Lao-Tse? Do you have the answer as, out in the wilderness of vacuum, oh, way, way, a heartbreaking way from this blue and white oasis, three men wrestle hope amidst infinity, a spark amidst the darkness, sweat amidst instantaneous boiling blood, control against bursting bubble of shriek, of pain, of darkness sucking away life? Oh, God! How much before a spider's silk snaps? How much? Oh, Apollo 13 stretches that silk so thin, so thin – oh, hold silk, hold, you must hold as thirteen heads back to earth, hold silk, hold, hold: and Sputnik sings its electronic song. It sings for it knows no fear of flesh. To be mechanical, orbiting workhorse. To be the mechanical hand, the sensor eyes. It's safe that way. So safe. It is not concerned about such matters as how much one can pull a spider's silk.

Gregory, Gregory, Gregory: keep your mind and heart earth bound. Gregory, Jeffrey and David: do not look skyward. Look to the ground. Look to the grasses waving, waving; look to the sea, washing, washing the beach. Look to the eyes of those around you; feel the messages, know the wonder. Remember 1967. Remember the four who died. Know that some years later, three more will die and three live by a spider's silk somewhere between Earth and moon. Look down, children, look down, look down, look down: there is your home, your feet on the soil, your hands touching bark. There. Stay there. Ah, but damn you! You look skyward again! Ah, but damn you! You reach again: your hands a wizardry of circuits: feeling, touching, grasping, letting go to grasp again. And your eyes, your eyes, how they keep scanning: peeling the layers of clouds from Venus, touching the planets with your intense and curious stare. Children, know you that there is a price to pay. Seven die while you grasp. Three will feel the fourth member of the crew, The Dark One, try to pilot the craft to infinity and oblivion. And more will die. Reach then! But know the price. Oh, but *know* the price . . .

1968. Gregory Bennet is eleven. He is in the fifth grade. His friend Jeffrey is in the same grade; David is in the sixth grade. And for three avid watchers of space exploration, they have much to talk about: Apollo 7, Soyuz 3, Apollo 8 . . .

Apollo 8: strange scene; Jeffrey and Gregory at David's house. A large, beautifully decorated Christmas tree with blinking colored lights and with some ornaments over eighty years old hanging from branches. Outside it is snowing: it is December 24th, 1968. In the background, the song, "O, Holy Night" is on the radio and on the color television, a silent picture: it is the moon. It occupies the left third of the screen. In the right third of the screen, very small, the crescent of Earth. Gregory watches and feels tears rolling down his cheeks. It is a brilliant and stunning moment. It will be years before Gregory, Jeffrey and David will understand their feelings at that moment; when they do, it will be described as an ache of love and loneliness, of the bleak despair yet the actualization of beauty; the Devil of vacuum and the God of life are there on the screen. The Yin of shadow, the Yang of sunlight – yes, yes, it is there. The smallness, the greatness, the coldness, the warmth, the desolation and the unutterable beauty – it is all there. It is a silent moment. It is a Holy moment; it is a moment that is the magic core of all people's souls: what is being celebrated on that evening, December 24th, A.D. 1968 is not the birth of a child of a minor religion. What is being celebrated is the birth of that which is greater for it encompasses all: the Birth of Awareness – of man looking upon his cradle.

O Holy night and everyone watches the television *the stars are brightly shining* outside the snow is falling *for yonder breaks a new and glorious morn* and on the screen, that thin and delicate crescent called Earth *Fall on your knees!* Blue and white in the abyss of black *O, hear the angels voices* Oh, Earth! *O, night divine, Oh, night, O, Holy night!*

And after Christmas, it's Soyuz 4 and Soyuz 5. Then Apollo 9, Apollo 10 and oh, God! Why can't they go the entire way? Why stop at nine miles above the moon? Gregory is angry. "What a gyp!" he says.

"Yeah," says Jeffrey, "that's really dumb."

But David is more reasonable. "Naw," he says, "they're doing the right thing. You want to lose more astronauts?"

"Next time," says Gregory, "next time."

"When?" asks Jeffrey.

"July, this summer," says Gregory.

"Sh!" says David, "an update!"

On the television, Walter Cronkite; the camera then shows a background scene of Mission Control. Again the scene is replaced, this time by a live transmission from the orbiting craft around the moon: the craters, the bleak desolation . . . and Jeffrey, Gregory and David stare.

It is July 16, 1969. David has been invited by his grandparents – who live in Florida – to come and visit them. The invitation is also open to his friends, Gregory and Jeffrey. Mention is made of visiting and touring Cape Kennedy.

David is enthusiastic. Immediately he invites Gregory and Jeffrey to go. They accept. It is the first time any of them have traveled without their parents.

The families of the three make arrangements; on July 17th, they are on a 727; they will arrive in Miami on the 18th of July, met at the airport by David's grandparents.

Gregory sits near the window. David sits next to him and dozes. Jeffrey sits across the aisle. He is reading *The Time Machine* by H. G. Wells. Both Jeffrey and David have, in a couple of hours, become accustomed to flying; looking down at the west, then the midwest has, at least for them lost its fascination. But not for Gregory. He looks out; the white clouds below, the land; it's familiar – but why? What?

Slowly, slowly he drifts off to sleep and below him, yes, the Earth turns. He turns to look at his copilots, Jeffrey and David. David points – the hand is coming; the hand is coming – that incredible hand made of satellites and space hardware and in the palm of that hand, something glows. The hand rushes past. The forefinger touches the moon but only for an instant; Gregory, David and Jeffrey are pulled behind that hand. They pass the moon, and leave the Earth far behind and Gregory thinks, what is that glow? What is in that glow? He wakens, is momentarily disoriented by being in the jet; he remembers, looks out the window. It is sunset. The sky is brilliant yellow-orange; the horizon burns with the fire of the sun and Gregory closes his eyes. The brilliant glow still fills his mind and a face seems to form in the glow but he cannot tell who it is or what it is. He tells David about the dream and that triggers a session – a lively, energetic talk about who had what dreams when and several hours later, the jet lands: Miami.

David's grandparents eagerly greet them, ask them about the flight, ask them if they were scared and Jeffrey says no, but he never could cover too well and Gregory is tired and David is the only one who has any energy.

Back at the grandparents' home, there are phone calls to let parents know that everyone has arrived safe and sound. There are also innumerable cans of Coke and pastry and snacks plus a large swimming pool in back of the house and Gregory declines all and just wants to sleep. It is humid and Gregory is not used to it; he sleeps restlessly and the glow, the glow, the face in something . . . early toward morning he sleeps better.

The next day, the 19th, the three boys watch television, read the newspapers and know everything about Apollo 11. They do, however, take some time for a swim in the pool later.

And the next day is the big day: July 20, 1969, the day man is to land on the moon.

Gregory, David and Jeffrey sit in front of the television. They eat their breakfast and lunch in front of it. When they go to the bathroom, they take as little time as possible and come back asking if they had missed anything; oh, never mind that much of the information is repeated and redundant. Man is landing on the moon! And hour creeps closer, closer; the ship lands. A long silence; Gregory, Jeffrey and David hold their breath. And then the words. And it is done. Then the pictures, live from the moon; Neil Armstrong stepping down the ladder: the foot of man stirs alien dust. And in Gregory's mind, he sees a face – his face? The face of a child? A face – looking upward at all the stars in the sky. A face: and the expression is shock, yet wonder, bewilderment, yet hope, fear yet courage. The sky parts like a curtain and Gregory's mind fills with wonder – and light.

Dr. Frederick's Last Task

DR. FREDERICK WAS forty-five, with an overabundance of wrinkles around his eyes and an aura of having-seen-it-all. He grimaced as he sat at his broad dark desk, making himself as comfortable as possible – considering his peculiar set of circumstances. He wore a gray suit with white shirt and subdued blue tie. Running his hand over his graying hair to make sure it was in place, he glanced at his appointment book, noting the patients coming for return visits and the brief summaries regarding several new patients. Dr. Frederick guessed it would be a typical day. He glanced at the clock – nine exactly – then pressed a button on the intercom and said, "Miss Leo, send Mr. Klotzky in."

"Yes, sir," came the reply and in a few minutes Mr. Klotzky, a tall, robust-looking fellow (who rather looked like a lumberjack) came sauntering in. His blue eyes were fierce as always, his blond hair a bit thinner, and the hatchet was still stuck in the back of his skull. "Howdy," he said to Dr. Frederick and smiled.

"Hello," answered Dr. Frederick, "please have a seat."

Dr. Frederick scanned the notes from the last session. "Well, how are you today? How's your wife?"

"Pretty good. She's on vacation with the kids to the mountains. Still has some chest pain though."

"Oh?" asked Dr. Frederick.

"Yeah, she hasn't taken the ice pick out of her chest yet."

"Mm," murmured Dr. Frederick, "I see. Well, how're you doing? Still have those migraines?"

"Yeah," said Mr. Klotzky, slumping a bit in the chair, "I sure do. Nothing seems to help. No amount of Excedrin or Anacin seems to help."

"Well," Dr. Frederick replied, "This has gone on for some time. Maybe you should think about removing that hatchet from your skull."

"Yeah," said Mr. Klotzky, gingerly touching the hatchet blade, "I suppose . . . but I'm afraid that if I do, I'll lose my brains or bleed to death."

Dr. Frederick nodded. "I don't think that'll happen, but, until you're ready to do that, just more medication I suppose."

"That'd be fine. And can you make out a prescription for my wife?"

"I guess that she's still frightened that if she pulls that ice pick out – "

Mr. Klotzky shook his head slowly, " – her lungs will collapse."

Dr. Frederick wrote out the prescription. "Here you go. Call me if your headaches get too severe."

Mr. Klotzky sighed, then stood. "Yeah, well thanks." He turned to leave.

"Mr. Klotzky?"

"Yes?"

"You really should hang a little red flag from that hatchet handle to warn people. You don't want to poke someone's eye out – you could get a ticket."

"I suppose you're right," Mr. Klotzky agreed, "I'll take care of that today."

After Klotzky left, Dr. Frederick noted in the chart: Headaches continue; pt. advised to remove hatchet. Prescription renewed.

Dr. Frederick filed Mr. Klotzky's chart in the desk drawer and pulled out another, glanced at it briefly then pressed the intercom. "Mr. Hotchins, please."

Mr. Hotchins was a splintery old man dressed in a blue suit, white shirt and very red tie. He wore a gray hat with a little feather stuck in the band. Over his right shoulder drooped a dead cat.

Dr. Frederick smiled. "Mr. Hotchins, how are you today?" He wanted to rise, but simply didn't have the energy to do so.

"I'm doing pretty good, but I've been bothered recently by very unpleasant odors."

Coughing, Dr. Frederick turned and opened a window. "There seems to be a lot of odd odors going around, Mr. Hotchins, but I think you're doing better – I mean last week you came in complaining of a crawling sensation on your left hand – "

"I know, and I did exactly as you advised – I took off that jar filled with spiders that I was wearing on my hand – it helped a great deal."

Dr. Frederick reached into a drawer for some pine-scented room deodorizer and sprayed it about nonchalantly. "And what do you suppose is causing the bad smells?"

"Dunno," shrugged Mr. Hotchins, "just don't know."

"Could it be that dead cat on your shoulder?"

"Feedie? My dear beloved Feedie?" Unconsciously, he lifted his hand to stroke the dead animal, unintentionally removing large chunks of fur and skin. "Never! It can't be Feedie!" Abruptly, Mr. Hotchins stood. "It just can't be! I'll never come here again as long as I live! Let's go, Feedie!" Mr. Hotchins turned, and the cat's tail tore off and dropped to the floor with a *fwump*. In an amazing move of awareness and agility, Mr. Hotchins snatched up the tail and was out the door, slamming it behind him.

Dr. Frederick sprayed the room with more of the aerosol, then opened the window wider. He wrote in Mr. Hotchins chart: Pt. complains of smelling strange odors. Advised to remove dead cat from shoulder. Pt. refused. Denial. However, other symptoms seem to be less problematic.

As before, Dr. Frederick put the file away and plucked out a new, empty one. "Please send in Mrs. Gallsworthy."

"Yes, Dr. Frederick."

He idly wondered what this Mrs. Gallsworthy's problem was and hoped it wouldn't take too long – lots of cases today, plus another new patient at two.

The door opened and a woman, short and wide – like she'd been compacted by life, her face lined by lances of stress – walked in, followed by a large green frog in a baseball hat. "Dr. Frederick?" the woman asked.

"Yes. Won't you have a seat? What can I do for you?"

She entered, fitfully clasping her purse and looking about furtively. The frog hopped once behind her and sat nearby. Mrs. Gallsworthy squirmed in her seat. "Well, it's like this – it's about my son, Daniel."

Dr. Frederick looked at the frog, "What about your son?"

Daniel nodded at Dr. Frederick then opened his mouth and with a long, pink tongue, flicked a fly out of mid-air.

"That's the problem."

"What's the problem?"

"Catching flies in public – he did it at church last weekend and the congregation was outraged."

Dr. Frederick frowned, perplexed. "But he's supposed to eat flies."

Mrs. Gallsworthy twisted in her chair and fidgeted with her pink purse. "Maybe I didn't explain myself clearly – " she began again, "I mean, I know he's supposed to eat flies, but he's doing it all the time – he can't stop eating. I'm afraid he has an eating disorder or maybe he's missing something in his diet – "

Dr. Frederick thought for a minute. Daniel opened his mouth, *flit*, a pink tongue zipped out and another fly vanished.

"Daniel?" said Dr. Frederick, "are you feeling well?"

"Breet," replied Daniel.

"Do you think your eating is a problem?"

"Bort."

"Hmm. Well, I'm still going to give you the name of a nutritionist. If you're only eating flies, it might be wise to expand your diet a bit – you know, moths, flying ants, mosquitoes – you are a growing frog and your body requires lots of calories. Could be an addiction-allergy, which means you crave food you're allergic to – like flies. A nutritionist can help you." Dr. Frederick wrote the name of a nutritionist on the back of his business card and handed it to Mrs. Gallsworthy.

"Oh, thank you, thank you," gushed Mrs. Gallsworthy, standing. "I think this will be most helpful and might solve our problems."

"I hope so," said Dr. Frederick.

Smiling, Mrs. Gallsworthy put the card in her purse and snapped it shut. She turned to Daniel. "Let's go, Danny." She walked out the door, Daniel hopping close behind her.

Dr. Frederick sighed. That was fairly easy and not too unusual. He hoped the rest of the day was the same, and it pretty much was.

There was Mr. Gleckin, a young man with dark eyes and black hair who complained of a burning sensation on his back. He requested burn medication without considering that his flaming shirt might be the problem. And there was Mrs. Enrod who, with pigeons nesting in her hair, said she couldn't understand where the white spots on her clothes came from. She liked Dr. Frederick's suggestion of wearing polka-dotted dresses until she could decide what to do about the pigeons.

Then there was Mr. Slather, a very fat, fifty-five-year-old man, who pulled behind him a red wagon filled with pastries. He complained he couldn't understand his constant weight gain and requested a weight reduction diet while sucking down a milkshake.

At the end of the day, at five-o'clock, Dr. Frederick sighed. Miss Leo brought in the checks for the day and Dr. Frederick stared at her. "Little blue flames on your blouse again."

She glanced down, "Oh yes, heartburn. Too much alcohol recently."

"You've been dealing with that ever since I've known you."

She nodded. "It's so hard to change. I just have to keep on working at it. Good night," she smiled, "I'll see you tomorrow."

"Indeed," he replied. "Have a good evening."

Finally, it was Dr. Frederick's turn to leave.

Slowly, and with great effort, he stood, and realized, as he had realized many, many times before, that someday he'd have to do something, *something*, about that twenty-pound anvil in the seat of his pants . . .

Coming Home So Cold

NO, NO. MY father is not the kind of person you would expect to see on a starcraft. On a farm, yes, on a starcraft, no. And even if you saw him on a farm, you'd wonder about him. From a distance, you'd see him as extremely tall, thin; wrists like flesh-covered wire and you'd think, "My Lord, won't the wind blow him away?" Or, "My Lord, won't a hailstorm drive him into the ground like a nail?" Or, "My Lord, won't the sun fade him to nothingness?"

My father: Jack Montgomery Hollingsford – but to me and everyone else, Jackie, wheat straw from eastern Washington, tanned by sun, scoured and blasted by Palouse winds that, in winter, etched icy fingers across the land.

Jackie always looked hollowed and gaunt; sunken cheeks, deep set green eyes and wrinkles across his forehead like furrowed earth. Hair white as sun and sparse as its warmth on a February day.

I guess if I saw him for the first time, I'd think: this man. This withered seed of a man. This man was covered by thin wrapper of old style clothing which covers stretched paper of skin . . . what is he doing – going into space, I suppose? What? But I was joking! Why, he's at least eighty-five! Aren't there age restrictions?

Or. This man! What is he doing here on Earth Station Four? He's what? He's waiting to board the shuttle from this station to the starcraft? What!? Isn't that just a little absurd? Where would he be going?

Or. Oh, come on! What? This man is on his way to where? Prandor? Sure. Sure he is. To see his son? You're serious? But Prandor is a colony world – it's still being explored! Man, not just anyone goes there! I mean, not him – you realize the restrictions? And the cost? Oh? Oh! He's the one? He did that? He's the one who got Hutchinson Stardrive to locate in Spokane, Washington? Oh, God!

I was on Prandor when I heard the news that my father had completed his part in the multi-billion dollar deal. I sat down hard on the ground.

"Son of a bitch," I whispered, "he did it!"

Big and hulking Stanly came over. "Shit. Just heard the news. Hey, rich boy! Wow! Son of *the* Jack Montgomery Hollingsford. Hey! Wow! Your daddy's quite the something, ain't he?"

"Yeah," I replied, "yeah, he is. He's crazy. Didn't I tell you he's crazy?"

Stanly scratched his vast red beard. "I'm more interested in how he played such a big part in it."

"Ever been to the Northwest?"

"Nope."

I picked at the grass. "There's always been rivalry between Spokane and Seattle. Seattle looks at Spokane the way a queen looks at a street-walker. All the main commerce, all the goodies, seemed to go to Seattle. My father learned, God knows how, that Hutchinson Stardrive was looking for Northwest factory space. Hutchinson was considering either Seattle, or Portland, Oregon. All this was hush-hush until my father found out and leaked it to the papers."

Stanly looked puzzled. "How did your dad find out?"

I smiled. "Jackie's hobby is real estate. When it comes to deals, I swear he's both telepathic and clairvoyant. And before he makes any deals, he consults the *I Ching*. Anyway, after he found out, however he found out, he told the papers and Spokane screamed. Jackie was the loudest screamer."

"So?"

"So this. Jackie was a prosperous farmer and had been buying land around Spokane."

Stanly smiled. "Oh, ho. Clever."

"Sure," I said, "Jackie screams, 'You bloody bastards! Isn't Spokane good enough for you?' and then turns right around and says, 'Now that I have your attention, I just happen to have six hundred acres of land you can buy for fifteen million; but, of course, if you'd rather settle for three hundred acres in Seattle at one billion dollars . . . ' "

Stanly looked impressed. "With that kind of money, he could easily afford to visit you."

"Yeah," I laughed, "but the irony is that the trip isn't costing him anything. Hutchinson was so pleased that they asked him what they could do for him. And he told them: 'I wanna look around the galaxy.' Hutchinson officials were a little – ah – aghast – and it meant looking at or bending some regulations, but Jackie got what he wanted and part of his trip is a stop here." I shook my head. "He's kept me well briefed – but to see him actually pull it off – " I laughed.

Stanly began laughing, too. "Well, Jesus Christ. When's he coming?"

"Probably some time next month, I imagine." I looked up at the violet sky. "Yeah, probably next month."

Sure enough, one morning some weeks later, silver glinted in the early sky and soon the shuttle ship from the starcraft landed. And out walks my father. From a distance, he looked as tall and wind scoured as he always did. His clothes were the same as I remembered: striped gray pants, white shirt, dark vest and a coat that matched his trousers. The shoes were shiny white and new as the suitcase he carried – red and yellow plastifoam. He set that down, removed his hat and scratched his head.

I walked up to him, extended my hand. "How you doing, Jackie?"

"Right well, Edward, right well." His handshake was firm and strong.

"You look good," I said. And he did. Could never figure out how a guy so thin could be so damn strong. Honest to God, it was like every cell in his body replaced itself with steel every day. That, or you have to be born with steel in your guts if you're from eastern Washington, home of Sahara summers and Arctic winters and constant sandblasting. Maybe it was the sandblasting which made him so thin.

"Nice place," he said as he set down his suitcase. "Anything get in my pants if I sit?"

"Nope."

He sat on the ground.

"Grass okay to chew?"

"Yeah."

He pulled a long sliver of grass, stuck it in his mouth, laid back on the ground and put his hands behind his head and looked up at the sky. Two large, reddish moons hung in the purple sky. "How many moons this place got?"

"Three."

"Huh." Long pause. "Sky's the wrong color."

"This isn't Earth, Jackie."

"Huh." Then he rolled onto his side. "Good to see you. How you like it here?"

"It's okay," I said. "Miss Earth sometimes. You come all the way out here to see me?"

"Ain't that reason enough? Ain't that a good reason for a father to come see his son?" Then he smiled – no, not so much with his lips; rather, with his eyes. Yeah, that's the Jackie I know. Yeah. Unless you look into those green eyes, you could be staring at chiseled rock. It's the eyes. It always was his eyes: the awareness, gentleness, toughness, sharpness, laughter, calculation – and the genius who gave eastern Washington a major manufacturing center and himself fifteen million dollars. He had that way: he had made a fortune growing wheat and fruit and somehow always made it. Others might fail – he would make it. It was like he had a subconscious contact with earth. It was as though he could put his hand on earth and feel its temperature, pulse, breath and knew, knew when the earth was ready for seed. He listed to the land and spoke gently to it and the land yielded to him and yielded and yielded again to him.

"Ain't no secret," he used to say, "just listen to the land and it'll tell you what you want to know but you got to listen, listen and listen hard."

And because he listened, the wheat was full and yellow. And the orchards thrived; oh, bumper crops of apples, peaches and cherries. Oh, God, the cherries, so black and the juice sweet and blood dark. The orchards were oases of green surrounded by scorched brown hilltops with protruding boils and pustules of ancient lava.

During winter, snow gripped and gripped again the crevices and cracks of rock. Yet, just below those tortured summits of rock, the trees were spared from icy onslaught. The winds never touched the barren trees though the boughs did not seem to have that much protection. Storms raged and the sky was black and gray, low and moving like a thick and tattered blanket, yet the trees, the trees seemed to sleep under delicate white, undisturbed, untroubled by the violence overhead. The serenity amidst chaos – it seemed to me part of Jackie's gift, too: protection and care. So often I thought, yes, yes, the land knew of him and felt secure by him and was, in turn, good, so good to him.

My father walked and the grass turned green and flowers bloomed. My father walked and the wheat turned gold and apples reddened. He walked and peaches became swollen and cherries heavy and black and boughs drooped under their heavy sweetness and bees stung the cherries and the black juice ran and amidst this, my father walked as one who had no extraordinary talents – simply out for a stroll; his hands in his pockets, stopping occasionally to gaze out over the land.

And now this man lay on the ground of Prandor, looking at me, smiling with his eyes. Then he sat up. "It's a rich world," he finally said. "The soil is good here. Could support a lot of people."

"Yeah," I said, "it easily could. Say – "

He cocked his head a bit and waited.

"The orchards, the wheat fields back home – they aren't going to be destroyed by Hutchinson – "

He then smiled with his lips as though his lips were finally catching up with his thoughts. "Ha. What do you think?" He stood and slapped his arm about my shoulders, and laughed. "Ha, ha! Hell, no. The orchards, the fields, they're for you. Remember now, it's only a small part of what was, but it's the best. It's yours whenever you want it, whenever you return."

I nodded and grinned.

"You think I'd have it any other way?"

"Guess not."

"Damn right. It's a good land. But remember, you got to listen to it. You got to listen to it, feel it, touch it and listen. And if you listen right, you'll know what to do and everything will be okay."

He then took out from a coat pocket a little leather bag. Opening it, he pulled out something round and colored – candy – no – I looked closely – a seed. A cherry seed.

"How did you – " I began.

"Shh!" he smiled. "Surprising what you can sneak on board."

"You know that's illegal – if you get caught – "

He grinned. "I won't." He knelt on one knee, found a stick, penetrated the earth, dropped in the seed and then covered it, pushing the dark soil together carefully, tenderly. When he looked up, there was a profound and gentle beauty in his eyes; I had seen it before when he would stand on a hill looking over waving yellow and gold oceans of wheat or when he'd walk through the orchards and touch an apple or a peach or a cherry; a profound love of the living, of caring and watching and nurturing things to grow, to become, to absolutely burst to their limits in making actual their potential.

Is that why the land responded? It knew when it was loved? My father. My father looked down at the ground. "Some day there will be a tree here. Some day a cherry tree. A cherry tree on Prandor. And on every world I stop, I'm going to do the same. I'm going to plant a seed."

My father stayed for three months on Prandor. We flew the scout ship everywhere. My father said little during all of this, but his eyes told so much – the wonder, the comprehension, the beauty. He understood the world in a way that I could barely grasp. He communicated with it every time we touched down; it was as though he saw the world as an entity, a total being, and knew just where to scratch it and make the whole thing roll over on its back and purr; ah, someone had discovered how to give it the love and attention it wanted. And needed. And deserved. And would probably get less than often enough.

Suddenly Prandor was an incredible place to be. My father's face became a mirror on which I saw the seas shining all silver and bright and shimmering. A mirror: and the mists rolled and boiled over the hills, the jungles. A mirror: icy crags soaring to the dark sky. And the colors! Oh, the colors! Blues, greens, yellows, the greys of twilight, the dark wash of dusk, the violet sky, the gigantic ruddy moons. My father said little, but his eyes told all: Wonder! Wonder! Wonder!

I had been on Prandor for two God damn years and suddenly, with my father beside me, it was as though I was seeing it for the first time.

Finally, on the third month, Jackie had to say it. "Well, I guess I gotta be gettin' on."

He said it at camp. He said it when the sky was high with thunderheads. Suddenly the world about us snapped and spit with lightning-white brilliance and the thunder crashed and whammed and boomed and everything shook. And my father, my father in the dusk nodded faintly. "Sorry," he whispered, gazing out over the landscape, "other worlds to see." The whiteness snapped and flashed again and again and against it, my father was a tall and lean silhouette and I saw his eyes: profound sadness. "Yeah," and he put an arm around my shoulders, "I gotta get going. Spent all my life in eastern Washington and before I kick off, I wanna see the universe."

The growling and roar of thunder abated and the storm moved on. The sun came out then, and in the distance, slender trees were brilliant yellow swords against the dark sky. Drops of water on trees and bush sparkled and shimmered. I walked my father to the shuttle. He turned and in the setting sun, one side of his face became the color of warm gold, the other half in shadow. "Good-bye, son. Next stop, Illyorya."

"Good-bye, Jackie. Thanks for visiting."

My father. Tall, windblown straw from eastern Washington. We shook hands; he turned, walked up the ramp and into the belly of the shuttle. He turned again and waved; then, automatically the ramp raised and sealed the opening. In the distance, more lightning flashed and thunder rumbled. The automatic pilot of the craft engaged the engines; the craft lifted, higher, higher: a golden bird, higher, higher, a glint of light, higher, then soaring, soaring closer, closer to the sun and then beyond.

I stayed on Prandor another year. Nothing was the same after my father's visit. Sure, there was the routine, but somehow, everywhere I went, or no matter what I did, there was the newness of the world that I had seen through my father. And when it was time for me to go back to

Earth, my part in the exploration over, I walked by the place where my father had first stopped and sat. And there, poking up through the soil, the sprout of the cherry tree. My father was here; it'll be a beautiful tree.

One month later, I was back in eastern Washington. It was April and the sky was a searing blue (it seemed so incredibly alien at first!). Already the wheat was green and waving like an undulating sea. After several days of settling in at the farm, I went to the post office to pick up a year's supply of mail. And there was a card, mailed on Mycrilia, two months earlier, that had arrived at the post office on the day I had returned to Earth. I stared at the card. On one side was a holographic image of a scantily clad woman up against a wall of rock while some horrible, presumably native, beast of Mycrilia – something of scales and fangs and claws and somehow lustful look in the yellow cat-like eyes – towered over the woman. On the other side of the card, a neatly written message:

> Dear Edward: Don't just stand there! Save the lady! Having a wonderful time. I've forgotten how many cherry trees I've planted. How's the one on Prandor doing? Never felt so well in all my life. Best wishes to you and say hello to Dale."
>
> Love, Jackie
>
> P.S. Wish me Happy Birthday. I'm 87 today. Celebrating it in the middle of the galaxy is an experience. But I *do* miss Earth.

I smiled. As I walked the two miles back to the farm, I must have looked at the card a dozen times. And smiled and laughed nearly as often.

When I got back to the farm, I was hot. I went into the house, tossed the mail on the table, got a beer from the cooler and then sat on the porch. I looked for Dale. In Jackie's absence, and in mine, Dale McHanney, a cousin, had been running the farm. In the time I had been back, I had seen him several times.

Dale was as fat and as plump as a peach and his eyes were as dark as Bing cherries. At thirty, he was prematurely bald and he always wore a hat, even on the hottest days ("Pertek 'gainst cold." And on just right days, he would say, "I like to wear hat.") and he never said he wore it because he was bald.

Dale kept pretty much to himself and, like an obese bumble bee, he bumbled through the orchards or fields, seemingly without much direction. Yet, the farm seemed in good shape and it appeared that Dale did the necessities to keep the farm going, although I suspect he did not do much more than the necessities.

Once in a great while he might instigate a conversation – one with a lot of holes and spaces in it. It was as though it took him an hour to think up the words, fit them together and another hour just to pronounce them and make sure they came out all right. The longest talk I had with him was when I first returned – and even that conversation didn't last more than five minutes.

I drained my beer and went in for another one. When I returned, Dale had started to mow the lawn. I waved to him; he nodded. The sound of the mower; a thousand drowsy bees. The wind cool . . . beer . . . good . . . mower, the . . . mower . . . a thousand drowsy . . . drowsy bees . . . and when I awoke, it was late afternoon. The smell of freshly cut grass was an exotic and rich perfume. Beyond the yard, the road, unpaved and dusty, and on the other side of the road, the orchards and the steep hills with outcroppings of lava.

To the right of the orchards, the hills parted and the valley opened out into the vast, now green, sea of wheat fields.

Sunset. The top of the hills changing colors from yellow to amber. Dale came ambling through the orchards. It was cool, the last week in April, the trees rich and white in blossoms. Their fragrance along with that of the cut grass created an intoxicating nectar and I drank and I drank the air and drank it again. I looked to the sky, still surprised that it was blue, not purple, and that at the most, I'd see only one moon, not three. And the moon would be white and very, very far away.

Dale finally clomped across the road. Every time he stepped, a cloud of dust billowed out from his large feet. He came up on the porch and sat on the railing. He wiped his face with his shirt sleeve, but did not take off his hat.

"You really need that hat tonight, Dale?"

Slowly he nodded, finally he said, "Pertek 'gainst mosquitoes."

"Oh." I hadn't heard that one before.

"How . . . how's your . . . your daddy?"

"He had a birthday the other day, Dale. Eighty-seven. Doing real well."

"Huh?"

"Jackie had birthday. Eighty-seven. Doing good."

"Oh! Oh." Long, long pause. "Where . . . where he is?"

"Traveling about the universe, Dale. Visiting all the planets he can possibly visit."

"Huh?"

"Traveling. Space ship."

"Oh, oh."

Another long pause. The sun set more, the hills turned darker, the fragrance of blossoms, grass, heavier, overpowering. Twitter of birds. Distantly, in the house, *click-hummmmmm* as the cooler came on.

"Your daddy comin' – comin' home." He looked at me, his eyes dark.

I shrugged. "I don't know Dale. He must have visited about every planet there is to visit by now – " The eyes continued to stare, darkness, darkness. "Don't know. Soon maybe."

Dale nodded and looked away.

He was calm. I was suddenly unsettled, for Dale hadn't asked a question. Jackie coming back? Then I was aware that Dale was talking in a low voice, " . . . he come back soon. Real soon."

"What?"

"He come soon."

"How do you know?"

Dale did not respond. Instead, he stood and as he walked past me, I suddenly felt a profound sadness. I shook my head and tried to compose myself but the feeling of sadness would not leave. Sometime later, I went to bed. The feeling still had not left.

Jackie came home.

He had been coming home slowly, slowly, all night long until the small hours in the morning when the sun was a heartbeat below the rim of the world. I awoke suddenly. It was so very, very early in the morning and dad had finished coming home and I clutched the bedsheets Jackie had come home and trembling, trembling, I looked out the window and the sky was a cold, cold pale blue and Venus as white as ice in the sky Jackie had come home and all around outside, sudden frost was thick and white and things just bloomed and plants fresh and newly greened bended, bended, embrittled; the crystal spiders with cold bite penetrating and drawing away the warmth, the life, Jackie had come home and the air was dry as ice and the rising sun's warmth was as though fed by ice fires, the fire which makes your fingers burn and tingle and Jackie had come home but he did not stay. No, no. He passed through here and would never pass through here again and the land that loved him knew why the cold had come; wherever Jackie drew his final breaths, he drew his last one here; oh, no, no, he would not die away from Earth. He came home, passed through, and gone else where to another home; and life mourned him and let settle the frost of his death – yes, yes, it would evaporate in the sun, but the grasses would lay low; the blossoms from the apples, the cherry and the peach trees; the blossoms would snow down, a blizzard in April. Jackie had come back, yes, come back and passed through and gone home somewhere deep, deep in the earth from where he was born and I looked out the window at the ice blue sky so cold and the frost was white so cold and the moon was as thin and as white as a sliver of frost so cold and the sun, rising, gleamed and gave no warmth so cold Jackie had come back and gone home, my Jackie and I shivered and I trembled and I shuddered so cold so cold so cold.

Onions

EDWARD HAS ALWAYS been fascinated by onions. Strange things, onions, he thinks as he cuts one up for a salad. You cut them and you cry, you peel them and layer after layer comes off. How strange onions are.

The doorbell rings. He goes to the door, opens it, and there is a little blue alien dressed in a silver suit and carrying an attaché case. "Extril calling," says the alien. "Would you care to see our wonderful display of games, tricks and products from all over the Empire? We have items that will thrill, delight or teach every member of a Terran nuclear family."

Edward ponders this. He smiles. "Won't you come in. We have Christmas coming up and I really would like to pick out something unusual."

"Wonderful!" says the alien and he walks in; Edward has him sit down while he, Edward, clears the coffee table of magazines so that the alien has somewhere to put his attaché case. The alien then opens the case and Edward stares at all the merchandise made on hundreds of worlds throughout the Empire.

The alien smiles. "Ah, you do look interested. What appeals to you the most?"

Edward sits down near the alien. "What's that?" he points to a clear glass ball, about the size of a large marble.

The alien smiles. "From my home planet, Yiggle. A Weather Reflector."

Edward looks dubious. "A what?"

"Weather Reflector. Tells you what the weather is going to be like an hour in advance." The alien reaches into the case and takes the object out and places it on the table, "Now," says the alien, "look outside. What do you see?"

Edward looks out the window. Low, brooding clouds move across the sky. Edward frowns. "Looks terrible out."

"Well," says the alien, "let's see what the weather is going to be like an hour from now."

The alien touches the ball with a long blue finger. The ball stirs, a miniature gold sun appears in the middle; the little ball suddenly sprouts hands and feet and begins to do a tap dance.

"Ah, says the alien, "it's going to be fair and sunny. A perfect day to have fun and dance." The alien hands the ball a short piece of string. The Weather Reflector takes it and proceeds to skip rope: *click-click-click* go the little feet on the coffee table top.

"Amazing," says Edward. "Just amazing."

"When the weather will be gray and gloomy, a little dark cloud will appear in the middle of the ball and it will rock back and forth, making dark little sounds. If it's going to be windy, bits and pieces of paper and grit will whirl around inside it. If stormy, the ball will walk as though leaning into the wind while also trying to hold an imaginary hat on its head.

"Ah," says Edward, genuinely pleased, "my sister can use that. She never gets the weather forecast right. Maybe this will help her."

The little glass ball with the miniature sun inside resumes tap dancing and whistles a gay little tune.

"What else do you have?" asks Edward. But he answers his own question when he sees a key ring; the ends are little hands locked in a tight handclasp.

"Ah," says the alien, grinning, "one of our most popular items. Made on the planet Klud – a planet on which they have just discovered locks and keys – and a population which has also discovered how easy it is to lose keys." The alien picks it up. Instantly, the little hands break their grasp and hang on to the alien's finger. "For the being which cannot afford to lose keys," says the alien, "I present the Insecure Key Ring. Instead of looking for your keys, this key ring comes looking for *you!* It also screams and yells at you for mislaying it and dearly hangs on to belt loop, finger, button hole; the fingers also have retractable claws which, when extended, will hang on to fabric."

"Cousin Alfred is always losing his keys. I'll take it."

The alien removes the key ring from his finger. It screams in a high little voice; the hands become fists that shake threateningly. The alien places the key ring on the table; the two hands become as feet and the ring scampers across the table, leaps toward the alien and grabs the alien's sleeve.

"No, no," says the alien, "you have a new owner now."

The alien plucks the ring from his sleeve and gives it to Edward. The ring, with a squeal of joy, grabs hold of Edward's sleeve, happy at finding someone else to latch onto.

"Dependent, isn't it?" murmurs Edward.

"Yes," says the alien, "very much so. It simply can't stand being alone. That's why it makes such a wonderful key ring."

With frightening intensity, the key ring's little hands clutch Edward's sleeve.

"Yes," says Edward, "cousin Alfred definitely needs this." Then, "What else do you have?"

The alien looks over the many items. "I've noticed that your species wears socks."

"Yes."

"Well, here we have socks that can never lose each other; socks that love to be worn, love to be washed, tumbled dry and they never lose each other."

Edward thinks of all the mismatched pairs of socks he has and how many have walked out of his life; he is at once skeptical. "How is it possible for socks never to lose each other?"

The alien smiles. "At the risk of making a pun, they can never lose each other because they're always mating."

A silence follows while Edward ponders this. He thinks back to his own inconvenience. Yesterday, he hunted all morning and never did find the mate to a blue sock. "Yeah," he says, "yeah, that sounds pretty good. Maybe I'd better buy a few – I'll take six pair," Then, "Uh – do they eat?"

"Sort of." The alien picks out the socks. "They seem to survive very well on a diet of sweat. They also repair themselves so that they never get holes."

"Very nice," says Edward, "very nice indeed." And then, thoughtfully, "but do you have anything a little less active – you know, something nice like soap or perfume . . . "

The alien studies the contents of the case. "Well," he finally says, picking out a small vial of amber-colored fluid, "how about some nice hallucinogenic perfume?"

Edward just looks, uncomprehending.

The alien smiles, screws off the cap, dabs some on his finger and then rubs it across the back of Edward's hand. "Smell," says the alien and, hesitantly, Edward does. It is the smell of roses and he sees himself standing in a vast, open field, the sky the color of an early June day, the grass up to his knees in vivid, green youngness, oh, the smell of roses, roses and Jennifer comes walking through the grass, her smile sun radiant, her hair buttercup yellow and she walks, swinging her arms in a leisurely, relaxed way and suddenly they are running to each other, oh, roses, roses, he can feel the grass whipping about his legs, the tops of the grass kissing his fingers, the world all blue and green and shining sun and then their arms around each other, oh, roses, roses, and kissing and the air the smell of roses, and falling into the grass, falling to the damp earth, the sun so white, the sky so blue and the world smells of roses, roses, her breasts against him, she breathing in the ear, whispering, "Now, Edward, Edward, now, now!" and Edward looks at the bottle and says to the alien, "Good Christ! How many bottles you got? I'll buy them all!"

"Just have the one," says the alien, obviously pleased.

"Can I have another smell?" asks Edward, leaning forward.

"Not now," says the alien. "I've got something else to show you."

Edward leans forward even more; he is having a difficult time controlling his hands, as if, at any second he would lurch forward and grab the perfume. The alien pushes the bottle a little farther out of the way and says, "It's not that I don't want you to have fun with the perfume, but – ah – some customers get so taken by it that they go off into hallucinations for hours, sometimes days, and I don't get paid. After I leave, you can hallucinate however way you wish for however long you wish. All right?"

Edward sighs but still leans forward. "All right. What else have you got?"

The alien looks into his attaché case once more. "Hm!" he says. "I thought I had at least one more thing – but I guess – " The alien stares at something. "Oh, yes, yes, I thought I had something else here – " He picks up a rectangular object and gives it to Edward.

Edward feels it. "Soap?" he says. He sniffs it. "Doesn't have much of a smell." It is pale green and does indeed feel like soap. Edward looks at the alien. "It is soap, right?"

The alien looks somewhat perplexed. "Well, I guess you could call it soap. It's from Opayknon."

"Opayknon?"

"Yes," says the alien. "Some of this universe's greatest and most profound truths about existence and self are formulated there. And whenever they bathe, they all use this soap."

Edward still looks askance at the soap, "But – it's still soap – isn't it? I mean, it's supposed to get you clean, right?"

"Oh, yes," says the alien. "It does indeed get you clean." Then, nodding to himself, "Yes, yes, it does indeed get you clean."

"Well," says Edward, looking at his treasures, "thank you for dropping by. I'm sure all these gifts will come in handy for someone."

"Oh, yes," the alien says, closing his attaché case. "We usually have something for everyone. Now, let me see how much this will be."

He reaches in a side pocket of his suit and produces a black cube that fits into the palm of his hand. He concentrates and little blue numbers appear on the top of the cube. The total appears on one side. He puts the cube back; from another pocket, he produces a small receipt book and as he fills it out Edward gazes upon his treasures: the little, gaily dancing sphere with the miniature sun inside (Edward glances out the window and indeed, the sun is breaking through the clouds); the key ring (hanging so tenaciously to Edward's shirt sleeve that the fabric is wrinkled); the six pairs of socks (red, blue, yellow, green and two plaids) lying in tight little balls twitching this way and that in ecstasy (Edward is glad that they are mute – it simply would not do to be sitting on a public transport and having your socks lusting after each other and making dirty little noises as well); and nearby is the perfume which Edward wants to try again as soon as he can – and there is the soap. Edward smiles. It is going to be a good Christmas. All these neat and wonderful goodies! He idly wonders if he is going to get as many interesting things as he is giving. He would not mind having a Weather Reflector or an Insecure Key Ring. And at that point, the little blue alien gives Edward a bill of sale.

"Twenty-two fifty Terracredits; twenty base total, two-fifty to take care of tax and currency differences."

Edward takes the bill of sale and finds the Terracredits in his wallet. The transaction completed, Edward and the alien stand and shake hands.

"Thank you," says Edward. "These will make great gifts. But – " and he looks thoughtful, "in regard to the soap, do I just use it as soap? You know, water, wash cloth and so forth?"

The alien nods. "Yes. And take it from me, for the first time in your life, you're going to feel truly clean."

Edward does not reply. He just picks up the soap again and looks at it with curiosity and suspicion. He shows the alien to the door; they shake hands once again, and all the while Edward holds the soap. After the alien leaves, Edward goes back and sits on the davenport.

Click-click-click. The Weather Reflector is jumping rope again.

The Insecure Key Ring still desperately clutches Edward's sleeve.

With an effort, he pulls it off and says, "I'll be back."

The ring howls mournfully, then pounds on the table with little fists. Edward sighs. Maybe he won't wait until Christmas to give cousin Alfred the Insecure Key Ring. He stands and is torn with indecision as he looks to the perfume and the soap. He thinks a moment longer, then goes to the bathroom. The kitchen, the onion, can wait. The soap is the only thing he has not really understood.

And so: into the shower. He lets the water spray over him a few minutes while he thinks, so, I have the soap that all Opayknons use. Edward tries to think of what he knows about their culture and remembers a comment he heard long ago: "To them, Dostoevsky is an idiot."

Edward holds the soap a few more minutes. Maybe he really shouldn't do this. Just *what* would such a culture as the Opayknons put in soap? What miracle ingredients? Would he be shocked? Surprised? He smiles to himself. Only one way to find out. He wets his wash cloth and tries to make a lather, but not much comes of it. It is more like some sort of abrasive. He shrugs and applies the bar directly to his skin and behold! It is as though a shell of something washes off him – no, not skin, but a layer of something almost transparent, like, yes, skins of an onion. And, as whatever it is washes off, it forms images on the bottom of the tub as it runs to the drain – one image is Edward seeing himself being intimidated by his father. "God damn!" he mutters and he stomps the very vivid image with his foot. The image breaks apart and washes to the drain.

With a strange eagerness, Edward scrubs himself again with the soap. Another image forms at the bottom of the tub; this time, his profound manner of feeling guilty and wanting to keep people away. And he stomps *that* image with his foot. And that image washes away down the drain. Yes, he thinks, scrubbing himself down a third time, yes, like peeling away layers of an onion until you get to the heart of the matter.

And sure enough, another layer of something washes off Edward and pools in the bottom of the tub: his inability to express anger directly and he sees it when a waiter gives him the wrong wine and instead of saying something, Edward takes the wine but leaves no tip. And Edward stomps *that* image with his foot. And he scrubs down a fourth, a fifth, a sixth time and then something strange happens. His skin takes on a translucent, then a transparent quality and there, in his heart, he sees a small image of himself, a childlike image who waves back at him and says, "Thank you for shedding all the bullshit! You had me under so many layers of self-distortion, I was beginning to wonder if you'd ever let me come out again."

"Dear God," mutters Edward, looking into his heart. He drops the soap and the water splashes over him.

"You know," says the figure in his heart, "I think we ought to go to Opayknon."

Edward smiles. "You know," he says, "I think you're right."

Edward shuts off the shower, gets dressed, packs a suitcase. He writes a brief note to his cousin Alfred, explaining that the key ring is for him, the perfume is for Aunt Agatha whose depression might be helped by it (if, of course, she wants to be helped), the socks for her son who has a terrible time keeping his socks together and the Weather Reflector – that goes to Edward's sister. And the soap? There isn't much left of it; just a small wedge.

With suitcase in hand, Edward looks around the house. The Insecure Key Ring is screaming and running frantically around the coffee table, desperately looking for something to clutch. The perfume sits there, ready to intoxicate and bring about a being's wildest fantasies. And *click-click-click* – the Weather Reflector is dancing again while the socks twitch in constant delight. It should be a great Christmas for everyone, he thinks. As a last, perhaps symbolic, act, Edward goes to the kitchen and throws the onion away. Then, smiling, he picks up his suitcase, walks to the public transport that will take him to the spaceport and eventually to Opayknon. As he walks, he feels for the first time in his life truly clean. And the small childlike image of himself in his heart smiles widely, closes its eyes and sighs luxuriously.

Of The Odd Events In Regard To Mr. M.

IT WAS THE favorite pastime of Mr. M., an older gentleman with a rather plump belly and a very red nose and small eyes that nonetheless saw adequately and everything that he needed to see, it was the habit of this man to sit outside his rather meek house but which, of course, had a very large porch as houses did in this part of the country which was rather warm for much of the year, and with a wonderful view out to the valley and to the long, dark road that lead up to his place. It was the habit of this man to sit out on the porch in the evening, in his jeans, drink a big beer and read over the day's events in the newspaper from the town, the lights of which twinkled like a swath of the Milky Way in the sinuous valley far down below.

Mr. M. enjoyed this habit of reading the paper that was delivered by young Roman, a man of dark hair and eyes with a sense of impulsivity but, thought Mr. M., I was that way when I was young. And on this particular day, there was the paper on the porch and Mr. M. had finished his dinner of legumes and chopped onions, carrots, and celery too, then went with his beer, sat in the rocking chair, and sighed, ah, so wonderful to be alive, to look out and see the sun's rays slanting yellow and making the dusty brown hills glow like a smoldering low fire and the air was warm. Not far away, he could hear the barking of the Vera family's dog and the laughing scream of the Amanda kids and Mr. M. sighed luxuriously as he opened his paper and slowly scanned the headlines: *Governor Decrees No Leniency on Thieves,* and over there, *President Orders Commission To Study Railway Problems* and he was about to turn the page when, down in the corner, a most curious headline: *Death of Mr. M. Saddens Community* and the story read, "Mr. M. of so and so address was found dead of apparent heart attack." What a coincidence, Mr. M. thought, as he read, a gentleman with coincidentally the same address as myself somewhere in the city. How odd, and he read further, "Mr. M. was a well known banker several years ago in the blahblah Bank in the west side of the district in the city of Suchandsuch and so forth and so on" – and Mr. M's eyes grew very wide. A joke, he thought this is but a joke, why, he'd call that newspaper office and have the paperboy fired immediately and maybe he might take a suit out against the paper for such a slanderous joke and angrily he turned the paper and there was another story about half way down, *Mrs. Soandso Remembers Mr. M.* and he read, "He was always so studious in school and a very serious boy, we always knew that he would go somewhere in our community. " And Mr. M. stared at a picture of the woman: yes, it was his old school teacher, the one who had the brown stringy hair and the smudged glasses that always strayed down her nose until they looked like they were going to drop off. And the colors that she wore – oh, they always clashed. Mr. M. read further, yes, and there was the minister of the parish who said that Mr. M. " . . . would always be remembered as a pillar of the community with fine upstanding values and who never hesitated to give money to the local chapter of the Anti-Liberal League – " Well, thought Mr. M., reading this over, at least this gentleman who certainly *sounds* like me, was well regarded in his community. Thank goodness for *that*. And he read the paper some more and there, on page five, a picture of a man and a woman taken some years ago. Slowly Mr. M. reached down and picked up his beer, vaguely noticing that his hand was shaking and only dimly did he notice spilling beer on himself. He looked at the picture of that man and that woman and he sighed as he thought, Yes, that was Marcia herself, quite a few years ago . . . the headline read, *Well Respected Couple Took Frequent Trips Abroad.* "Yes," he whispered, then sipping the beer, "yes, we did much traveling then. Ah, yes we did." And he closed his eyes tight, Marcia, oh, how, how I've missed you, oh, Lord, how I've missed you. And he sighed and turned the page. Another small article, *Mr. M.'s Son To Eulogize Father*. The story went on about how his son, Thomas, was going to talk about his father's distinguished military record in the Great War – ah, he thought to himself, Thomas, how could you know that I fought more with the paperwork than I did at the front lines but I am honored that you respected me or, he smiled to himself, that I stretched the facts so well. And by the time he got to the end of the paper, he did not know what to think. This must be a joke but who would go to such an elaborate extent to make such a joke? He sipped his beer and looked out to the hills now bathed in the red hue of a just-set sun and overhead he saw Venus, glowing like it was molten burning silver, and he said to himself, "I don't know what to think of this – honest to God, I really don't. It must be a joke it just must be a joke, what else could it be?

Who would do this to me? And he thought back. Had he made any enemies recently, for surely this was a joke, he was alive and he pinched his flesh on his wrist and watched it slowly flatten out again and he still heard the Vera's dog and he took a deep breath, yes, that was still air filling his lungs and he closed his eyes, yes, that was honeysuckle on the wind – then this would have to be a mistake. It would just have to be. And he began to laugh. He put the paper down and began to laugh and he thought about the plans for tomorrow – yes, he would get up early and go into town as he usually did and he would stop at the cafe and visit with old Marteen who had a bit of a wheezing laugh but always had something good to say and always good humor danced in those green eyes and there was Rosie, yes, she always served him first in the cafe and he could hear her voice now, "Ah, Mr. M., down for your morning stroll are you? What will you have today? Some coffee like you always do? Cream and sugar, of course?"

"Of course," he would always reply.

He smiled at the memory of so many days spent that way and so too tomorrow. Opening his eyes, he looked at the paper once again and drank the beer. Yes, he could go in to the newspaper office and ask to talk to Mr. Rasio directly. He would say, "Mr. Rasio, I don't know who wrote this story but I do not consider it humorous at all. Whatsoever. Whatsoever at all. Do you understand? I have hardly died. I am standing right here before you and how dare you say that I have died? I want you to print that you've made a mistake, that I am hardly dead – " He smiled at the look Mr. Rasio would have on his face, a look of shock, of Mr. Rasio stumbling about with his words, saying, "Oh, Mr. M. we are truly sorry! We don't know how this could have happened! We really don't! Yes, yes, we will print a correction immediately! We will put it right on the front page with the headlines of the World – it's that important to us that we have your good will." And Mr. M. rocked back and forth, and in the twilight he looked out to the lights beginning to sparkle in the valley, and he could make out the cars pulling up that long road up the hill, noting with interest one that slowed, then turned up his long driveway, noticing, noticing the long shape first – and then staring – at the oncoming hearse.

NAPTIME

MR. SMAERD ALWAYS enjoyed talking about dreams. Having had a life filled with dreams, some of which came true and others which did not, he considered himself an expert. Of course, he considered himself an expert in other things as well: for example, fashion, with a taste for smart, different-colored black jackets which contrasted hideously well with his large green bubble pipe and his precisely sloppily cut blue hair. He also considered himself very well learned about many things and looked very professional. A professional dreamer, perhaps. And while he considered himself an expert, his neighbor, Mrs. Onions, who lived right next to him in the apartment building, considered herself an expert as well. Frequently, when Mr. Smaerd stepped out on his balcony, she was there, a glass of something or rather in her hand. She had a small nose, her hair was always untied neatly in back and she had a fondness for print dresses, usually with the colors of blue, yellow, orange, pink and green and somehow, Mr. Smaerd always had the sense that she looked like a walking flower garden, especially with all those bees crawling over her dress.

As far as what she did, Mr. Smaerd really didn't know. She was fifty or eighty and enjoyed looking out over her balcony to the stars beyond.

Whenever she saw Mr. Smaerd, she said, "Oh, did I have a good dream last night."

"Really," Mr. Smaerd said, "tell me about it."

"I was in a store and bought some toothpaste and several books." She shook her head. "Figure that one out."

Mr. Smaerd looked joyfully uncomfortable. "Tsk. That is a strange one. What is toothpaste and what are books?"

Mrs. Onions smiled. "I don't know. Has me totally by surprise. Then I had another one several visions ago – I was sitting in a boat on a river. Fishing."

"Boat?" said Mr. Smaerd, "River?"

Mrs. Onions just shook her head again. "I don't know."

"Really," said Mr. Smaerd, somewhat inappropriately, "sometimes I worry about you. Your dreams make utterly no sense to me. When was the last time you had a dream that made sense?"

"Well," said Mrs. Onions, dropping her glass to see it explode on the pavement below, "it's been a while, let me tell you." She leaned on the railing which yielded reluctantly to her hefty arms. "The most recent one was that I was dancing on top of a sand dune, watching the sun go by on roller skates."

"Hm," said Mr. Smaerd, "at least that makes sense. But what are roller skates?"

Mrs. Onions just sighed and her breath brought tears to Mr. Smeard's eyes.

"Tsk," she said, "I wish I knew." And she looked at him. "But what about you? What dreams have you had recently?"

Mr. Smaerd laughed. "Some very naughty ones. Oh, I assure you, some very, very naughty ones."

"Really," said Mrs. Onions. "Tell me."

"Well, one was that I was sitting at a desk, dressed in blue jeans, a white, red and black plaid shirt with a maroon turtle neck, writing a short story about dreams on yellow paper at a green Hermes typewriter."

"Oh, my goodness," and Mrs. Onions blushed. "That is a naughty one."

"Not only that," said Mr. Smaerd, "but outside there was a wind howling, it was raining and the date was thirteen March, 1983."

"Oh, you nasty thing," said Mrs. Onions, looking away and pulling the top of her dress a little higher. "It sounds scandalous! Now if I just knew what a desk was or a short story or a typewriter – " and she shrugged, "but never mind; the story is filthy enough without all the details."

Mr. Smaerd looked away. "Oh, I don't know where they come from," he said. "I had no idea I had such filth in my mind. I'm almost ashamed to share them with you."

"Really," she said, "really. You ought to be ashamed of yourself." Her eyes twinkled. "Got any others?"

Mr. Smaerd pursed his lips and thought. "Yes, several visions ago, I dreamed – " and he deeply blushed, "I dreamed I was a bus driver."

"Oh!" said Mrs. Onions, delightfully offended. "How dare you, Mr. Smaerd! Oh, that is so delightfully pornographic!" She giggled. "Of course, I don't know what a bus driver is, but it certainly sounds nasty."

"Not only that," said Mr. Smaerd, leaning like he was sharing some utterly vile but juicy secret, "I was calling out directions!"

"Oh, my!" and Mrs. Onions howled with disgust and joy. She clapped her hands. "Oh, my, Mr. Smaerd, what lustful dreams you have."

"Had another one not too long ago." He laughed guiltily. "Dreamed I was a certified accountant."

"Well," said Mrs. Onions, "that certainly sounds lewd too. Certified yet. I don't know what that means, but I'm sure it's disgusting."

Mr. Smaerd laughed. "I don't know what it means either, but I woke up feeling disgusted. My, what goes through my mind. It surprises me. It really does. Do you know of anyone who has such strange dreams as we do?"

"Well," said Mrs. Onions, glancing to another apartment, "Mr. Egami told me one a few visions ago." She bit her lip. "He told me not to say anything and I think the poor man is a bit – " and she sighed, "you know. A shame." She snuffled back a tear. "He told me he had a dream that he was walking a dog in a park."

Mr. Smaerd looked delightfully sad. "It's a shame what happens to people when they get old. I mean their thought processes just – " He leaned on the railing which moaned slightly at the weight and he spread his hands in rage, "their thought processes – you know – they – " And he sighed from acute contempt, "thoughts just – " He shook his head and a tear of joy came to his left eye, " – processes – thoughts – can't – ood . . . pop . . . wup . . . "

"I know what you mean." said Mrs. Onions, "I know just what you mean. It's a shame to see what happens to people like that. It's so easy to see how he just can't think anymore."

"Indeed," said Mr. Smaerd, stretching. "Well," he said, glancing at the glazed sky, "I have to work yesterday. Did I ever tell you about the dream I had about working?"

"I don't believe so?" she asserted nebulously. Mr. Smaerd studied Mrs. Onions' dress and wondered idly what type of fertilizer she used to get those colors. "I'm almost afraid to say it," he said, "but I dreamed that I was a lawyer defending a very famous person."

Mrs. Onions looked mortified. "I'm so happy for you, that you would dream that." She grimaced. Then she looked a bit sure and secure. "I guess I'm not certain what a lawyer does, however."

Mr. Smaerd scowled neutrally. "Defends very famous people."

"Of course," said Mrs. Onions, understanding not at all. "Well," she said, "I must go in and see if my dinner is uncooked yet. It's been so nice talking to you – please, if you have any other dreams, do let me know."

"Will most certainly do that," he said. "Have a rough night of it."

“Thank you.” said Mrs. Onions and she went inside. “Same to you and more of it.”

Mr. Smaerd went into his apartment, ate a leisurely hurried meal and then fell asleep. When he woke up, he laughed. Dreams, he thought, such dreams. Mrs. Onions . . . Mr. Egami. He smiled, stretched and, as his usual habit, went outside, yelled “Vorp!” and ate the sky.

The Adman's Madman

WALTER P. PHILLIPS was thirty-five. Walter P. Phillips had a very large belly. Walter P. Phillips was balding and his nose was large and the skin on his face was rough and red. He had just bought a new house. He was deeply in debt. He had just had an affair with a woman at the advertising agency. The woman thought that Walter Phillips could get her a better job. Among other things.

"When did I say that?" he said as they lay in bed at the Tropics Hotel.

"You said that maybe you could do something."

"Well," he said, "there's nothing I can do."

She got dressed. "We'll see." She walked out of the room.

The next day, Walter P. Phillips came home.

"How was the convention at the Tropics Hotel, dear?" Mrs. Phillips said.

"Wonderful," he replied. He sat on the couch and as he sat, the air went out of the thick cushion with a *whoosh* and he sat back, secure in his excuse. "We came up with a whole new campaign."

His wife, in a maroon dress and her lovely dark hair as beautiful as always, walked out from the kitchen. "How was Fred Hutchinson?"

"He was in fine form. Came up with the best concepts."

Marion smiled. "And Ernst Packham?"

"Drunk as usual." He shook his head in sympathy. He looked at his wife; Gods, what a lovely! He really should stop messing around – to lose Marion –

"Okay," said Marion, still smiling, "he wasn't drunk as usual when he stopped by yesterday."

Something went *thud* in Walter P. Phillips. Like his heart had just dropped through his stomach, through the seat of his pants, through the couch and through the floor.

"Oh," he said. "I'm sorry. That was the *last* convention. He wasn't there this time."

"And Fred Hutchinson was in the hospital with a heart attack."

Walter P. Phillips looked at his wife. Marion looked at him. Inside, Walter P. Phillips was caving in, imploding like a too-dense star.

"How's Sheila?" asked Marion.

"Sheila who?"

"Shall I spell her name?" She smiled sweetly. "D-i-v-o-r-c-e." Then, with efficiency, she went to the closet, got her coat, walked out and slammed the door. Walter P. Phillips stared at the door for a long time before he got sick. And for a while, he stayed sick – so sick that the agency for which Phillips worked decided that since Walter P. Phillips was so good at creative content, he would have no trouble getting work elsewhere and that he really was underemployed there and so forth and so on and Walter P. Phillips, some weeks after all *this* had happened, was in bed and felt the closeness, the closeness, the terrible, closeness and he suddenly saw himself sitting on a hill. It was night and below him lights of the city flickered and as he watched, the sky began to pale and soften and the stars dimmed. In the distance, a bleak and black mountain range emerged from the darkness. As the horizon lightened, words became visible, words white and emerging in the sky. Walter P. Phillips read them: "This sky and the following reality presented as a special service to Walter P. Phillips by Sunn Cereals Incorporated." Just then the sun appeared over the horizon, a blazing white and bright sun, and Walter P. Phillips covered his eyes. The heat was intense and he found himself thinking, "So hot. So hot so early in the morning!" And he opened his eyes; the electric blanket was on.

He was sweating. He got up, changed his pajamas, and turned on the television. He looked out the sliding glass door; outside it was snowing. Outside it was very cold and on the eaves, icicles had formed, long and sharp and translucent, like slender, beautiful daggers, slowly growing. Walter P. Phillips shivered and went back to bed. Tomorrow, he thought, tomorrow I'll look for a job. Right now, I need to sleep. He crawled back in bed, the television his company, his lover, his friend, his identity; after all, some of what was on that tube – in terms of advertising – came from his mind as did the realization, as he dozed off . . . the heat of the sun was overpowering and yet, from somewhere, a wind blew; it blew and whispered, "Now, now for only fifty cents and two box tops from Sunn Cereals, you, too, can have a giant stone elephant with jade eyes in your back yard. Made of white marble, this elephant is the perfect conversation piece! Just think of what a marvelous gift this will be on Father's Day or for that hard-to-find gift for your student! Perfect to have outside near the pool! What more could you ask for!"

Walter P. Phillips turned and there stood the giant white marble elephant, the jade eyes green, as green as grass, as green as the skins of tiny frogs, and the white marble so white and bright and polished – and the elephant moved. Slowly it moved toward Walter P. Phillips, the eyes so green and bright and as real as Groovie Facial Soap for those troublesome years when skin blemishes blemish all hopes of peer group acceptance by anxious alienated teenagers – hey! Don't be left out in the social cold! No, no, no! Buy Groovie Facial Soap and be leader of the band, be class president, have a Corvette, get it every night *wowowowowow* dress in the best of clothes, be on the honor roll again and again! Groovie Facial Soap can give you this and *so* much more! Go to the store – for you there's hope with medicated Groovie Facial Soap! You, too, can have some fun! Scrub your face and *be* Someone! And the white elephant with green eyes moved and Walter P. Phillips stepped back; the sun was very warm on his back and he was sweating and the clothes stuck to him and his throat was dry and he suddenly remembered a conference he had with Hutchinson.

"Hutch! Aw, Hutch, Hutch, Hutch! You're too God damn sensitive! When you're in the selling business, you gotta kinda stretch facts."

Hutchinson, tall, black-haired, severe and hard-looking, shook his head. "There's a difference between stretching facts and outright lying."

"But it's not lying, Hutch! Look! Dig! The caption reads, 'You too, can get yours.' And you have a picture of Red Felt Liquor and a man and a woman drinking it. It's not lying. It's just association."

Hutch scowled. "It's dishonest. It really is."

"Look. Sex sells. That's the reality."

Hutchinson looked around the conference room as if he felt it to be unbearably cramped. "Oh, shit, Walt. You help *create* that image that sex sells. You help create a demand and then have the audacity to turn around and say that, 'It's not my doing that a demand exists! I'm just catering to it.' Jesus! That's downright irresponsible." Abruptly Hutchinson leaned forward and began gathering papers.

"Listen you asshole! Hasn't anyone told you about free enterprise?"

Hutchinson looked utterly contemptuous. "Hasn't anyone told *you* about exploitation! You don't see people as people. You just see buying power!"

"Look," and Walter P. Phillips spread his hands, "this is America. If people are dumb enough to buy bullshit, let them buy bullshit! No one's twisting their arms."

In disgust, Hutchinson slammed his briefcase shut, got up and left.

Walter Phillips shook his head, then shrugged as he thought, "Won't last. Won't last at all. Only the strong survive. Only the strong survive."

The elephant moved again. And as the elephant moved, it began to change. The eyes turned black and shining and there appeared more of them; the trunk changed to mandibles. Walter P. Phillips stepped back further. Overhead, the sun was intense.

Then he heard something and on the television was one of his commercials; ah, slick, slick, slick, and it was a commercial that was Walter P. Phillips' best; it was simple, ah, yes, so simple. The beach shot: an incredible sunset with the sounds of the waves crashing. No voice. In the middle of the shot, a low and sleek luxury sports car and a black- haired man in bathing briefs with his arms folded across a tan and hairy chest; a man looking arrogantly out at the world, a powerful man, a self-made man, a man who had competed and won and he stood leaning against the car and a woman walked up to him. A woman skimpily clad, she had long blond shining hair. She came up to him, sensually ran her hand across his stomach and he smiled condescendingly, arrogantly, and she got in the car on the other side and he smirked and climbed in and the camera zoomed in close to show her leaning against the man and running her hand up and down his bare leg just below the swimsuit and the car moved, moved off into the sunset and then the subtle, throaty voice: "Scorpion. Only for those who know how to *get it on*!" The picture began to flip and flip and flip and Walter P. Phillips got up and adjusted the set. As he came back to bed, he looked outside and the sky was black and the snow gray and the bushes and trees, shed of leaves, were outlined white by snow against the black sky and had the color of bone and looked like calcified dendrites, cold and still and dead, dead, dead. Walter P. Phillips trembled and climbed into the bed, burying himself in the covers just as a commercial came on in which a woman danced. The name of a wash day product appeared and the woman took sheets and pillow cases and held them up and the background scene was a country setting; all green and pure and the sky was blue and the wash so clean and the woman danced in a fit of existential joy and envious neighbors watched with pallid laundry, unable to join the woman in her joyful madness for she, she, *she* had the whitest wash around and was therefore a better person, a more acceptable person because *her* laundry was shades, shades above all others in the quest for perfect cleanliness and purity and therefore was closer to God, and the white elephant grew more legs and the body changed and became bulbous and elongated and darker and on its belly an hourglass appeared, a red, red hourglass and Walter P.

Phillips began to run and time began closing in on him; he could feel time scrambling behind him; he knew the bulbous, poisonous, ugly deceit was coming, coming, coming home and he did not have to turn to see the sunlight glittering off those eyes, all those eyes that saw him so clearly, that saw how the everyday dishonesty had permeated down, down, down past the skin, past the muscles, dawn, down, down to the marrow, into the white blood cells and then, like leukemia, the process had gone wild and poisoned the body and the body, so poisoned, became blinded to itself, became as a fly, blindly batting against a window, battling itself until, stupidly stunned, it fell randomly to the sill near a dark crevice where window met ledge, falling, falling onto sticky rope and from the darkness something moved and Walter P. Phillips looked out the window but there was nothing out there. He got up and turned the television off. He went upstairs and fixed himself some coffee and as he held the cup, he saw it shake and looking into the cup, he saw the little concentric rings moving back and forth, back and forth across the surface.

He closed his eyes and said, "No, no. This is not happening to me. It's all right. My wife didn't even wait for an explanation. It's all her fault." He smiled. And suddenly a memory:

"She sounds like a real bitch," Sheila said as they lay in bed.

"She is."

"You still plan on divorcing her?"

"Yes."

"When?'

"Soon."

"How soon is soon? A week?"

"Shhhhhh. C'mere."

But I never promised her a position, Walter P. Phillips thought, did I? No, no. I don't think so. He looked up from his coffee, looked out the kitchen window. Outside. There. Something. Something moved.

He got off the chair and something in the back of his mind whispered, "Now, for only fifty cents and two box tops . . . "

There. And suddenly a great white elephant with two very green eyes stared through the window and Walter P. Phillips dropped the coffee cup. He ran downstairs and slid the glass door back and was running; the snow was cold fire to his feet. A silly image came to his mind. The image of a fly trapped in silk on a window sill and from a dark crevice, something moved, something leaping out and scrambling toward him.

Suddenly it was not funny. Not silly. Walter P. Phillips, in his running, turned. There, behind him, blacker than the sky, with eyes glittering like black ice, came the spider and Walter P. Phillips tripped and was ensnared in silk as white and soft as snow and the spider came, the hourglass very red and Walter P. Phillips screamed but to his ears it sounded like a buzzing, a dumb blind buzzing and the great black spider drew nearer, nearer; the brush of the cold, cold mandibles, then the bite and with the poison came – the night.

The Coat

NOW, YOU SEE, it's like this. Little Nicholas Jackson was born into his father's heavy black coat. And soon those were the first memories of Nicholas, struggling and wearing that ill-fitting dark coat and trying like hell to love it even though he hated it. But his father, Nicholas Senior, saw that not only was his coat good enough for him and his name, but if it was good enough for him, then everything he had would automatically be good for his son, and of course, the son, young Nicholas – how could he know otherwise? So, of course Nicholas wore his father's heavy black coat – it was all he knew for it was all his father ever knew, for it was all *his* father knew. And that's all there was to it.

And so, here was Nicholas, hereafter called Nicholas Junior, wearing his father's dark coat.

And it really was a ridiculous coat. What strange first memories young Nicholas had: a strange mixture of a world of sunlight and bees, and blue sky and yellow sun and the coat – that immense, huge, suffocating, black, heavy coat.

Honest to God how absurd. The only place where he could feel the wind was on his face. No other place, save his hands and his feet when he tried to go barefoot (except he kept stepping on the coat). Nicholas Senior saw Nicholas Junior at times uncomfortable but simply said, "My father had to wear it. I had to wear it. I don't know what your problem is, but I'm sure you'll get used to it, just like I did."

By which Nicholas Junior knew that his father meant there wasn't anything he was going to do about it because if there was, he would realize he might have to do something about his own coat that he had to wear and, for whatever reason, he wasn't about to do that.

Oh, how absurd, but at the time, Little Nicholas didn't know what to do about it at all. He didn't have the faintest idea that he could do anything and whoever realizes that until they are many years along and then decide that the coat really isn't their style and then make a decision to take it off and drop or shred it, and leave it neatly at the parent's feet or sometimes necessarily throw it in their faces.

Ah, would it not be wonderful to decide one's wardrobe so early in life? But not so for Nicholas Junior. Not so for him at all.

Now, you might wonder where was Nicholas' mother in all of this? Did she not realize that Nicholas was wearing too heavy a coat for the occasion? Any occasion, actually. Did not she wonder when Nicholas was just a baby what that dark aura was about him? Didn't she wonder when he, in the baby carriage, kept getting lost in the heavy black coat that something was wrong? Didn't she ever say, "Nicholas, my baby and darling Nicholas, that coat will make you ill. That coat is much too heavy for your constitution." Now, how was it that the mother did not see? How could she be unaware that when Nicholas went swimming, he stayed and struggled beneath the surface of the water for really too long periods of time? (After all, such a heavy coat simply became waterlogged so that swimming was no fun, and was certainly just a struggle.) And where other children glided like pale fish through the sun-sparkled water, Nicholas just floundered and gasped like a fish out of water. Or how was it that on those lovely hot days, Nicholas, with face beaded and shining in sweat, almost suffocating in that black coat – how was it that she did not see Nicholas' discomfort?

That is indeed a good question. Perhaps she didn't really want him, and by him being miserable, that way she could justifiably love him. Doesn't misery always bring out the caring in people? But maybe that wasn't it at all. But she did not see. For whatever reason, she did not see and Nicholas, wearing that black, heavy coat, got his mother's love. Time moved on and you know how that goes. Even though Nicholas knew the coat was somehow the very worst thing he could wear, well, not knowing any better, perhaps he wore it anyway. He grew into it. Sort of. Now just because you grow into something doesn't mean it fits any better. No, no, oh, not at all. It just means you distort your body enough to fit the form – what else can you do? Poor little Nicholas, growing up, wearing a heavy dark coat that was anything but his own. But what can you do when you're a day old? Two months old? A year or so old? What choices have you about certain clothes that you have to wear for the rest of your life and no matter how ill-fitting, the only advice you can possibly get, given that it is given with love as it is known (which isn't really love at all but unconscious tyranny), the only advice you can get is that, "You'll learn to love it as you grow into it for there are no other alternatives that are love-defined in this family for you." So what are you to do at age two? Shove off the coat and risk rejection? And even Nicholas Junior, minutes after birth, knew the folly, the impossibility, the ludicrousness of that.

The black and heavy coat stayed in place, ah, sad, sad, anchored by survival need and quest for love, the coat stayed in place.

It stayed in place in spite of the admonishments of his best pals, Kenny for one, who wore clothes of bright colors and whose parents always respected his tastes and asked him what he wanted to wear, and so Kenny was quite the individual with a trust in his tastes and his own sensibilities and he always looked at Nicholas and said, "Gee, don't you ever get tired of wearing that coat? Look how black it is and how frayed the sleeves. The buttons are coming off and it's way too large. Don't you have other coats you can wear? Or other clothes? I can see this in winter when it's dark and gloomy and then everyone can't help but wear coats like this – but *all* the time?"

To which Nicholas replied, hurt and defensive, "But what's wrong with it?"

Kenny asked, "Is that really your coat?"

"It's the only coat that I know."

"But is it *your* coat?"

"Yes."

"And you choose to wear it?"

Desperately, Nicholas said, "Yes."

Kenny looked puzzled, unsure as to what to say for he saw the desperation, didn't know how to talk about it or much less what it meant and finally said, "Oh," but really meant, "I don't know what's going on with you, but that black coat that you always wear is a mean looking coat and I have a hunch you're wearing it for the wrong reason and it's not even your coat – what do your clothes really look like beneath that old coat? What are you really wearing? Polyester? Cotton? Wool? Plaid? Blues? Greens? Red? My friend, what are your clothes and true colors beneath that black coat?"

Ah, poor Nicholas, what was he to say? For everyone's worst fears are such that if they have been taught that they must wear a dark coat, it must be because that which is beneath the coat is so worthless or so secondhand, or so colorless, that if they showed their wardrobe to the world, their clothes would be found to be utterly rejectionable; therefore, your worst fears about that which is beneath the coat are thereby confirmed. So of course the coat remained in place. Nicholas wore it at school dances and while everyone was showing off their glorious but (of course) adolescent wardrobes, Nicholas just assumed that once the coat was in place, it would always *be* in place and that was the only wardrobe he had, there were no other clothes to wear. But oh, how hard it was to dance in an ill-fitting black coat that enshrouded Nicholas like a great black sack of space. And oh, how that coat made it so hard to dance; Nicholas might try to turn but the momentum of the coat simply made him ungainly. He'd try a new step but the coat got in the way and he'd end up falling. He'd reach out to touch hands but the coat sleeve flopped over his fingers and the only touch anyone ever got was a fistful of fabric and a handful of darkness. And where everyone else danced and as they danced their new wardrobes became more lively in color, more solid in hue, poor Nicholas; it was as though his coat became heavier, the fabric denser and darker and what, what, what was poor Nicholas ever to do? And what a strange sensation to be wearing a coat that was one's own but did not fit or really belong to one at all. Oh, what a strange and strange sensation that was. And to make it even worse, whenever he went home, his father always said, as he sat unconsciously distorted and destroyed by his own coat, "My, my, what a fine looking coat that is. You should be grateful that I gave you that coat. Why, if it weren't for me, you'd not have that wonderful coat at all. Wear it well and make me proud of you."

His mother, still, for whatever reason, unable to see that black coat even now, did notice his discomfort and always gave him much loving concern.

Who can refuse? Ah, that parental love is the strongest there is, and who can refuse. To such overwhelming love and concern, of course he said yes, and yes, and every time he said yes, it was as though the coat became darker and fit closer or like tender meat crammed into a shell, he made the coat fit as best he could, but oh, the pain, the sense of pain was always there. Nicholas could only guess that was the way it was – but his friend Kenny appeared very happy and Melissa, she always wore bright colors and had gay and happy parties and his other friend Jackie, my how he loved reds and yellows and on the dreariest of days, he wore the brightest of colors as if defying the clouds, the very dark side of the moon, the unending dark and deep well of space, to try, just to try to snuff out that blaze of bright fire known as Jackie.

At what point does one make a decision to remove one's coat? At what age? At what time? How is that decision made? Perhaps it was when Nicholas was sixteen. Perhaps it was because of Meredith that things began to change.

Meredith MacKenzie was as sweet a young lady as you could find anywhere, what with long blond hair and delicious smile. She liked Nicholas and Nicholas could not figure out why.

All this came about because she was in his art class with him and tremendously enjoyed the sketches he made, although to him they seemed of small consequence, even though everyone else liked them, too. It was the only thing he could do without the coat getting too much in his way, but the long sleeves did make it hard to draw, and frequently the vast folds of the coat made it difficult for him to sit and be comfortable, or draw without smudging the lines or colors. But in spite of the coat, that at least, was one place where Nicholas could accept a little color into his life, though how colorful it really was was as yet rather beyond him.

But one day, while sitting in the lunch room, sitting in his vast coat and trying to be as comfortable as possible in that dark and thick hand-me-down, Meredith came over and said, "Hi, I really liked the sketch you did."

And Nicholas, almost choking on his cold corned beef sandwich said, "Uh, oh, gee, uh, thanks – it wasn't really anything all that good – "

Meredith smiled. "Everyone liked it."

Nicholas smiled a grim little smile and it was though somehow the coat felt closer and bigger than ever before.

"Uh, well, gee," he said, "um, thank you – "

"May I sit with you? Can I join you for lunch?" Her look was gentle and patient.

"Oh, uh, yeah, sure," said Nicholas.

And she sat.

And he did not have the faintest idea what to do and he seemed to lose himself in that coat even more.

"Don't you ever get tired of wearing that coat?"

"Huh?"

"That coat. That heavy black and dark coat. Why do you wear such an awful coat?"

Nicholas looked at her with a mixture of shame and guilt as if there was something terribly wrong with the coat and not only was the coat wrong, but what was beneath it was also wrong. And he did not know what to say so he sat there, but with very dry mouth eating a corned beef sandwich and feeling very unhappy indeed. But she was patient. And she kept smiling. She dug in her brown bag and brought out a tuna fish sandwich, a big red apple, and a small bag of potato chips. She ripped open the top and offered them to Nicholas. "Care for some?"

Guiltily, Nicholas accepted.

"It's okay," she said.

"Thank you," he said.

"You know," she said munching a chip, "my father used to wear a coat just like yours."

Nicholas stopped eating and stared at Meredith.

She crunched another potato chip. "It took a lot of work for us to help him take it off. He just couldn't believe that the natural clothes he wore beneath the coat were actually okay." *Crunch*, another potato chip, and she offered him some more. From the depths of his coat, he looked at her, comprehending but no, not comprehending at all.

"Of course," she said, "the hardest thing for him to realize was not only that he was wearing a coat in the first place, but that he could take it off." She sighed. "He just did not understand. But after you've known someone who wears such a coat, you see it on others."

Nicholas shrunk even further into his coat.

"I know you probably don't understand," she said, "my father didn't either, not for a long, long, time. But finally he let us become close to him because he finally saw that he was okay – " And before she knew it, she had her hands up to her face and began to cry.

Just then, without even thinking, Nicholas, in spite of the heavy and dark coat that he wore, he right then reached through all that fabric and touched Meredith right on the arm and as he moved, his coat pulled away from him, oh, just a little way for him to look down to see a shirt he was wearing beneath suddenly become a blaze of reds and yellows and greens and blues; and Meredith, suddenly looking at Nicholas, looking through her own tears, said simply, "Thank you, Nicholas," and then softly, "Thank you very much."

Nicholas, still blinded by the colors of what he really wore beneath that dark coat, began to grasp the nature of the decision that he had to make.

CARS

YOU'RE SITTING BY the road beneath that pale dawn sky and she drives by you in her junker '62 Fairlane 500 and slows way down and says, "Wanna ride?"

You look at her. Yeah. Nice lady she seems to be, what with the red hair, the freckles, the granny glasses and – um – are those empty beer bottles in the back? Well, we can't all be perfect and you say, "Yeah, that's what it's all about isn't it? Helping each other out on this strange journey."

"You bet," she says.

"Thanks," you say and you climb in and she punches the accelerator like she's trying to get to the nearest galaxy by out-warping the Enterprise. You're pressed back into the seat by the mounting g's and she says, "This old heap does pretty well for a '62."

"Ak," you say.

"What's your name?" she yells to be heard; you must be reaching mach three, and outside, things blur.

"Ak," you say.

"Ak, it is," she laughs. "Oxygen is below the dash. We're about to go through a thermal layer."

You didn't have this in mind.

"Some asshole men I pick up are just like my fucked up old man," she says. "They beat me and if you lay a finger on me, I'll punch you right in the nuts."

"Ak," you say.

"Abuse!" she screams. You don't know who hits the ejection button first; you think it's you. Your section of the Ford blasts upward and you get a stunning view of Saturn before you flip topsy turvy, still anchored in the passenger's side and somehow you can hear her voice give one long, slurring accusation, "I know what you were thinking fucker eat shit and *die*."

"Ak," you say but you think that this was a good thing and for some reason you cannot comprehend, maybe the atmosphere is thicker here, the seat slows and slows and why it doesn't disintegrate and burn up is beyond you. Maybe your head is too impervious these days; maybe your skin has turned to titanium alloy that can withstand the extreme temperatures you have withstood from the intense friction with other people way back in the past. Maybe you were born on the sun with sun beings whose primary purpose was to take energy and give nothing back. Maybe you're used to all this; you don't know. But gently your seat settles sedately down by the interstate once again and you breath out a sigh of relief. "Ak," you say, "My God, I'm still alive. Still alive."

You unbuckle yourself from the seat and look about the reddish desert, the immense wastes of sand and in the distance a dust devil dances and the sky is that pale blue and the moon is like a crescent Cheshire smile. You haven't the first idea where you are and as you ponder this, someone else pulls up in a '58 Edsel, the color of earth and she, the driver, says, "Hi, stranger, going my way?"

"Sure," you respond, and this looks better this time around; nothing in the back seat and it's it clean inside, but boy it's dark, like you're sitting in the dark of Jupiter, of Pluto's night side and in the shadow cold of the interior, you can vaguely make out her face, the curly dark hair, the dark eyes, the earth-colored clothes.

"Climb in," she says.

"I thank you," you say, "getting a ride is sometimes a difficult task way out here. It's nice to have company along the way."

She nods. "My mother hated me."

"Gee," you say, "that's too – "

She does something to the gear shift; she pushes it down; the car vibrates and you accelerate. Down.

"She beat me all the time," she says and she begins to cry. Down you go, down, down, down, there goes the daylight, and you can't imagine how many layers of history you are sinking through, "1988, she beat me so hard that I landed in the hospital. 1986, she forced me out the window of a second story apartment – I broke my teeth and my leg."

"I'm sorry," you respond, and of course, in the car, it is utterly and totally black as Cretaceous mud underneath the feet of a Brontosaurus. Oh, man, it's *black*.

"You fucker," she seethes, "how can you know? You had it so good – "

"No, I didn't," you respond. Jeeze, you can't see her face but her energy field surges, withdraws and punches you again and again, like an airy fist.

"Oh, my mother was such a bitch," she says, "and my father he was never there. You're just like the rest, aren't you? You're just going to leave – "

"What?" you say. "What? I don't even *know* you, we're not even friends, but I have to admit, it's difficult to be close to you right now – "

"You're going to abandon me, you're going to leave me – "

You sigh. "Well, I'm beginning to think, for my sanity, that may not be a bad idea – "

Suddenly, light. You're blinded. You blink, look around, oh, my God, you wonder, broad canals, a crystal city in the distance and it's a 1950's Mars and *whamph*, the car lands on the paved side of a broad canal.

"Get out," she says, "you're just making me depressed."

It's strange, even in the light, her face is dark, dark as the backside of the moon, dark as the silk chamber of a spider, black as the tar in a tar pit and you get out and watch her drive away and suddenly her car explodes way down there on the horizon where sky and land and canal seem to merge at some vanishing point and you watch the smoke curl like a question mark, only to turn into an exclamation point and you sit on the side of the canal.

"Oh, shit," you mumble to yourself, "this does not look like Detroit, or Tacoma or any other place I know." And you sigh again. "And it doesn't look like the local traffic may necessarily go that way. Oh, isn't this strange indeed."

You stare out at the landscape, to the lichen fields beyond, to the fear moon, Phobos, stumbling, falling through the sky and think, a lesson. There must be a lesson here. Wonder what the hell it is. You close your eyes. Deeper. You go deeper. You sigh, focus, and on the side of the canal, with the wind singing through the spires of Syrtis Major, shining, white and pale green and blue in the sun, you go deeper, deeper, much, much deeper, focusing on the inner world and *wham!* you see the hatred of your ancestors, see the rage and the bitterness of the women, of all the mothers in your past and coming back up, up to the present and you simply say, "Of course." You look into the canal. It's deep enough and combined with your depth of hopelessness, you could drown.

"Yes, I could," you say, "maybe I should," but you shake your head. "Who am I to sign, seal and deliver my fate while I still have breath?"

Abruptly, you turn around and there she is – a Martian. You shake your head. A Martian but she looks okay. The amber eyes are a little odd; the four fingers to a hand – um – well – and are those nubbins on her forehead – ah – antennae? Pale orange skin – too many carrots perhaps?

She sits there in her Mars machine or car or whatever you want to call it and she does something absolutely marvelous. She smiles. "Il yakatat," she says.

You shake your head.

She opens up the side of the machine in which she sits. She gestures. "Dweur ga."

You shake your head again. The city of Syrtis Major gleams and shines like a promise and the wind ripples the surface of the canal. Something weird breaks the surface, flies for a minute, then dives down and you turn to her. You turn to her amber eyes, to her smile, and you climb into the car; she touches you with her strange hand and says with the softest voice you've ever heard, "Gwee pas pa, gwee pas, pas pa. Gwnell. Sha sa."

And you want to cry, wanting so much to trust that which seems so strange.

THE FINAL TRICK OF FUNNYMAN

FUNNYMAN COMES STRUTTING into the big top with the galaxy spinning on his fist, and the crowd goes wild. The announcer yells to be heard: "And now for the main event, what everyone has been waiting for: Funnyman and his spiral galaxy!" And again, everyone cheers, applauds and yells. And Funnyman, big, rotund, bearded Funnyman in the white suit with black diamonds that sparkle like stars in the lights, Funnyman holds one hand up in a gesture of mastery and showmanship. "Thank you," he says, "you're all too kind, too, too kind."

Several people in the audience go "Awww!" in mockery of Funnyman's self-abasement. He smiles. Yeah, he knows what he's doing. He manipulates the audience like it's a mass puppet show. The spiral galaxy spins around and around on his left fist.

"Now," he says, as the spotlight focuses on him, "for my first trick, watch carefully."

Slowly, Funnyman pushes the stray wisps of gas and stars inward on itself until he has the spiral galaxy into a sphere. Then, with both hands, he compacts it. The audience is silent as he does this, except for someone coughing in the upper section and a child crying because he has to go to the bathroom again even though he already went (actually, the child is more fascinated by the bathroom fixtures than the magic act). And Funnyman proceeds, and oh, how the light sparkles off that suit. An old woman nervously turns a handkerchief around and around in her hands. A man loosens his necktie. Funnyman continues to pack the stars and gasses closer and closer. When everything is into a tight ball, he smiles impishly, his expression seeming to say, "Don't you just wonder what I'm going to do?" And he prolongs his actions and the audience is impatient and loves the suspense and suddenly Funnyman yells, "Yes!" and throws the ball up; it expands, explodes in brilliant light and stars shoot out; it is a magnificent display, thoroughly wonderful and everybody stands and applauds and yells, "Bravo! Bravo! Wonderful!"

The children clap their hands with exaggeration and look up eagerly to their parents; oh, the expression: "Mother! Father! Isn't it wonderful? Isn't it? Isn't it?"

Slowly the galaxy settles on Funnyman's right fist; it settles and slowly spins, around and around. The audience sits and quiets.

"For my next trick," says Funnyman, "I'll need a child from the audience."

Scattered cries from the audience: "Me, mommy! Me!" and "No! Me! ME!"

Finally, someone lowers a child over the railing and, at first, the child runs toward Funnyman – then stops, and begins to run back to his parents. "Ohhhh!" murmurs the audience sympathetically. Funnyman smiles, drops down to one knee and says, "C'mere. I think you'll enjoy this." Timidly, the child responds and goes over to Funnyman. Funnyman takes the galaxy off his fist, lowers it, spreads it out so it is as thin as a sheet of sparkling frost. Then he picks up the child, places him in the center of the glowing sheet and the child floats up, up on that sheet of stars and brightness, slowly, slowly spinning about. The child peers over the edge of the brilliance; on his face, immense wonder and surprise. And, as though by command, the sheet of stars drifts back down, until it is but a meter off the ground. Funnyman lifts the child off and again the audience stands and applauds. "Bravo! Bravo!" the crowd yells. The child happily runs and skips back to his parent's arms. The galaxy rises, settles on Funnyman's left fist, spins slowly about and the audience calms once more.

Funnyman smiles. Oh, that impish grin – what is he going to do now? After a few minutes (while the audience waits with rising frustration and curiosity), Funnyman tosses the spiral galaxy up; as it rises, Funnyman claps his hands twice. *Flash!* The galaxy splits in two. The audience gasps. Funnyman then has a galaxy spinning on each fist. He tosses up the galaxies again, claps his hands twice – two separate bursts of light – four galaxies now come drifting down, two on Funnyman's right, two on his left. As they drift down, he takes the top one on the right, pulls it over to the left, takes the bottom one on the left, pulls it to the right and repeats the action until all four galaxies are circling about. Funnyman's juggling is purely masterful. When the galaxies are rotating at a constant speed, Funnyman backs away and by their own momentum, the galaxies continue to rotate by themselves, over and over and when, at last, their momentum begins to slow, Funnyman steps in, gently catches each one and allows them all to fall into each other and each time one does, a tremendous burst of light occurs until, at last, one spiral galaxy is left spinning on Funnyman's fist. There ensues a profound and awed silence. Then the audience explodes! Wild applause! Cheering! Cries of "Wonderful!" and "Magic! Bravo! Bravo!" resound and people stand. Funnyman smiles dolefully and bows.

Again, the people become silent. Suddenly, outside the tent, screaming! A yell: "The beast! The beast! The beast has escaped! Run! Run! The beast has escaped!"

Inside the tent, the silence lasts but a second more – then, chaos! Some yell, "The beast! The beast is loose! Run!"

Others yell, "No! Stay here! It is safer here! Don't go out there!"

But before anyone can do anything, the beast appears. It comes in the main entrance of the tent and changing shape and form and is pure black. It screams and howls but not like a creature that bellows by blowing breath out – no, this howl is the creature sucking in, but not just air, oh, no – it sucks in everything; it extends its darkness like long pseudopods – one reaches up (it looks like a tornado) and sucks away the top of the tent to reveal the pale and starless sky. The audience stands as though frozen.

The beast advances toward Funnyman and he, with the galaxy rotating on his fist, he stands his ground and does not move. Oddly, he does not look frightened; rather, he looks as though he seeks the beast as a challenge, something that should be, yes, can be overcome. Funnyman steps forward with the galaxy rotating on his fist and he says, "Come beast, come beast, attack me, beast, take me in your darkness, beast."

But the beast is strangely wary. It advances, retreats, it circles. It is fascinated, afraid, hateful, vicious and yet it circles and circles and Funnyman holds out the galaxy to the beast and oh! how the beast howls in sucking rage and fear! Funnyman advances. "Come beast," he says, "come, take this light from me, you howling bastard son of despair. Come beast, come, come, smother this light in your sucking and howling nothingness. Come beast, come, dissolve me in your endless night."

Again, Funnyman holds the galaxy out to the beast. The beast extends pseudopods now like clutching waves, waves ready to crash down and drain and drain and suck away.

Again, again, the beast circles about and it is as though it has totally forgotten the audience which sits utterly spellbound by the battle before it.

"Ah," says Funnyman, "you wish to dance, do you? How then shall we dance? Shall you approach and I recede? Funnyman follows through with the action – he steps back and the beast approaches. Funnyman laughs. "Then I step forward and you step back?" Abruptly he steps forward and instantly the best retreats and yanks back pseudopods. Funnyman laughs again. "Oh," he says, "but this is fun!"

All about Funnyman oozes the beast; sometimes low and stalking, sometimes high and overwhelming. But always there, always waiting, always advancing, retreating, advancing again. And in step with it, Funnyman with the galaxy on his fist, cajoling the darkness, "Come, snuff me out, squeeze into nothing. Come. Come. Are you weak, oh, beast? Why is it you cannot, will not destroy me?" At that moment, the beast does not move. "Could it be that we need each other, beast? That, if I were to destroy you, I would destroy myself? That if you were to destroy me, you would destroy yourself? Begin feeding on yourself?" Funnyman and the beast dance around each other, threatening, baiting, advancing, retreating. This continues for a few minutes more. Then, Funnyman turns to the audience and says, "I grow weary. I grow very weary of this." He looks directly at the beast. "You tire me." He tosses the galaxy up, claps his hands and *flash!* The beast sucks a howl and backs away and Funnyman has two galaxies, one on each fist and he laughs gleefully, uproariously, which contrasts fearfully with the beast's sucking howl and moan.

Funnyman jumps, arms and galaxies outstretched and with a mighty cry, a massive inhalation of pain and fear, the beast leaps skyward and attaches itself to the heavens, spreading out to fill the sky like some wing of a vast black bat, and the pale and starless sky vanishes.

Silence. Then, someone in the audience yells, "You did it! You did it! You saved us! The beast did not devour us!"

Funnyman nods, but looks wary, wary, indeed wary. "Oh, don't be so sure!" he says, "Oh, don't be so sure at all! You forget that right above you, the beast hangs, ready to drop on you at any moment. And when he does, he will suck you right into his darkness until there is nothing left of you."

A mother of a small child cries; her face is imploring. "Oh, please, please, is there no way to stop the beast? Have you no power to keep it at bay?"

The child, at the mother's side, clutches the mother's dress and looks fearfully at the black sky.

But Funnyman laughs. "Oh, dear, yes. I understand your feelings very well. And let me share something with you. I'm old now, and my days as a funnyman at this circus – well, I've known for a long time those days were numbered." As he talks, he joins the two galaxies and then packs the one down, down, smaller, smaller, until it can be enclosed by his fist. "Yes," he sighs, "I'm tired now, and it is time for me to do something different." He pauses. "Now I see what it is that I must do." He looks up to the beast. "It's not over, you know," he says to the beast. "Do not be so confident. It's not over at all." He then looks to the audience. "All of you are blessed because now you are going to see my last and most magnificent trick."

Ah! Still the master showman. He looks around waits until everyone is looking at him, listening, wondering, watching. And at the last possible moment, before the crowd explodes in frustration, Funnyman does the incredible. He opens his mouth and tosses in the incredibly compacted galaxy, and swallows it.

For a few seconds, nothing happens. But suddenly, brilliant light seems to engulf Funnyman. And when the light fades, all that people can see is the outline of a man filled with the spiral galaxy. And then his voice, "Oh, but my, you've been such a fine audience and I love you all. But now, let's see if there is something I can do to make sure our dark friend keeps a proper perspective on the situation."

With a mighty leap, Funnyman (remember, now, he is just the figure of a man whose every square centimeter is a splash of stars in a galaxy), this man leaps to the sky and, suddenly, the entire sky is alive with fire and explosions and a sucking screaming! And when people are finally able to look to the sky, no one says anything; children look up uncomprehending of what they see. Some adults shake their heads in confusion for now the sky is no longer blank; no, not only is it black with the body of the beast, but now, against the black of the beast (or perhaps in it?), ah, yes, Funnyman stretches the spiral galaxy clear across the sky in every direction. And it is suddenly clear that the beast is never going to overwhelm Funnyman and his spiral galaxy – but also, Funnyman and his galaxy can never totally overwhelm the beast.

And so: the battle is a draw, and somehow it seems a truce has formed between Funnyman and the beast; the heavens appear stable as though a compromise has been reached.

But will it be forever so? That is difficult to know and the crowd puts further thought on this aside. Instead, people stare with love and wonder at their new skies, their brilliant, shining yet despairing black skies. The people are so quiet; they stare at their skies for a long, long time and admire how Funnyman, with the galaxy in his gut, keeps the beast at bay.

Acknowledgments

First of all, many thanks to those who have read these manuscripts and critiqued them; I am referring specifically to the wonderful people I have met through the Seattle Chapter of the National Writers Club, in my critique group, and specifically the friendships of Marie Landis Edwards, her husband, Si, and Brian Herbert, as well as Calvin Clawson, Phyllis Hiefield and Linda Shepherd. A special thanks to my friends Jez and (the infinitely patient) Bob Blair. Thanks also to the fine staff on Five West, Harborview Hospital where I have worked lo, these many years, who have always been supportive and encouraging of my writing. Thanks to Julia Cameron for her book, *The Artists Way*, in addition to the Seattle meeting of Artists Recovering Through Twelve Steps that enabled me to break through the self-lies and embrace the truth of myself, and accept myself as the fine artist I am. Thank you, John Dalmas, for your long time friendship and willingness to write an introduction to this collection; thanks to Jack Cady who, as a teacher of mine at the University of Washington, had faith in my writing (in spite of the times, I think, when I tried to prove him wrong), and to the memories of Jack Leahy and Avram Davidson. Also, thanks to Robert Silverberg for my professional debut in *New Dimensions 9* and Jon Gustafson for inviting me and introducing me to the world of science fiction conventions. Thanks also to Terry Brooks and Jack Cady (again), who took time from their busy schedules to read and comment on the book. Additional thanks to Jack Evans, Mike Jaymes as well as Edward Bryant for his usual sage and wise advice, Lisa Jean Bothell, editor/publisher of Three-Stones Publications, Ltd./Heliocentric Net, and Roberta Gregory for her fine editing skills for the new edition. Many thanks to all.

A little story about "Onions," included in this collection. I received a phone call one December evening. "Are you the Bruce Taylor who wrote that story, 'Onions'?"

Not quite knowing what to expect, I said, " – uh – yeah – " I also wanted to say, having had many strange calls, something smirky like, "What'd you have in mind?"

"Oh, thank goodness," came the voice, "thank goodness. We read that story when it was published in the *Seattle Post Intelligencer* in 1980, and, well, we're in a retirement home, and, well, you know – we just wanted to make sure we said thank you for writing that. We've Xeroxed so many copies of that story and sent it to so many people – everyone liked it – we just wanted to say 'thank you' – "

?? These things really happen to writers?? How nice! "Well, uh, well – gee – um, thank you, I mean, really, thank you very much – I'm glad you liked it."

"Well, we just wanted to make sure we told you that – " Mentally, I completed the sentence and felt flattered, honored and – sad, sad, very, very sad.

"Thank you for that," I said. "That means a lot. Guess that's one of the reasons I do this – sure ain't for the money – but I had a great time writing it and I'm glad you enjoyed it."

"Please," came the woman's voice, "please tell me that you won't stop writing and getting these stories published. You're so good."

By this time I was feeling like I was going to cry. "I promise," I said. "I do indeed plan to keep writing and keep my stories out there."

"Thank you," came the voice. "Thank you for writing 'Onions.' "

"Thank you for letting me know you liked it."

"Good-bye," and a pause, "and God bless you."

"Good bye," I said.

And there was a sense of Something That Had To Be Done Being Done. And a few days later, a Christmas card. And I haven't heard from that person since. Alive? Dead? I don't know. But such a gift that person gave me that Christmas – because they had considered what I had written a gift – to them.

About The Author

Born in 1947, Bruce Taylor was raised in Seattle, Washington, his current home. Early in his life he was drawn to science fiction, particularly the works of Jules Verne, H.G. Wells, C.S. Lewis, and Ray Bradbury. Later, he became equally familiar with Dostoevsky, Flaubert, Steinbeck, Chapek, Kafka, and Chekov.

Taylor attended the University of Washington at Seattle, where he received a B.A. degree in Sociology while also writing for the *University of Washington Daily* and studying fiction with such teachers as Jack Leahy and Jack Cady. After leaving college, Taylor worked a number of odd jobs before taking his current job at Harborview Medical Center on the locked inpatient psychiatric unit as a counselor. After a great deal of work in the field of hypnosis and hypnotherapy, Taylor now teaches classes at Harborview on stress management techniques.

In 1972, Taylor attended the Clarion West Writers Workshop and since then has had work published in, among others, *New Dimensions, Tomorrow, Pulphouse, Twilight Zone, The Silver Web, Magic Realism*, and a number of foreign publications. He has also served as writer in residence at Shakespeare & Company in Paris, where he was filmed reading his fiction for an NBC program on American/French relations. Taylor is currently working on a novel entitled *The Humphrey Bogart Blues* while marketing two other novels, *Edward, Dancing on the Edge of Infinity* and *Kafka's Uncle.*

When not writing, Taylor enjoys hiking through New Zealand, Yosemite, The Swiss Alps, and the Cascades; he has an absolutely *smashing* view of Mt. Rainier from his writing loft.

Also Available From
Fairwood Press:

<u>Our 1st Trade Paperback:</u>

Other Voices, Other Doors:
A Collection of Stories, Essays & Poems
by **Patrick O'Leary**
Cover art by Rick Lieder. $17.99 USA postpaid.
Available through Ingram
ISBN: 0-9668184-0-7

<u>Chapbooks</u>:

The 10% Solution:
Self-editing for the Modern Writer
by **Ken Rand**
Cover art by Keith Boulger. $5.99 USA postpaid.
ISBN: 0-9668184-0-7

ZOM BEE MOO VEE
& Other Freaky Shows
by **Mark McLaughlin**
Cover art by Paul Swenson. $5.99 USA postpaid.
ISBN: 0-9668184-1-5

<u>Our First Paperback</u>:

Welcome to Hell:
A Working Guide for the Beginning Writer
by **Tom Piccirilli**
Cover art by Chris Whitlow. $6.99 USA postpaid.
ISBN: 0-9668184-2-3

Send to Fairwood Press; 5203 Quincy Ave SE; Auburn, WA 98092
add $1.00 /2.50 each item for Can/Elsewhere

Printed in the United States
758200006B